THE COUP

THE COUP

A NOVEL

JAMIE MALANOWSKI

DOUBLEDAY

NEW YORK   LONDON   TORONTO

SYDNEY   AUCKLAND

PUBLISHED BY DOUBLEDAY

Copyright © 2007 by Jamie Malanowski

Published in the United States by Doubleday, an imprint of The
Doubleday Broadway Publishing Group, a division of Random
House, Inc., New York.
www.doubleday.com

DOUBLEDAY and the portrayal of an anchor with a dolphin are
registered trademarks of Random House, Inc.

An excerpt originally appeared in *Playboy* magazine.

LIBRARY OF CONGRESS CATALOGING-IN-PUBLICATION DATA
Malanowski, Jamie.
    The coup : a novel / Jamie Malanowski. — 1st ed.
        p. cm.
    1. Vice Presidents—United States—Fiction. 2. Political fiction.
3. Satire. I. Title.
PS3563.A422C68 2007
813'.54—dc22

                                        2007007519

ISBN 978-0-385-52048-5

PRINTED IN THE UNITED STATES OF AMERICA

10 9 8 7 6 5 4 3 2 1

FIRST EDITION

To Clem and Irene Malanowski,

my dad and mom

THE COUP

1

GODWIN POPE CHECKED his watch. Seven minutes left. He won't be late for this, Godwin thought. There's a legion of handlers and the mighty magnet of free air time on five broadcast channels and five cable networks to keep him on time for his first State of the Union address. His first real one, anyway. Jack Mahone had delivered one a year ago, but at that point, he'd been in office less than three weeks and was still keen on making a good impression. Since then, Mahone had on various occasions proved capable of keeping his wife, his children, his staff, the joint congressional leadership, the other seven of the G8 leaders, the Dalai Lama, eighteen gold medal–winning Special Olympians, and the Chicago Bears waiting while he flossed, did a crossword puzzle, played with his dog, finished his calisthenics, and talked to George Clooney about nuclear proliferation, but it seemed much too much to believe that he would dare shamble in late on a vast national audience equipped with remote-control channel changers and a hundred choices.

Or maybe he would.

Parked high in the vice president's usual spot behind and above the podium, Godwin surveyed the House of Representatives Chamber in the Capitol Building. The panorama wasn't his uniquely, of course; on Godwin's left, Herman Vanick, the fleshy, cunning former gym teacher who had elbowed his way into the Speakership of the House four years ago, had nearly the same perspective from his seat, though Godwin doubted the ass-patting towel-snapper saw what he did. Vanick looked at the room and saw pretty much what Jack Mahone saw—a dung hill populated by ants who loved, hated, feared, or owed him, but who were basically merchants, here to buy and sell favors, markers, pork. Godwin looked at the room and saw history—John Quincy Adams and Henry Clay and Sam Rayburn, a beardless Lincoln and a callow Kennedy, measuring themselves within the room's quiet magnificence. Well yes, okay, those men, along with an army of ambitious sharpies who had managed to maneuver their hands in the people's business—and their pockets.

But hey, Godwin thought, there's no point being glum about it. That's civilization, right? The strong and smart and clever have always tried to get something out of the credulous and besotted—and not only get something out of them but make them think giving it up is the right thing to do. The divine right of kings, Godwin snickered to himself. Now there was a sell job.

Of course, a big part of anybody being able to pull off a theory like that—that any single ordinary-looking goofball, whether you call him president, king, kaiser, sultan, or whatever, should control the fate of thousands or millions or hundreds of millions—was being able to perform well in meetings like this. Because ever since *Homo sapiens* slouched out of the caves, people have had meetings like this. Not always in a great high-ceilinged hall scrutinized by fourteen television cameras and the eyeballs of a global audience. Sometimes it has been by the big rock or the big sequoia or the carcass of the mastodon. But always we've gathered, ready to listen to the Top Man try to map out the road ahead. And as always, Godwin noted, the customary members of the tribe attend:

On the right, the guardians, our military chiefs, the members of the Joint Chiefs of Staff. Not our most valiant warriors, mind you, or our bravest, or our most bloody-minded, or our most efficiently lethal, but six professionally accomplished, ribbon-bedecked commanders who have learned, through decades of bureaucratic maneuvers, that the answer to every military question, whether it's about money, time, firepower, or troops, is "We need more."

Next to them are our great justices, the members of the Supreme Court, resplendent in their robes. Nine judicial pashas, with nary a shred of practical experience among them, mystical high priests trying like a fat woman with a pair of bicycle shorts to stretch an eighteenth-century document around twenty-first-century issues, while at the same time wriggling to cloak partisan positions under the guise of nonpartisan precedent. Godwin remembered the pretty young attorney who had been parked across from him at a dinner party—at Freston's house, that's right, Freston of Frest-Tel Construction. Yes, in fact it was Freston's stepdaughter by his third marriage, Rochelle, the Frest-Tel heiress. She'd just finished a stint clerking for the elderly, musty Associate Justice Pinturabo—look at him down there, his fat belly bulging even under his robe! She had disclosed the most amazing fact: seven of the nine ultimate arbiters of the laws of the world's richest, most innovative nation had never Googled a thing—not even themselves.

To their left sit the cabinet, a group of men and women of medium accomplishment and a superabundance of caution. The president's friends. His fund-raisers. His donors. His bootlicks. Forgettable, interchangeable people whose proudest accomplishment, now and for all their lives, will be to say "I headed a government agency." *Headed.* Like Pelé.

And filling the room, stretching from side to side, are the mighty solons of Congress, the 535 wise men and women of the Senate and House, the Jacks and Jills and Shaniquas and Billy Bobs, the ex-fraternity house presidents and prom committee chairgirls, the former school board members and state assemblymen who learned their trade debating liquor laws and zoning regulations, 535 egotists superglued to corporate interests, who now get to kick around the great questions of war and peace, poverty and abundance, enrichment and enslavement. Living dinosaurs, Godwin thought, creatures whose tiny minds stand in inverse proportion to their wide, spreading butts.

All waiting for . . .

The back doors of the chamber opened, and the sergeant at arms of the House, Woody Lynn Grant, a thin, tiny, pinched-faced man wearing huge aviator glasses and a glen plaid suit with ginormous lapels, called out to the assembled throng.

"Mr. Speaker! Mr. Speaker! The President of the United States!"

Will wonders never cease? Godwin thought. On time!

His annual speaking part in the great national dramedy come and gone, Grant, who had been making that announcement for twenty-eight years, and who three years ago was rumored to have thrown a letter opener at an underling who had, without a sufficient tone of mournfulness in his voice, noted that Woody was now four years past retirement age, stepped aside. Into the vacuum strode John Bartholomew Mahone, wearing a navy Hart Schaffner & Marx suit and a professionally triumphant grin. He moved down the aisle, slowly and yet somehow at the same time vigorously, pumping the outstretched hands of those members of his party who had managed to finagle aisle seats in an effort to get a split second of face time on national TV while backslapping the passing prez.

Look at him, thought Godwin. Good old Jack Mahone. Smilin' Jack. Happy Jack. Crafty Jack. President Jack. Big Jack Off. We rise and salute his entrance, his presence, his very perambulation. It's an act a great many one-year-olds have mastered, Godwin thought, but let's applaud him nonetheless.

Herman Vanick leaned close to Godwin. "How long do you think this windbag is going to gas on tonight?"

"I understand they did run-throughs at the residence yesterday and the fastest time was seventy-two minutes."

"Ke-rist on a crutch!" moaned Vanick. "I was hopin' to get home in time for the second half of the USC game."

"If he left out all the pork barrel programs they put in just to get in on your good side, Herm, he could cut it by a quarter."

"Yeah, right. Say, is your buddy Ralston going to sign any free agents? Everybody knows the Redskins need a fullback. People in fucking Mongolia know the Redskins need a fullback."

"Don't spread it around, but I hear they're going to go after Marco MçChesney."

"Ah, shit, McChesney'll be as big a bust as this asshole Mahone."

Godwin had no opinion on the relative merits of Marco McChesney, but he wasn't going to exhaust himself defending this asshole Mahone. The president was a Louisiana man, Baton Rouge, fifty-nine years old, ex-governor, ex-senator, passably handsome, garrulous, louche, a man who possessed a common touch, a man of the people. He came out of the convention nine points back and won thirty-six states on Election Day, almost a landslide, mostly by correctly and successfully painting his opponent as dismally out of touch. Thirteen short, fast months later, he's managed to plunge to the lowest favorability rating that any president ever had at the end of his freshman year.

The poor stupid bastard never had a honeymoon, Godwin thought. He let his good old buddy loyalists from Baton Rouge manage the transition, and they rewarded him with a slow, slovenly, amateurish, leak-filled process that left most of the key cabinet appointments in limbo until they had to get bum-rushed through the vetting process as Inauguration Day loomed. Corners were cut, disastrously, as it turned out. Mahone's first attorney general nominee, a pompous federal judge from Minnesota, was revealed to have been employing a teenage Guatemalan houseboy for six years. The jurist was thrilled to be able to plead guilty to various tax violations and ship young Esteban back to Quetzaltenango before the hard-ass lifers in the Justice Department got the chance to ask too many questions. The furor over that blunder hadn't quite died down before Mahone's replacement nominee, an esteemed law professor and mother of four from Baltimore, famous for her many television appearances, was paraded before the media. The president's friends in the press gushed at this model of modern womanhood and wondered how she managed to do it all; virtually at the same time, his enemies wondered why she possessed seventy-two separate Prozac prescriptions from physicians in Maryland, Pennsylvania, Virginia, West Virginia, Washington, D.C., Ontario, and Grenada. She very quickly decided she needed to spend more time with her family, and Mahone elevated a bland deputy from the previous administration, just to stop the hemorrhaging.

Or, to be more precise, to stop the hemorrhaging from that particular wound. Jack bled elsewhere. There was the gay ambassador being married in Barbados confirmation thing, and the First Lady's clumsily phrased expression of sympathy around the crippled kids thing, and the ex-daughter-in-law's nude Web site thing, and the eighteen marine peacekeepers being killed in Malaysia while Jack was skiing in Sun Valley thing, and the Hurricane Fatima recovery debacle thing, and the NASDAQ collapse and the economy teetering on the verge of recession thing—zing, zing, zing, all in a row. The president of Fox News busted his overtime budget for the year in just over six months because he had to put on so many extra people in order to maintain the network's flow of fair and balanced outrage. But it wasn't just Fox that didn't think Jack was up to the job, and it wasn't just Godwin. The tone of the editorials in the *New York Times* and the *Boston Globe* and even the home state *New Orleans Times-Picayune,* which had begun at apologetic, had evolved into dismayed, and had lately turned south into exasperated. There were thumb-sucker pieces in the opinion mags about the decline of executive power and features in the conservative mags about Herman Vanick and the rise of congressional authority, and there were murmurs among Washington's permanent plutocracy that Jack was simply unlucky. The unspoken question behind such comments, of course, was how long could an unlucky man be left in charge before his unluckiness sickened them all.

Godwin kept applauding as he watched Jack effervescently run the gauntlet of cabinet cheerleaders, reach the podium, and bound up the steps. Godwin extended his hand, but Jack reached past his vice president and grabbed the Speaker's outstretched arm. Vanick's name recognition was lower than Mahone's, of course, but his favorability ratings were higher, and Jack wanted the cameras to have a good long look at the president having a warm, smiling, bipartisan clutch with the Speaker, the better to make it look like Herm's fault when the president's legislative program hit the shit can on Capitol Hill.

"Hey there, Herm, how they hangin'?" Jack fairly bellowed, loud enough that Godwin was afraid the whole room would hear. "Think you'll stand up and applaud for anything I say tonight?"

"My guess is you'll say something I agree with, Mr. President," replied Herm, his professional bonhomie in perfect form.

"One thing I'll bet you'll agree with is that I probably shouldn't have had those chiles rellenos before a big event like this. Man, I got gas something awful!" At that, Jack snapped off a fart. "You fellows will have to forgive me if I have to let a few go up here. Better out than in."

"No problem, Mr. President, I've been there myself," Vanick replied, but Jack was already reaching for Godwin's hand.

"Hey there, Godwin."

"Good evening, Mr. President." Godwin loathed the man, but he knew the rules: polite at all times, deferential in public.

"Chet went over everything with you, right? When to applaud, when to lead a standing ovation—"

"Yes, Mr. President."

"And how to look. You have to look confident."

"I will."

"And proud."

"Yes, sir."

"Very proud and very confident."

"Yes, Chet and I went over this."

"And interested! For fuck's sake, look interested. No yawning in the background."

"Yes, Mr. President."

"Oh, and one more thing—" Mahone motioned Godwin closer, and Godwin leaned way over so that their heads nearly touched. On TV, commentators were remarking on this as a sign of the close collaboration that the two men enjoyed. "Godwin," Jack was asking, "are you coming back to the residence after?"

"After the speech?" The question stunned Godwin. Mahone tended to reserve such invitations for his closest cronies, a small category of humanity to which Godwin neither belonged nor aspired.

"Well, I hadn't planned on it, sir. I don't think I was actually invited."

"I guess I'm going to have to make a point of speaking to somebody about that. In fact, I'll kick Chet's ass. Because it would mean a lot to me if you came."

"Really?"

"Yes, really." A wide, warm smile lit Jack's face. "Isn't this the Mahone-Pope administration?"

"Yes, sir."

"Well, let's act like it."

"Yes, sir. And thank you, sir. I'll be there." How weird, Godwin thought.

"All righty. Now, could you do me a favor?"

"Certainly, sir."

"A friend of mine came in from out of town unexpectedly— you see her? Up in the gallery? About four or five rows behind the First Lady? And over—to the right?"

The two men looked into the gallery. The plump, extravagantly coiffed First Lady smiled sweetly and waved, and the men waved back. And indeed, over and to the right, Godwin could see a heavy-lidded blonde whom he took to be the president's out-of-town pal.

She had two large Tupperware bowl–shaped mounds of flesh prominently emerging from the surprisingly low-for-the-occasion neckline of what seemed to be a rather clingy dress, and she was using the long red fingernail on her left pinkie to daub at her mascara.

"The lovely blonde, Mr. President?"

"That's her. You didn't bring a date to this thing, did you?"

"To the State of the Union address?"

"Why the hell not? I know you like women. And it's cheaper than the movies."

"Well, be that as it may, I brought no date."

"So there wouldn't be any problem if we kind of said she was your date when we went back to the residence, would there?"

"None."

"And that's all you have to do. Bring her by, and then you can bug out if you want. Or stay if you want. Whatever."

And with a wave of his hand, Jack turned and at last faced the microphones and TelePrompTers and the business at hand—namely, attempting to right his already perilously off-course administration, leaving Godwin to settle into his seat and, behind a good soldierly facade, slip into a sulk worthy of Achilles. Christ, he thought, after all I've done, after all I've accomplished, it's been bad enough being stuck in an invisible, empty job like vice president. Now on top of that, I'm the president's beard to boot. I'm an idiot for being here, an idiot, an idiot, an idiot. And I have no one to blame for me being here but myself.

NO ONE WOULD ever have predicted that Godwin Pope would someday become vice president. His earliest progenitors on these shores had been flinty, suspicious Yankees who possessed a certain ingenuity and clever heads for business. As their contemporaries vied fang and claw to build and operate the best wool and cotton mills in New England by conniving to run one another out of business, the Popes were happy to sit back and supply them all with pins and needles. At one point, the family controlled 87 percent of the pin and needle market in North America, and still Great-Great-Grandfather Obediah undercut incipient competitors as ruthlessly as a Rockefeller. Over the years, the family fortune rose and fell, depending on whether it was one of the periods when the heirs boldly and successfully led National Metal Fasteners, Inc. into paper clips or staples, or whether it was one of the periods when the heirs—different heirs, of course, wastrel heirs—threw chunks of the family fortune at a promoter of commercial seaweed farming, or a maharishi from Philadelphia who preached the Tao of free love, or one of about a hundred dealers of fine cocaine.

By the time Godwin enrolled in Princeton, National Metal Fasteners, Inc. was owned by a mid-level Japanese copier company, and the family's riches had dwindled to the minimal point where Godwin still had enough money in the bank to be able to choose between one family tradition or the other. Godwin had begun sizing up the cocaine dealers when fate interceded and assigned him Tom Ralston as his freshman-year roommate. Ralston was a precocious fourteen years old, didn't much like to wash, paused in the middle of conversations to pick his nose, and thought everyone else was stupider than he was. Which was largely true, and in the case of mathematics, incontestably correct. Tom Ralston could solve foot-long algorithms in his head in seconds. And Godwin, who even at that early age had an alpha cool, who in his first week at school walked onto the varsity tennis team and talked three freshman girls into bed, for some reason between pity and affection, adopted the smelly, brilliant runt. He bought Tom clothes. He took him to parties. He got Tom laid. It may well have been considered the first purely altruistic act of Godwin's life, if only Godwin himself hadn't been so terribly, desperately alone. His mother, tragically claimed by cancer, died before he was old enough to form an independent memory of her face. He and his father, the difficult, severe, mocking Chesbro Pope, were never close, and all possibility of a gradual rapprochement evaporated on New Year's Eve in Godwin's senior year in prep school, when Chesbro perished in a private plane crash in the Pyrenees, taking with him the bitterness with which his many setbacks had soured his life. Also lost was his much younger second wife, Minerva, the chic, vivacious, probably alcoholic art dealer, whose attraction to his father Godwin could never fathom, and on whom Godwin carried a total crush.

Halfway through Godwin's last year at Princeton, the relationship with Ralston paid off with more than an emotional reward. With breathtaking ease, Tom had graduated two semesters early and gone to work for IBM in Palo Alto, where Godwin visited him over spring break. They were both complaining. Godwin had been accepted to half a dozen law schools, none of which he had any interest in attending. And Tom found IBM distressingly boring. "They're so fucking slow!" Tom screamed. "You can't get approval for anything without fourteen people signing off!"

"Approval for what?" Godwin asked.

"To do stuff," Tom told him.

"Like?"

"Like, to write programs."

"Television programs?"

"No, software. This personal computer thing is going to take off. Any moron can see that. People are going to buy these fucking things. Ordinary people. My mother's going to have a box in her living room that'll have more computing power than was on board *Apollo Eleven*! People are going to want to use them."

"What the fuck for?"

"To do stuff—their taxes, to play games, to run small businesses, I don't know. People will think of things. But to do any of that, they need programs."

"What makes you think you can write programs?" Godwin asked.

"They're just algorithms," Tom said, and showed him: there

were algorithms for an address book, and algorithms for an appointments calendar. There were dozens, dozens of algorithms that yielded pages of code that caused the computer to do things.

"What do you want to do with these?" Godwin asked.

"Sell 'em. Look, it's like fucking stereos. Most guys out here want to build stereos. Better woofers. Better tweeters. Bigger speakers. But people don't buy stereos to own stereos. They buy stereos to hear music. Well, that's where I come in. I want to be the Mick Jagger of the computer industry."

At that point, Godwin made up his mind to invest what was left of his share of the Pope family fortune in Tom Ralston's ability to solve equations, and his desire to do so like a Rolling Stone. He never returned to Princeton. He and Tom formed Zephyr, Inc., and even after the school awarded him an honorary doctorate in 1996 for endowing a computer sciences research center, which he did in Tom's name, Godwin's college transcript continued to show an incomplete for his senior year.

They set up shop in a strip mall in Mountain View. It was a brilliant partnership. Tom, with his technical virtuosity and head for product, designed the programs; Godwin, with his taste for competition, ran the business. He proved surprisingly adept at charming partners, at paying suppliers a few pennies less per unit and wheedling buyers into paying a few pennies more, and at working small concessions into deals that later paid off lavishly when new products or new markets were developed. Moreover, he showed real aptitude playing the cutthroat: lopping off the deadwood, terminating the threatening, abandoning at the last minute beloved suitors for arms that held more profits.

Seventeen years after that spring break conversation, Zephyr was swallowed whole by the Microsoft Corporation, leaving Godwin and Tom each worth $1.63 billion. Tom bought the Washington Redskins, and under his whiny, demanding, infantile, free-spending ownership, the team won two Super Bowls. Godwin wasn't so easily entertained. For decades he had been the public face of the company, and he had come to enjoy being quoted and cited and pictured and courted in all of the power centers of the globe. Suddenly, he discovered that he had nothing to do. Chesbro Pope, who surely would have been forced to hold his tongue during the years of his son's stratospheric success, certainly would have found a way to fling a zinger or two. "Nothing to do today, big shot? Maybe you should mow the lawn."

Tom suggested he start a venture-capital firm, where he could use what he had learned in the Valley to get in on the ground floor of the next big things. Nah. Where was the pleasure of getting in on the ground floor of the handheld computer market when you'd been in on the ground floor of the whole goddamn digital age? The thought of working bored him. Of course, so did leisure. He did some adventure traveling, scaling the sacred summits of Bhutan and hiking the Galápagos and riding horseback in Patagonia. It was all right. He also took flying lessons, which he liked—loved really, but it's not like one can build a life on flying around in an airplane until you reach a living postcard. It's true that he remained interested in women, or at least in having sex with them, but the fact that when in their company he seemed distant and mildly cranky until it was time to hump prompted the most desirable women to pursue other, more attentive high-tech millionaires. This irritated aimlessness lasted until the night he allowed Ralston to drag him along to a dinner party thrown by Shohreh Pashvalavoo, the voluptuous raven-haired political pundit. A glamorous Iranian emigrant who had parlayed her beauty into three strategically well-placed marriages and three highly remunerative divorces, Shohreh took a particular interest in Godwin, and to the neglect of her other guests, she spent the evening hanging on his every word. Later that night, straddling him in her bed, dangling her perfumed breasts in his face, she asked if he would mind answering a question. He expected she had something freaky in mind.

"No, of course not."

"Why are you wasting your life?"

Needless to say, he was caught off guard. "That's hardly the sort of question guaranteed to bring this evening to a happy climax," Godwin replied. He tried to keep his exasperation to himself, but wasn't entirely successful.

"Ah, you do mind. Well don't worry, darling, I promise you that you'll be quite tumescent again when we need you to be. But please, answer the question."

Her directness and her curiosity disarmed him. After some thought, he told her that he didn't know why he was so aimless. Had he been worn out by running the business? Did he feel unmanned when they cashed out? Lying on her satin sheets, he questioned himself for a while, and might have gone on for hours, exploring his innermost feeling with this dark-eyed beauty, had she not surprised him again.

"Cut the bullshit," Shohreh abruptly said. "Whatever reasons you come up with, they're all bullshit. You are rich, healthy, tremendously intelligent, enormously sophisticated, at the peak of your powers in the prime of your life, and beholden to no one. You should share your gifts. You should run for public office. Every day the world is at a crossroads. I can think of no one I trust more to determine in which direction we should go."

Whether it was what she said or where she had then put her mouth, either way he felt a dam burst of motivation. Hell yes, he thought, she's right. I could make a difference.

Eight brisk, busy, free-spending months later, Godwin got himself elected to the Senate. Four years after that, long after Shohreh left Washington and hied off with her lesbian lover to operate a sandal and candle shop in Northhampton, Massachusetts, Godwin glumly concluded that she was wrong. He was making no difference whatsoever.

That's when he decided to run for president.

At first he thought it was the most brilliant decision he had ever made, and he floated on an ebullience the likes of which he had never experienced. Sex, skiing, attaining business success beyond his father's wildest dreams, issuing an IPO that left him richer than all his Pope forebears put together—none of that quite matched the feeling of having the whole country focused on him. He found that he liked campaigning, liked getting up in front of crowds and spouting off. What surprised him was that they listened. He refused to talk about flag burning or creationism or homosexual marriages, issues he disdainfully described as twentieth-century concerns. "Why are we fighting over the scraps of these old issues?" he'd say in his stump speech. "Who cares? We are literally mere years away from a pill that will double your memory, from microrobots that will be fit into your arteries and clean up your bloodstream and lengthen your life span, from getting an implant behind your ear that will enable you to get E-mails in your head. We are in the midst of unbelievable developments in genetic engineering, robotics, nanotechnology, which will change our lives as thoroughly as the invention of the car and the lightbulb and the airplane did. Let's stop tearing ourselves apart over the leftover questions of a bygone age. Let's move on."

Let's move on, he said, and establish a health-insure program that holds down the cost of insurance and relieves business of the cost of providing it, which would instantly make American products more competitive. Wait a minute, his rivals balked, what about the costs? Let's move on, Godwin said. Can't we figure out a way to pay for education so that a young person doesn't graduate from college with a $100,000 debt? Can't we help families by increasing the tax credit for children? Promises, promises, his opponents chided. Tomorrow is right around the corner, Godwin replied. Ask yourself if you'll be ready. Or will you be unpleasantly surprised?

Godwin's challenge caught something in the zeitgeist. Almost overnight, his campaign became a vehicle for a whole range of dissatisfactions with the incumbent administration. All of a sudden, he became something larger than life, a champion, a man on horseback, the great hope, an independent insurgent who could reject the party, redeem it, ride at its head to victory in November. He took on the look of something new and interesting, and people responded. Donors gave him money, volunteers clogged his storefronts, bloggers drooled, surfers jammed his sites, and the news networks and the newspapers assigned correspondents. Once he took the lead in the preprimary polls in New Hampshire, the nabobs of the media came to him, tugging their forelocks, chuckling at his quips, solemnly digesting his views on the great issues of the day. They loved that he was different, that he had been a successful businessman, that he was a bachelor known to have dated some of the world's most desirable women, and that he had new ideas. In short order, basking in his celebrity and buoyed by a lavish media buy, Godwin won the Granite State primary, the Sunshine State primary, the Show Me State primary. Commentators began to proclaim his nomination inevitable, and it was barely Washington's Birthday! In his Silicon Valley period, he had had the experience, more than a few times, of appearing on the cover of a magazine, but now there were weeks when he was on the cover of six, eight, ten of them at once, and newspaper front pages, too, and it was intoxicating. He found himself having to divert his gaze to keep from staring at newsstands in airports, where images of his face stretched wall to wall, limited only by displays of Grisham novels on one end and the start of the Sun Chips rack on the other.

Poor Godwin. He didn't quite realize it, but he was in the Build 'Em Up phase of the American media's interest in a subject. The next phase, the Tear 'Em Down phase, would follow, as inevitably as night after day.

It began on the stage of an auditorium of Towson State College, at the end of a perfectly routine debate a week before the Maryland primary. On the stage were Godwin, Jack Mahone, and a couple of insubstantial small state pretenders. None of them had made any news in the discussion, which certainly worked to Godwin's advantage. No news, no switches in momentum, no more time on the clock for Mahone, no way to stop Godwin's nomination, no way for Mahone to keep raising money, no way for him to prevent Godwin from winning Maryland and rendering the rest of the primaries moot. Asked for closing remarks, Godwin, with professional polish, pushed through his final remarks to his usual vigorous finish.

"And that's how I plan to conduct my presidency," he said stoutheartedly, "with an open heart, a determined will, and one eye firmly planted on the horizon." The applause was on cue, and just as hearty as expected.

Had the pattern of the previous four debates been followed, Jack Mahone would have then begun detailing the lessons of hard work and honesty and community he had learned during the summers he spent working on the deck of his daddy's sunbaked shrimp boat on Lake Pontchartrain. Instead, new words spilled out of Jack's mouth, surprising the audience, surprising the media, surprising Godwin so much that seconds passed before he realized that Jack was actually speaking to him.

"Well, all I can say is, that sure sounds pretty. But gosh, almost everything Godwin Pope says sounds pretty. 'Let's move on,' he says. Okay, sure, we all want to move on. But first I have one question: How come there ain't any almonds in my chocolate bar?"

The audience roared with laughter. Even Godwin's supporters roared with laughter. Even Godwin's highly paid handlers roared with laughter.

"Can you tell me that?" Jack insisted, extending his open palms toward Godwin in an invitation to respond. "How come there's no almonds in my chocolate bar?"

Godwin had spent hours preparing for every gambit he could imagine Jack trying to pull, but he had no idea what Jack was talking about, and his ignorance terrified him. A vague, pregnant "Uuum" escaped his lips.

"How come?" Jack sarcastically demanded. He sensed Godwin's confusion, and realized that there was a chance panic was merely a prod away. "How come, Senator? How come there ain't no almonds in that chocolate bar you're trying to hand these good people? Yeah, I know why." Jack later said it was like when he played quarterback in high school in the big Thanksgiving Day game against the Renegades of Our Lady of Perpetual Peace, and the coach called for a sneak; he hit the line hoping to get a yard and a safe landing, but following a bing and a bang and a bump he was still on his feet, and the next thing he knew, he was facing eighty-five yards of green grass and a wide-open path to the end zone.

Minutes later the debate would end, and mere seconds after that Godwin would learn what Jack was talking about, why the audience was laughing, why Jack lingered through one postdebate interview after another wearing a shit-eating, victorious grin. He was talking about a Hershey's commercial, a fucking candy bar ad in which the cutest four-year-old girl in North America stands on tiptoe and peers above a candy counter and asks a vinegary-looking proprietor, "How come there's no almonds in my chocolate bar?" In the days that followed, Godwin would see the ad maybe five hundred times, would see the girl's picture, would see her in his dreams. But at the moment, Godwin had never seen the commercial, and the secret of her identity, let alone of her existence, might as well have been buried in a milk can under a rock in Tierra del Fuego.

"What are you saying, sir?" Godwin had finally sputtered. "I want to talk about the issues. Why do you want to talk about nuts?"

And the audience roared anew.

"The Chocolate Bar Debate," as it was swiftly dubbed in political lore, returned easily to his mind; indeed, others insisted on bringing it up long after Godwin had hoped to lay it to rest. But just like Ed Muskie after he cried or Howard Dean after he screamed, Godwin was a zombie candidate, bravely campaigning on despite having been instantly and irrevocably killed. "Didja see the debate last night?" Jay Leno asked. "Jack Mahone asked Godwin Pope how come his candy bar didn't have any almonds. Pope said it was because he was planning to ask Mr. Peanut to be his running mate."

Mahone's supporters showed up at every rally; Godwin couldn't get two words out before they began chanting "Where are the almonds? Where are the almonds?" Godwin tried to punch back. "I think my teacher-training program is a pretty big almond," he said on *Meet the Press*. "My investment tax credit for small businesses? You don't think that's an almond?" There was a lot voters liked about Godwin—no one doubted that he was smart—but deep in their heart of hearts they had always feared that anyone who had been born rich and who made himself richer just might not really know them. Now Jack had showed the voters that their fears were well founded, that, sure enough, Godwin Pope not only wasn't a guy who ever had to worry about how many almonds were in his chocolate bar but when he wasn't going to the opera and running around with rock stars and yachting in Barbuda and going to conferences about Third World development in Davos, Godwin Pope wasn't even a guy who ever watched television. In a single evening, with a single turn of a phrase, he had lost the One of Us Primary as well as the Laughingstock Primary, and he never won another.

"And that's why it's fundamental that we return America to its rightful place as a leader in international trade," Godwin suddenly heard Jack intoning. That's my cue, he thought, a frightened sweat breaking out at the realization that he had almost missed it. Godwin leaped to his feet and began applauding, just ahead of the Democratic senators and representatives on the floor, who did the same. I have to stop daydreaming, Godwin thought. It was very important for Godwin to look like he approved of Jack's plans to improve international trade, however half-assed and beholden to special interests they were. Godwin had actually run a company that engaged in international trade, as all of Jack's handlers would stress. Of course, it was important for Godwin to look especially approving of all of Jack's goals, as well as proud, as well as confident, all in equal measure. He did not want to hear through the grapevine or, God forbid, on a political talk show that the president thought Godwin was approving, proud, and confident about some things and more approving, proud, and confident about others.

Godwin passed the four months after the Maryland primary in an emotional netherworld. First there was the curious death-in-life experience he went through as his campaign desanguinated and died. There was so much to do when the wound first opened— more strategizing about how to get back on course, more activity to right the ship, more speeches, more appearances, more media, more frantic late-night phone calls for money, support, patience, more and more and more activity yielding less and less and less support. The energy faded, the crowds thinned, the money trickled off, and his aides moped, wept, bickered, argued, and quit. People kept leaving in tears. In those sudden dying days, as he lost primaries in New York and New Jersey and California and Illinois and Mahone amassed enough delegates to win, Godwin kept thinking about a spectacularly lurid book he had in high school, a large-size book chock-full of true stories about exotic tortures and picturesque dismemberments, all accompanied by gory full-page illustrations. It had an entire chapter on executions, including a passage on the French Revolution, which said that sometimes the blood that remained in the vessels of the head of a guillotined man would have enough oxygen to keep him functioning for as long as a minute after the blade had fallen, thirty or forty or fifty seconds where the Comte de Merde-Tête would look and blink and try to talk, and the cold-blooded crew who'd just chopped him would, out of some sense of late-manifesting decency, wait patiently for these last epiphanies to dissolve soundlessly before dumping him into a wheelbarrow and hauling him off to a ditch. In the last days of his campaign, Godwin knew exactly how he felt.

Of course, that was better than the following phase. Never in his life had he ever really lost at anything, never at anything he cared about, really. Godwin was surprised that there wasn't any kind of pain in this defeat, no real sense of personal denial or rejection. He resented the whole candy bar business, of course: losing an election because of such a bogus stunt—what was fair about that, what was sensible? But in truth, the lack of fairness, the utter bogusness, the lowness of the crude bumpkin who had pulled it, the cupidity of the media who had latched onto it, the stupidity of the voters who had bought it—all these thoughts were the analgesics, the tiny capsules of psychological ibuprofen, that kept Godwin from feeling his pain.

They proved powerless when eventually he entered the next phase, the pity phase. He found himself moving through a hallway or an airport or at a dinner party, and people kept coming up to him, people of every stripe, saying how sorry they were, kept telling him to cheer up, kept asking him if they could get him anything, talking to him like he'd been diagnosed with a malignant brain tumor. Their kindness angered him; he felt insulted. Godwin thought himself as a man who would have become president of the United States if not for a goofy underhanded joke. He was not a man who was small or broken or whipped, and it galled him to realize that thousands and thousands of people—pathetically ordinary people, people who'd never tried for anything, let alone accomplished it—now regarded him as a loser who might want, and surely deserved, their pity.

But at least they spoke to him. Most of the rest of the big parade, the presidential campaign parade of which he was once the grand marshal, had now moved on, his role usurped. It paused only occasionally to see how the ex-candidate was doing.

The ex-candidate.

God, how that annoyed Godwin. The ex-candidate, the ex–Silicon Valley tyro, the ex–important person. Always a man fast to scorn the moaners and whiners who forever lined the drainage ditches along the highways of his life, Godwin was now horrified to find himself dumped in their midst, and often speaking their excuse-studded lingo. The realization disgusted him, and he began to think of doing something sharp and decisive to break the mood, something cleansing. The thought of spending the summer looking at the steaming volcanoes and leggy blondes of Iceland was beginning to appeal to him, until he got a call from Tavis Whouley, the chipmunk-faced chairman of his party.

"Y'all will be coming to Miami, right?"

"To watch the coronation of Jack Mahone? No thanks. He'll manage fine without me."

"Y'all do need to come to Miami, Godwin. All the losing candidates are, and all of y'all are gonna get seven to ten minutes of prime time—I'm sure it would be more ten than seven in your case. I'm sure I can promise you ten to talk about anything you want in regards to how bad those Republican bastards are and why we need to elect Jack Mahone."

"No doubt you think that's an unrejectable offer, Tavis, and I thank you. But you know more people are apt to be watching bird documentaries on one of those nature channels than a tableau of also-rans."

"Now Godwin, that's precisely the kind of attitude we're trying to avoid. Now let me tell ya—y'all have been a pretty good sport up to this point about your recent disappointments, and surely that's no easy thing. But y'all are gonna have to do this one last duty, because the money-grubbing networks have given me a shitty four hours over three nights to produce our party's big infomercial, and I'll be goddamned if I'm going to let y'all do anything that's going to let them hair-sprayed pretty-boy anchors spend even a minute of that time wondering why y'all are off somewhere moping. Look, Godwin, y'all are young. Couple years, you might think it's better to have friends helping everybody forget that unfortunate candy bar incident than to have enemies who keep bringing it up, bringing it up, bringing it up every goddamn minute of the day. Do y'all get my drift?"

So Godwin went to Miami and was soon surprised to find that he was enjoying himself. The delegates were friendly and the conch was good, and Godwin spent much of his first night there salsa-dancing with an attractive state senator from Del Ray Beach named Joan or Joanne—Juanita!—a lovely woman, although he was a bit disappointed when he discovered that her breasts, which cantilevered so captivatingly above her belly in her silver cocktail dress, flapped like beagle ears as she flip-flopped around his bed. She sounded like a beagle, too. Still, it was as fine an evening as he could have expected, and he was just about to turn out the lights, when he got a phone call from Chet Wetzel, the manager of the Mahone campaign.

"Senator, please forgive my nosiness, but are you alone?"

"Yes."

"Governor Mahone was wondering if it might be convenient for you to see him."

"I guess I don't have too much planned tomorrow."

"The Governor was hoping you could see him now."

It was after twelve, and Godwin was about to gripe about the hour, when it dawned on him that there was something in the urgent understatement of Chet's voice that betrayed the very, very heartfelt hope that Godwin would agree.

"I'll just get dressed. I'm sure a cab could get me to your hotel in about fifteen minutes."

"We've taken the liberty of arranging a car for you, Senator. A Lincoln Navigator. It's on the third level of the garage under your hotel. The driver will blink his lights twice when he sees you coming. And Senator, we'd be grateful if you made sure nobody followed you out."

Godwin's driver drove in silence for ten minutes, jumping on and off the freeway and then back on again the other way, crosshatching the nearly deserted downtown streets, actually cutting, somewhat to Godwin's amusement, the wrong way down a dark alley, all to thwart pursuers who gave no indication of existing. The car eventually came to rest on the top floor of the parking garage of an empty mall, next to another Navigator parked under a big neon

T.G.I. Friday's sign. The driver jerked his head toward the other vehicle, and Godwin got out and got in, careful not to hit the closely parked car with his door.

"Hello, Godwin."

"Jack."

"Nice of you to come. How are you enjoying the convention?"

"Pleasant. Tending toward boring."

"Yeah?" Jack said in a tone of genuine concern. "Have you been over to South Beach? Those thongs, man. I tell ya, it's like wall-to-wall ass. I'd give this all up in a minute to be a cabana boy over there."

"Really? I don't think it's too late."

Jack's lip curled momentarily, and then he laughed. "Hah! Good one. You're a funny guy, Godwin. You should let that funny side out more."

Godwin didn't know if that constituted a compliment, but it was lame if it was and condescending if it wasn't, and he felt himself growing stony, the way he always did in Jack's presence. A small silence blossomed and began to grow uncomfortable, until Jack plunged in.

"Do you know why you're here?"

"No."

"You really have no idea why you're here."

"No!"

Godwin could see Jack pondering the likelihood of that being true. "Whatever," he said with a shrug. "You've seen the polls, haven't you?"

"Yes," Godwin said. "You're behind."

"Yeah, I'm behind. Worse, I'm perfectly positioned to get further behind. None of the metrics are working for me. Right track, wrong track, registration trends, what the public sees as my relative strengths and weaknesses. The money's getting iffy."

"Well, I hate to be the one to break it to you, Jack, but I never thought you could win this election."

"See, but I can. I can. I need to give the voters a new reason to look at me. If they could see me fresh for a minute, then I'd have a chance. And there's just one way I can do that—by picking a good running mate. And in all our surveys, there's only one name that unites the party, that surprises people, that gives me some momentum."

Godwin was thunderstruck. "You cannot be serious. Do you remember the primaries? I do. I remember them as a time when I was humiliated by a man I don't like very much."

"You don't like me?" Jack's face clouded over. "I like you."

"Please."

"Okay, you don't like me. You don't like some of the things I do, you don't like some of the things I stand for, and you don't like some of the people who back me. You think we're all afraid of change, that instead of preparing for the future, we're afraid of it and are trying to resist it. And you think that's shortsighted and wrong."

"And dangerous."

"And dangerous. We sure don't want to forget dangerous. Well, you know what? Let me tell you something I've never been able to tell you before. You're right, Godwin. Your ideas are right. Your vision of the future is right. And the things you want us to do are the things we sure as hell are going to have to do, because they're the right damn things to do. But not everybody gets that yet, see? Your Silicon Valley pals, your Ivy League pals, they get it. They understand why outsourcing the job of a tech-support worker in Wichita to some guy in a turban in Bangalore, India, is a smart, competitive move, not just for the guy in India but for the guy in Wichita, because with a little training, he can get into a new field that has a bigger upside. I see that. But the guy in Wichita don't see it, and his wife don't see it. They look at the mortgage bill, and they look at the retraining program, and they wonder if she's gonna have to get a job to make ends meet until he's finished, and they wonder who's going to hire him, and if they're going to have to move, and who's going to watch the baby if he's in a program and she's at work, and who's going to take care of his mother when they relocate a thousand miles away. And when you, with all your wealth, stand there and try to convince them that it's for the best, they don't like you for saying it. And you find that hurtful, don't you? Because here you are, with a real idea for how we should prepare for a tomorrow, a real vision that's only going to end up giving them more freedom and more choices and more money in their pockets, and they won't listen. Why? Because all their lives smooth-talking men in fine suits have been telling them what's best for them, and whenever that happens, they feel like they end up holding the shitty end of the stick. And you're being blamed for those lies. And that hurts you, doesn't it?"

In his whole life, no one had ever spoken to Godwin this way. He felt unsettled. This man whom he had never considered as anything but a rank buffoon was talking like he really knew what Godwin thought and felt.

"They're like children, aren't they, Godwin? They don't know what's best for them or who's best for them. They can't recognize how a person's going to help them, because all they pay attention to is his look or his personality, the way he talks, his Armani suits, how low-cut are the ball gowns on the movie stars he dated. They've decided very unfairly that there was something about you that they just didn't like. That's why the almond trick worked. They already had it in their heads that for all your obvious abilities, and for all they wanted to be like you, there was just something about you they didn't like. All they needed me to do was give it a name."

"Right."

"Because they like me. That's the thing. They don't think I'm so brilliant and they're not sure if I'm all that trustworthy, but they like me. They may not always know it when they meet me, but sooner or later, they will like me."

Jack sat back and exhaled. There suddenly seemed to Godwin to be a certain authenticity about Mahone. For eight months on the campaign trail, Godwin had seen nothing but a carnival huckster, a salesman, someone who was always on, always selling, always trying to be bigger than he could possibly be. But now, here, on the roof of this garage, in this car, just the two of them, the real man was suddenly present.

"Sooner or later, everybody likes me. Can't really say the same about you, Godwin. Jesus knows, we admire you, we respect you, we're awestruck by your damn brilliance, and we envy your money, your looks, your education, the fine women you squire around. But you're out of reach, babe. We can no more like you than we can like, I dunno, a Greek god!"

"Oh come on, I'm no god!"

"Me, on the other hand—I'm as human as can be. People think they could have a beer with me at a barbecue, and talk about their dog or the new point guard at LSU. But soon they'd be talking about their kids, and their schools, and what they're hoping for, and everything they're afraid of. And because they feel that connection, I can take them wherever they need to go—and that can be to where you know they need to go. But I can't do that without you, Godwin. I need you to show me that path, and I need you to get me that fresh look. The people need to see me as a bigger man, and only you can help me do that."

His meaty paw swooped down and grabbed Godwin's hand. "Will you do it, Godwin? Will you help me build a better world?"

THE PASSAGE OF eighteen months had done nothing to dull Godwin's embarrassment. Mahone played me like a child, Godwin thought. He even made a show of having to mull over the few flaccid conditions Godwin, in the shock of the moment, had managed to come up with, as though giving a couple of Godwin's people White House jobs and assuring Godwin of a seat at every meeting were serious terms. The romance lasted through the election, which Jack, having correctly gauged that the gravitas Godwin's intellect would lend, plus the credibility Godwin's business success would convey, plus the sexiness Godwin's bachelorhood would sprinkle in would add up to a small but significant change in the election's momentum, went on to win by a handsome margin. But after the inauguration, Godwin was all but forgotten. There was a presidential commission on technology to which Jack could have appointed Godwin, but didn't, and legislation involving encryption and the Internet on which Jack could have sought Godwin's insights, but didn't, and so on. Soon Godwin concluded that his influence amounted to nothing, that he had become an unwanted man in an unnecessary job.

"Thank you, ladies and gentlemen," Godwin heard someone saying. "God bless you, and God bless America!"

That's the finish, thought Godwin, and leaped to his feet, applauding heartily. Below him he could see all the Shaniquas and Billy Bobs applauding, too, and Jack, smiling warmly, raising his hand in a final presidential benediction before the cameras cut away. Keep applauding, Godwin thought, keep applauding. Suddenly, Jack turned around and shouted above the applause, "Don't forget the blonde!"

God, he thought as his stomach clenched, this so sucks.

2

GODWIN HAD INSISTED that he have a seat at every meeting in the White House, and he grudgingly admired Mahone for never trying to wiggle out of the deal. At first, Godwin attended everything the president had scheduled, showing up sharp and on time, having studied up on the background material. He needn't have bothered. Jack's meetings were loose and free-wheeling, except when they were abrupt and severe, or angry and operatic. What they never were was anything but Jack's meetings, directed by Jack, starring Jack, and despite the very best efforts of Chet Wetzel and the other members of the staff to stage-manage the content, they were produced by Jack, as well. And what they never, ever were was on time. Such it was that after awhile, Godwin began to cut back his attendance at these confabs, and then again, and again. It was painful for him to sit there and listen to Jack yell, listen to Jack complain, listen to Jack tell dirty jokes, listen to Jack rant about the many conspiracies his enemies were weaving against him. The present meeting, the 7:30 A.M. scheduled, 8:15 A.M. convened meeting with Chet Wetzel, the White House chief of staff, and National Security Advisor Serge Broyard, a political scientist from the University of Chicago, whom Godwin found insufferably vain, concerned a deal to sell the Chinese some communications satellites. Godwin, who now basically went to meetings only to make sure that it could be truthfully said of him that he in fact went to meetings, picked this one because the issue seemed to be all but settled, thus suggesting that the meeting was likely to be short, to the point, and unlikely to provoke Jack into any egregious antics. As it turned out, the matter was not settled, and although Jack had so far behaved himself, his tone was growing increasingly surly.

"All I'm saying, Mr. President, is why rush?" Chet was saying.

"Because we announced the sale, goddammit!" Jack said.

"Well, let's simply unannounce it," said Broyard, in what Godwin perceived to be one of his attempts to sound delphic and wise.

"Oh what kind of shit is that?" snarled Jack.

"We'll just say we've made a prudent reexamination," said Chet.

"Sure, and hand the Speaker another PR victory. We'll look so lame."

There was no reason on earth any sitting president should be having trouble with something like this. Not that it would have been unanimous by any means. The members of the opposition in Congress—whichever party was in opposition—would object, if only for the pleasure of getting a few column inches on page A22. It was completely predictable that Herman Vanick and his claque would pipe up and begin arguing that the sale would weaken our national security because the Chinese would surely use the satellites to help target their long-range ballistic missiles. True, the Chinese were a bunch of bloody-minded schemers who had been patiently planning for the day when they would overtake us as the world's leading superpower. Everybody knew that. But if the United States of America stopped doing business with everybody in the world who hated us or who wanted to eat our lunch money or who had a few human rights blemishes on their dockets, we wouldn't be able to buy or sell with anyone. Besides, Godwin thought the threat was ridiculous. He'd been doing business with the Chinese for years. They didn't want to blow us up. They were all more interested in getting better cell phone reception, pirating our software, hacking the Internet. But whatever the Chinese thought they could accomplish, they weren't going to be able to do anything without these satellites. Godwin thought it was a good deal, a no-brainer.

"Mr. President, we don't literally have to reexamine anything," said Broyard, attempting to sound soothing. "We'll just say we will. And then after awhile, we'll say we reexamined it and still found nothing wrong, and we'll look more prudent than ever."

"We'll look like a bunch of pussies," barked Jack, and began rubbing his temples. It must have brought him some relief, because he kept it up for nearly a minute. Finally he looked at Chet. "And the Pentagon is positive there's no way these satellites can be converted to military purposes, right?"

"Absolutely sure," said Chet.

"There's no way," Jack insisted.

"Absolutely none," said Chet firmly.

"On the other hand," chirped Broyard, "every day some kid with a laptop and some alligator clips pulls off something nobody thought was possible."

"What the fuck is that supposed to mean?" roared Jack.

"Nothing, sir."

"Nothing, my ass. What's that mean?"

"All the departments at the CIA are fine with the deal—the China desk, technology, space. Only one analyst has written up a dissent."

"So?"

"He's smarter than the other people. He's younger, he's less experienced, but he's got more imagination."

"So he could be right."

"Exactly. Nobody thinks he's right, but he might be."

"Jesus H. Christ! Everybody wants to cover his ass. Okay, do this: put a hold on this deal until the CIA gives it a full A-OK. And once they do get their act together and give it a full A-OK, make sure Mr. Imagination's minority report never sees the light of day. Got it?"

You have to feel for Jack, thought Godwin. Here he is, trying to make a decision affecting the lives and safety of a billion people, it involves technical gobbledygook that you'd need a Ph.D. from Cal Tech to evaluate, and he's got as his national security advisor, Serge Broyard, a man who can't make a recommendation without thinking about how he's going to portray the meeting in his memoirs. As the angry Mahone strode toward the door, Godwin gave him a sympathetic look. Mahone stopped short.

"What?"

"Nothing, sir. Tough decision."

"Yeah, tough decision. And you didn't say a fucking word. You know these people. You know this arena. What do you think?"

Godwin hadn't expected this. He paused. What the hell did Jack expect of him? "Mr. President, I think . . ." He hesitated. Take the middle ground, he decided. "I think all these things come down to leadership. Whatever you decide, just be strong. Show your strength."

"Show my strength?" Jack laughed. "Show my strength? Godwin, I know you despise me, but do you have to mock me? Fuck you, you arrogant ass-wipe."

And with that, he departed. Broyard hustled out as well, his eyes everting Godwin's. That left it to Chet to make amends.

"He doesn't mean it, sir," said Chet. "He just gets stressed."

Godwin, smarting from the slap, looked at Chet with a kindly half smile. "No, he hates me, Chet. He really, really hates me."

3

"OF COURSE he hates you!"

With a dark and suspicious view of life that usually prompted him to think the worst of people, Tom Ralston wasn't the best person to try to nudge Godwin out of the brooding funk into which he'd fallen after the meeting. It wasn't that his judgment was always tainted; after all, it was Tom alone among Godwin's associates who warned him against accepting the vice presidency, not for any political consequences but because he thought Mahone smelled like a rat. On the other hand, it was Tom alone among Godwin's associates who retained bodyguards and who had taken Krav Maga combat training and driver evasion courses and who hid an illegally modified assault rifle under his bed, which he used to keep the great lawn in front of his Virginia estate clear of squirrels, rabbits, and other furry living creatures.

"Look at him, then look at you—it's obvious why he hates you."

Like nearly all people except those in middle school, Godwin had a sufficiently high regard for his attributes and sufficiently developed justifications for whatever he chose to do with them that he seldom realized others held what would generally be called "a balanced view" of how others perceived him.

"What's obvious?" Godwin asked.

"It's obvious you're handsome, rich, smart, and that he's not. Your very existence is a living reminder of his shortcomings. Plus, there's that way you look whenever you're around him."

"What way?"

"You know—like you can't stand being in the room with him."

Tom's bluntness was making things worse. First, Godwin had felt bad that he was in this position; then he felt bad that he had to keep pretending he wasn't in this position. Now he felt bad that his pretenses were so transparent.

"By the way," said Tom, "there's Marco McChesney." He pointed to a television monitor, on which a shiny-helmeted, brightly uniformed man-beast of a fullback was dragging four manifestly ineffectual Vikings down the gridiron. The monitor was one of twenty Tom had mounted against one of the floor-to-ceiling, wall-to-wall mahogany bookshelves that lined all four walls of his personal study in his mansion in Fauquier County, Virginia, not much more than a stone's throw from Mount Weather, inside whose massive subterranean Emergency Operations Center Godwin, as vice president, had to waste so much time. One of the screens—the one upon which Marco McChesney currently could be seen stampeding about, was dedicated to the NFL Channel, which was broadcasting a highlight show featuring this year's free agents. One was given to playing a constant loop of the first of the Redskins' two Super Bowl victories in Ralston's regime, and on its neighbor, the second. Ten of the monitors were dedicated to a satellite TV system that brought him all the games that were being played in the NFL, one was set so that he could video-conference with the Redskins' general manager, another with the coach, one to a set of video cameras arranged around the Redskins' practice field, and another to a set secreted in the team's locker room. Tom told Godwin the other screens weren't connected to anything, but Godwin didn't believe him; it was Godwin's experience that Tom was always connected.

"He's a big 'un, all right," Godwin said, mostly by way of being polite, even though it made him feel bad to placate Tom. Things were better back in the days when he didn't bother. "Did you brush your teeth today?" was the sort of thing Godwin never used to hesitate to say to Tom. "It's like you've got Spanish moss hanging off your gums." He'd bugged Tom like that in snack bars at Princeton, and he'd bugged Tom like that while they sat in the waiting room at Kleiner, Perkins, Caufield and Byers in Menlo Park just before they requested their first round of financing. They had been like brothers—like Godwin imagined brothers to be—fighting, bitching, plotting their deals, hacking into the computers at Pizza Hut, fantasizing about how to spend their fortunes, actually spending their fortunes. They had grown up together, made mistakes together, learned how to be powerful together. Godwin was terribly proud of what Tom had accomplished with the Redskins (and Tom was even prouder of what Godwin had accomplished in running for office), but that success meant Godwin could no longer tell Tom when his breath stank or when his clothes didn't match or when he was letting one or another of his more pathological fascinations get the better of him. Which meant nobody could.

"So why don't you quit?" Tom asked. "Your resignation would hit him like a torpedo in his engine room. You're one of the few things propping Mahone up. You go—he goes."

"Ah, my resignation would be a two-day story. Then all the coverage would be all about my successor. Mahone would let himself be seen interviewing sterling role models from every racial and ethnic group in the country. He'd play the story out for weeks. I'd become the nut outside the gate throwing spitballs at the window."

"You could use it as a kickoff. Start mounting your challenge."

"For an election almost three years away?"

"Yeah. You'd have all that time to build an organization, and state your case against him."

Godwin tried to envision standing in South Dakota a year hence, trying to get people to listen to him harangue about Mahone. "It wouldn't work. Nobody likes a critic, even if everybody agrees with him. I'd just be blamed for bringing him down."

"We ought to be like the fucking British," said Tom. "If Parliament votes no confidence, out the prime minister goes."

"I guess the Founding Fathers thought we should live with our mistakes."

"Unless we wanted an impeachment."

"And we've had our impeachment for this hundred years. It got bad ratings, as I recall."

"They stank!"

"Plus, it's not really a very effective tool," said Godwin. "The Republicans used every underhanded trick in the deck, caught Clinton in a bald-faced lie, and still couldn't convict him of perjury. It's not enough to catch a president doing something wrong anymore. You can't even catch him doing something awful, like dereliction of duty or overstepping his constitutional powers or wiretapping people without a warrant or something. No, to impeach Mahone or anybody these days, you'd have to catch him doing something astonishingly bad, like selling out our national security or something."

"Or appearing to."

"What do you mean?"

"Or appearing to," Tom repeated emphatically, to no effect. Sighing, he elaborated. "Some things are just so bad that even their possibility is too terrible to consider. Like a child molester. You can get acquitted of that, but you ain't gonna be teaching any more gym classes. Look, whatever it takes, we've got to get rid of him and get you in there. The country needs you."

Godwin drained his drink. "Well, I'm afraid the country's going to have to wait. I don't see any magic trick that can make Mahone disappear."

"No, probably not. Look, it's getting late. Are you ready to meet Marco?"

"He's here already?"

"Yep. He's up taking a swim."

Godwin wasn't much of a football fan, but when Tom had asked him last year if he'd mind choppering over for lunch to meet the prospective free agents he was trying to sign, Godwin felt he could hardly say no. Not only because in many ways he owed so much of what he had become to Tom's native brilliance; Tom continued to be a unique and invaluable resource. During the presidential campaign, it was Tom who had trekked up and down Silicon Valley, wringing contributions out of tech execs. And in a city where the power elite treasured a chance to sit on the Supreme Court less than a chance to sit in the Redskins owner's luxury skybox, Godwin possessed an open invitation. Chatting politics and pigskins for an hour with some young behemoth seemed like a small price to pay for all Tom had done.

"Anything you want me to be sure to mention?" Godwin asked as they approached Ralston's indoor pool.

"Tell him you think he'll get fifteen carries a game and make All-Pro if he plays in Coach Klosterman's offense."

"Wouldn't a comment like that have more credibility coming from Coach Klosterman?"

"No, nobody believes anything he says. Everybody in the league thinks I'm going to fire Klosterman unless we have a great start. But you're not in the league. You're a politician."

"And that's why people believe me?"

"Yeah, if you're speaking to them privately. Everything you say privately carries a ton of weight. Like, you may not believe in God, but if you have a private audience with the Pope and he gives you his blessing, you don't say 'What the fuck good is that, you old witch doctor?' No—you feel blessed. Nobody wants to think 'I just had a private meeting with the vice president and all he did was piss in my shoes.' "

"Interesting point. Anything else?"

"Well, I wouldn't mention this part."

They had entered a small glass-enclosed sitting area overlooking the pool. Below them, in the shallow end, was Marco McChesney, the raging fullback Godwin had seen moments before draped in defenders. Now he was draped with three astonishingly attractive young women, an African American, a pale pink blonde, and the most drop-dead beautiful Asian woman Godwin had ever seen. All of them were naked.

"Not exactly the backstroke, is it?" asked Tom with a giggle. "Don't worry, it's one-way glass. They have no idea we're up here."

Godwin was hardly shocked. He'd been in business. Entertainment was just part of the process. "Is this the standard hospitality package you use to court free agents?"

"A nice fruit basket goes only so far. Hell, this goes only so far. These guys have been getting pussy thrown at them since high school. This is just keeping pace. I keep the black girl and the blonde on retainer. I haven't seen the Asian girl before."

Godwin couldn't take his eyes off her. She had a small birthmark by her mouth. It was unique, unmistakable. "She's really striking."

The ménage à quatre shifted positions. "What's that on his ass?"

"Tattoo."

"Of what? It looks like a lot of *m*'s or *w*'s."

"Fire," said Tom. "Tongues of fire. Hey, come here and let me show you something." He raised the cover of what had seemed to be a table, revealing a bank of monitors, on which Marco and the girls could be seen coupling from different angles.

"Oh please, don't," said Godwin.

"But it's so great! I've got six cameras! Underwater! Look at Marco's ass!"

Camera five afforded Godwin a view of Marco's massive buttocks, covered in what from this angle looked a whole lot more like tongues of fire. "Tom, old boy, I'm sure I'm violating some federal law just standing here."

"Naah," chided Tom. "Not according to my attorney. This is completely for the personal amusement of me and my guests. Oh look, he finished. Let's head over. He's very excited about meeting you. He wants to talk to you about funding youth programs. He wants to run for office when he retires."

As they left the little room, Godwin stole a glance behind him.

The Asian girl was sitting naked in a chair, her long black hair now wrapped in a towel. She was putting on lipstick. She paused, pursed her lips, touched the beauty mark with the long fingernail on her pinkie. Abruptly she looked up, toward the one-way mirror. Godwin quickly turned away and chased Ralston through the doorway.

4

THE RECEPTION AREA of the offices of *Newsbreak*'s Washington bureau looked pretty much the same to Maggie Newbold as it had when she left it behind her a decade ago: Confederate gray carpeting, dove gray walls, black leather and chrome furniture showing the marks of mid-career wear, walls decorated with covers of previous issues shouting out the great stories of the moment—gas crisis, Chernobyl, desert war, terrorist attacks—to which *Newsbreak* had attached itself like a small, loud bird to the back of a charging rhino. Maggie was twenty-six when she'd left these premises, a precocious star in these relatively staid precincts, moving on to become a foreign correspondent for the *Wall Street Journal.* Old Bryson Berger, the venerable managing editor, already ill with cancer, moved heaven and earth to try to keep her, but, truth be told, once she decided affection for the old bird wasn't enough to hold her back, he never had a chance. She wasn't interested. She found the newsweekly to be yesterday's medium. During Maggie's early years, she could already see that the newsweekly, once a source where bright and curious people could turn for news in an age before twenty-four-hour news channels and bloggers with BlackBerrys, had become at best a ratifier whose cover could most effectively be used to reassure people that the thing they'd been talking about all week was indeed important. It told her a lot that her bosses clapped and chortled whenever some iconic luminary kicked the bucket, and they could put out a special keepsake issue that would cause amateur collectors to buy extra copies and slip them into plastic and hoard them in their attics pure and unread. She didn't want to hitch her wagon to a place where people could be happy being unread. Even at her tender age, she knew she had the looks and talent she'd need to parlay a bigger shot. Now she was back, crawling back, really, and God, she hoped they'd offer her a job.

Maggie nervously picked some tiny lint pellets off the skirt of her Donna Karan suit. She had loved the suit when she bought it three years ago as part of her post-Pulitzer, postbook deal wardrobe splurge. Now she hated it, hated its boxiness and its pleats and how it clutched at the arm holes and was shiny in the rear, hated most of all that it was the best she had left. Not that it would have mattered to most of the men she'd have met while wearing it; they would have been far too focused on her still-wide blue eyes and duvet lips and generously curvy figure. Nor would it really matter to Linda Archer, the bureau chief she had to impress today, Linda being a woman who always dressed in corduroy jumpers or khaki slacks, as though she took her fashion cues from the perky teachers at her children's elementary school. But it mattered to Maggie. She fantasized about the day she could give it to Goodwill.

"Ms. Newbold," the receptionist said, "Ms. Archer will see you now."

They headed down the corridor toward the bureau chief's office. It was all the same—the same colors, the same covers on the wall, the same gauntlet of small offices out of which streamed the endless chatter of CNN or CNBC or one of the numerous other information channels. They passed her old space, now occupied by a pretty mocha-colored girl, first name on her nameplate Ayisha, last name *M* something—too long to grasp at a glance—young like Maggie had been, probably as precocious as Maggie had been. Might have been the same desk! Might have had the same Sweet 'N Low and Cremora packets in the drawer!

Linda's office was different—differentish anyway. Maggie's last chief, Bryson Berger, had been a nautical buff, and he kept a lot of sailing stuff, ships and sails and things, all over the desk and win-dowsills. Linda, a working mother who grieved at virtually never seeing her children during any of their waking hours between Wednesday morning and Saturday night, posted their drawings all over her walls and covered her desk with toys that had caught her kids' fancy, Cookie Monster figures that had been packed with Happy Meals, Harry Potter on his broom. Maggie thought the chil-dren's art was lousy, lousier than most kids' crap, tumbleweeds of angry scribbles and tableaux of stick spacemen ray-gunning stick aliens to death.

"Come in, Maggie, have a seat. Been back long?" Linda's greet-ing was spoken evenly, with a small smile, and Maggie knew that was about as bad a welcome as she could have feared. Linda was a bit senior to Maggie, in age and experience, and they had never been really close. But they had worked together for a couple years, had been colleagues, and in a list of potential greetings topped by a huggy "Hey Maggie, welcome back!", "Come in, Maggie, have a seat" was about as cool as it could get.

"Thank you, Linda. I've been back for a month or so. I have an apartment in Kalorama."

"Lovely," Linda said.

"I like what you've done with the space. I guess Sara took all of Bryson's seagoing paraphernalia home when he died."

"Yeah, Sara . . ." Linda's voice drifted into air, leaving no clue about what Bryson's widow had done or hadn't done or whether Linda even remembered who Sara was. But her mouth tightened, and she looked down at her lap and then right in Maggie's eyes.

Here it comes, Maggie thought.

"Loomis has asked me to take you aboard," said Linda. "He thinks you can still be an asset."

Maggie waited to see if Linda had something more to add, but Linda parked on that thought, and now Maggie knew it was her turn.

"I'm glad to hear that," she said. "I agree. It's only been four years since I won the Pulitzer. I'm sure I—"

"Let's not discuss the Pulitzer," said Linda, holding her hand flat like a traffic cop's. "Frankly, I think you're lucky the questions about you were never raised in public. From what I know, I'm not sure why it wasn't rescinded."

"No doubt it would have been, had there been any proof against me."

"Half the leaders in the Middle East kept your panties as a souvenir. If sleeping with a Western woman wouldn't have incited a Wahabbist rebellion, I think the proof would be there."

Maggie thought of unspooling her usually effective line about successful women and the tales that get spread about them by people jealous of their success, but she looked into the face of Linda Archer, a grindstone who had climbed through the ranks writing earnest and detailed articles about subcommittee reports on educational policy and national health insurance, and who now worked seventy hours a week and who, in return, was forty-one and gray and lined, with a remote husband and whiny children and a boss who was never, ever satisfied, and she doubted that Linda would sympathize. Instead, Maggie muttered, "It's just not true," certain that no empirical investigation would ever show that half the leaders in the Middle East, an exact 50 percent, had kept her panties as a souvenir. Hell, to a lot of those kinds of meetings in those years, Maggie hadn't even worn panties.

Had Linda Archer's ensuing silence lasted much longer, Maggie would have picked herself up and departed in a huff. But just as Maggie's huff was nearing a critical mass, Linda blinked.

"The thing is," she said, "I work for Loomis, and we have one rule here, and that's whatever Loomis wants, Loomis gets."

Hallelujah, thought Maggie. She had been banking on the Loomis card working for her. She knew he liked to surround himself with the people with whom he'd started out. He hated all the old-timers, Bryson Berger and all the others who had made the mistake of misreading his smug, cocksure, know-it-all attitude as evidence that he was doomed to fail, and he'd enjoyed mocking them as he clawed past them up the masthead, just as he'd later enjoyed mocking them when he let them go. But it did Loomis only so much good to be considered merely smarter than all who had gone before him; hell, how smart did you have to be to be smarter than they were? No, Maggie knew that it burnished Loomis's reputation all the more if he was regarded as the most special member of a whole special generation. That explained why he promoted the cohorts who had come up with him, surrounded himself with them, awarded them rank and title and pay. In truth, though Loomis may have been special, the rest were not, but he liked having his loyalists around to reassure him. Maggie wasn't going to be spending enough time with Loomis to wage a relentless campaign of flattery, but she knew she mattered to him in a different way. Loomis liked to think everything about him was special, and he enjoyed the idea that the pretty twenty-five-year-old reporter with whom he had spent a torrid weekend in Virginia Beach after they had closed the 1992 election issue had gone on to win the Pulitzer Prize. Maggie knew it did nothing for Loomis's ego if in his one great interoffice romance he had fucked a future disgraced has-been. No, he'd want her to be a star. She knew that when she asked, he'd say yes.

"But let me be plain," said Linda, "Loomis or not, if I think you're sleeping with your sources, you're out."

Having won the game, Maggie knew she needed to make Linda feel good about losing.

"I understand perfectly," said Maggie, dropping her head in a look of contrition. "What's my first assignment?"

"No assignments yet. I think you should just meet some people. Just get reacquainted. There's a new assistant secretary at Veterans Affairs. We got an interesting press release about a reorganization at the Federal Housing Administration. I've been meaning to have somebody talk to Godwin Pope."

She's burying me, Maggie thought, and despite her best efforts, something in her face must have betrayed what she thought of these ideas, because the lines around Linda's mouth tightened even more.

"One day sooner or later, Godwin Pope is going to want to get something off his chest," she said. "If you're lucky, maybe he'll get it off his chest to you."

Maggie quickly nodded her assent.

5

IN THE WEEKS THAT FOLLOWED, Maggie Newbold was the best little girl in class. She met, as instructed, the deputy secretary for Veterans Affairs, and came out with a couple of quotes that she gave to another writer to use in a story on government spending, and then turned her appointment with a housing administrator into a nice little sidebar to a business section story on mortgages. She made suggestions at meetings, shared phone numbers of sources, made the coffee in the morning and filled the dishwasher at night. Heading out late one Friday, her minimal contributions to the week's efforts all wrapped up, she found young Ayisha with the long last name—Mumenyori, as it turned out—on deadline with her very first cover story, weeping in the bathroom. "Come now, dear," she said firmly, "let's get this sorted out." Looking over her shoulder, perusing her first draft, Maggie gently coached the rookie through. "You've buried your lead, dear," she said quietly. "Move this paragraph up. Use this for your nut graph. Now, do you have a nice quote to stick in here, perhaps something from some alarmist on the Hill who thinks the administration's failure to act on this matter will cause the end of the world? Yes, that one will do nicely." She hung out sipping Snapple in the younger woman's office until Linda signed off on the piece with unexpected enthusiasm.

Monday morning, she ran into Linda on the elevator. When the bureau chief said, "That was a nice thing you did," it look Maggie a moment or two to understand what Linda meant. "Oh," Maggie said, dismissing the effort, "everybody needs a hand from time to time."

"The Maggie Newbold I used to know would never have done anything like that," said Linda, and Maggie was at first shocked by Linda's ability to take a compliment and turn it into a shot. She was about to remind Linda of a time back in the day when a furious Bryson Berger had handed her a California wildfires piece that a sobbing Linda had turned into hash. "Make some sense of this shit," he'd told Maggie. But as soon as Maggie had done so, as soon as she saw the admiration in Bryson's eyes and the coup she had scored, she pushed him into giving her the sole byline, leaving Linda no credit for a story that she had slaved on for two weeks. Maybe that was the difference Linda meant. Maybe because this time Maggie wouldn't have to think about clawing up the ladder or falling off the ladder or crawling back onto the ladder, maybe this time she could just be a good reporter, a member of the team.

That afternoon, she went to the White House to see the vice president.

"MS. NEWBOLD, how do you do? Please have a seat."

The name hadn't really jumped out at him when he saw it on his schedule, just one of a hundred bylines that managed to strike him as both vague and familiar at the same time. Surely there'd be nothing vague about it any longer. Washington was full of women who were said to be beautiful, but most of these women were just poised and glossy versions of nice-looking girls, all with shellacked hair cut ten years behind how ever women in Hollywood were styling theirs. But Maggie Newbold was genuinely striking. She led with a smile that was wide and bright and frequent. It seemed to Godwin to float on her face, and she rose up behind it. Not too tall, Godwin observed. Curvy. Nice legs. Patterned stockings, a nice professional way of whispering, Look at me. He wondered why she wasn't on television. Maybe she had an allergy to hair spray.

She reached into her purse and removed what appeared to be a fountain pen and laid it on the desk before her. "Do you mind if I record this? Strictly for my files."

"That's a recorder?"

"Yep. A friend in the Mossad turned me on to it. Voice-activated, crystal-clear, stores seventeen hours of conversation without missing a syllable. He says it would work through the hull of a destroyer. I never leave home without it."

"Nice. I'm glad you told me. So let's do this. You're at *Newsbreak* now, yes?"

"Yes, sir."

"And before that the *Journal.*"

"Yes, sir."

"I haven't seen your byline in awhile."

"Yeah, I took sort of a break. But I'm happy to be back at *Newsbreak.*" Let's move this along, she thought. I don't know what he thinks he knows about my past, but this is no place to discuss it.

"And so they've given you the vice presidential beat."

"Sort of," she said, "but not quite." He's making jokes with me, she thought. Flirting? she wondered.

"Planning a cover on me?"

"No, sir, not even an article, necessarily. It's just that my editor thinks you're an interesting man."

"Hah!" Godwin fairly boomed. His loudness startled her. "Your editor thinks? What a fine old reporter's evasion. Your editor thinks something. You yourself are reserving judgment."

"Something like that." He's definitely flirting. "But enough about me," she said. "How do you like your job?"

"My job? Very exciting. To be part of this administration? To be able to devote oneself to improving the lives of working families across America? Very exciting."

A big smile spread slowly over her face. "We're not on the record here, you know," she said, smiling and offering the tiniest of winks. "We're not even on background."

"So what does that mean—that I should start spouting controversial comments that would make you wish we were?"

I'm glad he's relaxed, she thought, but I wish he didn't find this so amusing. "Let me try it this way," she said. "Is this a job that's making the best use of Godwin Pope's talents and abilities?"

He didn't expect that one, she thought. Look at the way that jaunty smile left his face. Look at how his brow furrowed up. Seconds passed, the equivalent of a long, silent "Ummmmm."

"You have to realize," he finally said, "making use of Godwin Pope's talents is not what the job's about. It's a service job. And sometimes one serves by making the best use of one's talents. And sometimes one serves by—not."

All right, she thought, and smiled slyly. Try this. "Is Jack Mahone making the best use of his talents?" she asked.

A look of satisfaction captured Godwin's expression. He seemed very pleased with the question. "There's not a doubt in my mind that there's a very good chance that we're all going to look back and say, 'This was one of our greatest presidents.'"

Come on, now, she thought. Godwin Pope, you must think I'm an idiot if I'd swallow that one. "If what?"

" 'If what?' "

"Yes, sir. You said there's a very good chance that we're going to look back and say, you know, 'Put him on Mount Rushmore.' But what has to happen before we do that?"

"What do you mean, what has to happen?"

"What has to happen. He's not one of our greatest presidents now. What has to happen?"

"He just—he just has to be himself. Look, we may have had a bad inning or two, but it's a long game." Abruptly, she laughed at him, almost a snort. "What?" he said, exasperated.

"Sorry, Mr. Vice President. I never figured you as a sports cliché kind of guy. But let's go with that. Did you know that in most baseball games, the winning team scores more runs in one inning than the losing team scores during the whole game? It's true. If Jack Mahone's had a couple bad innings, his game might be all over."

Suddenly, Godwin's face clouded over. Uh-oh, she thought, he's not having fun anymore. "It's really all about leadership, isn't it?" he said firmly. "The administration's been buffeted a bit, that's true. That's when you have to stand up and seize control. You just have to act decisively and seize control."

"Have you told this to the president?"

"I have one rule: my advice to the president is always confidential."

The usual dodge, she thought—pretty disappointing. "But if I may extrapolate a bit—would it be fair to say that Godwin Pope wouldn't have pulled back that satellite deal for further study?"

"Just because of a little congressional criticism? No comment."

"I don't suppose we could go on the record with that 'No comment,' could we?" She flicked her tongue to the inside of her cheek.

"Sorry, Ms. Newbold," he said, and wagged his finger at her. "And now I have to go."

"Just one more for the gossip pages," she said. "How's being the Bachelor VP working out?"

"Honestly? You'll never hear a bachelor say that he isn't having fun, but as you get older, you start thinking about having a relationship, and frankly, this isn't the kind of job where you have a social life conducive to that."

"And here I thought you were going to say that it was just great."

He escorted her to the reception area, and they shook hands. "Are you over here often?" he asked. "I wouldn't mind if you dropped in. Or if you have some question in the evening . . . You know, they've put me up over in the old Naval Observatory."

"Even though you still have the town house in Georgetown you bought when you were in the Senate. Yes, I know about that." She shook his hand. "Thanks for talking to me," she said. Let's flirt again some time.

Godwin watched the slow roll of her hips through a glass-paneled doorway as she walked away. He couldn't believe how his heart was pounding. Geez, she was something. The number of interviews to which he'd been subjected was beyond remembering, and they were all pretty much the same, all starting off with an attitude somewhere between the chilly hostility of a dental appointment and the adversarial competitiveness of a wrestling match. At best, you ended up having a reasonably enjoyable conversation with the reporter; often enough, you ended up shoveling quotes at the guy so that he got something mutually advantageous to the both of you and you could call an end to the session.

But this woman had something, some combination of warmth and skepticism that had made talking to her, well, fun. Plus, there was the matter of her looks—that smile, those cheekbones, those expressive eyes. She reminded him of Minerva, who always seemed to be smiling, who had a way of never letting you treat yourself seriously, while at the same time making you feel that there was no one on earth with whom she'd rather be. Come around again, he was thinking. The conversation wouldn't have to be so one-sided.

He turned to go back to his office.

"Maggie Newbold, huh?"

"Mr. Richie Platt! How nice to see you. Coming by for a visit? What brings you over from your cell in the Old Executive Office Building?"

"Some of your guidance, sir, if you have time."

Richie, now twenty-seven, was a graduate of Boston College Law School. During the presidential campaign he had served as Godwin's body man—the loyal mutt, that is—who carried his schedule, charged his cell phone batteries, fetched his sandwiches, carried his ChapStick, and who alone among the horde of people who had supported his candidacy had won some measure of affection for his efforts, which explained why Godwin had gone out of his way to secure young Richie a job in the Mahone White House.

"For you, Richie? Oodles."

They took a seat in Godwin's private office.

"That Ms. Newbold's some beautiful woman," said Richie.

"With a gift for imagery like that, no wonder you're a speech-writer."

"She working someplace?"

"*Newsbreak.*"

"Ohhhh. I wondered where she was going to surface."

"What do you mean?"

"There were all those rumors—you don't know about the rumors? There were all these rumors after she won the Pulitzer Prize about her having slept with her sources. Then she just sort of disappeared. Left the *Journal,* although I don't recall any kind of announcement or retraction or apology or anything. Probably nobody could prove the allegations."

"Ah, the unprovable allegation, the most malignant kind. If you can't prove something, you can't ever disprove it, either. What's on your mind, Richie?"

"Well—have you heard of any good jobs opening up?"

"Jesus Christ, Richie, you work at the White House! How good a job do you want?"

Richie made a face. "I'm, like, the fourth speechwriter at the White House. I never get to write anything good. No speeches, no addresses, no remarks for the World Series winner."

"What do you write?"

"Birthday messages. I do a lot of them. Mostly to people who gave the president money. It's boring. And nobody likes me. Let's be realistic. I'm not one of the original Mahone people. I started with you, and everybody thinks I got my job only because you pushed for it."

"Which is true."

"And everybody also thinks the only reason I've kept my job is because I get girls for the president."

"Which is . . ."

"Which isn't true. At least not since the campaign ended." For part of the campaign, Richie had been drafted to accompany Mahone on the trail, part of his advance team that plotted entrances and exits and other aspects of his campaign rallies. Godwin had never asked Richie to confirm or deny the stories that sprouted up about his ability to entice a certain brand of politically active coed to go upstairs and meet the candidate. He didn't doubt that they were true. Richie had wavy singer-songwriter hair and a loose, casual sort of vibe that had always seemed irresistible to members of the opposite sex.

"And now he's pushing me again. Kind of. Right now, it's subtle. He just, like, comes around and says 'Hey, old son, remember that tall redhead in Ann Arbor?' Stuff like that. I get the point."

"Has he asked you to travel with him?"

"Not yet. That would be the real test, wouldn't it? I think it's just a matter of time. I hear not everything's so hunky-dory with him and the First Lady."

"Well, what can I tell you? Try to leverage that into some better assignments. Meanwhile, I'll keep my ears open about jobs."

"Speaking of jobs . . ."

"Hear something good?" Godwin always enjoyed a bit of gossip.

"We've been asked to draft remarks announcing the appointment of Adrian Simone."

"To what?"

"Chairman of the Civil Rights Commission."

"Oh, by all means, let's name the most polarizing man of our time to one of the most sensitive, politically correct positions in the administration. Mahone's instincts are infallible."

"Please keep quiet about it, sir," said Richie. "Everyone's afraid it's going to show up on thewormreport.com, and I don't want anybody to try to trace it back to me."

"Everybody's afraid of the Worm Report," said Godwin. "It's just a blog."

"Yeah, by a mystery man with great sources. Who do you think Flip Stacks is?"

"I have no idea. Who's your suspect?"

"That guy who was fired by the *Times* last year. He's got a ton of contacts. Come on—who do you think?"

"Chet Wetzel."

"Oh, you're no fun, sir."

As Godwin ushered Richie to the door, Godwin's secretary, the arthritic Mrs. Gottschalk, padded in with Godwin's tuxedo. "What's doing tonight?" Richie asked.

"A party at the Vanatuas'. Silver anniversary of one or another of their companies. Construction this time, I think."

"Take me! I'll network!"

"Sorry, Rich. You're not in a league to go to these things."

"I'm not in a league to go to these things because I never go to these things. If I ever went to one of them, I'd be in the league to go."

Godwin found it hard to argue with his logic.

6

GODWIN HAD BEEN in more than a few fine homes in his time, but he always liked coming to the Vanatuas' house. A Stanford White original, it was built in Chevy Chase by Norbert Diebold, a Baltimore shipping magnate who wanted a place near Washington, the better to keep an eye on tariff policy. Norbert's son Cuthbert was born in a second-floor bedroom in 1898, and over the next decades, Cuthbert would win a Silver Star in the Argonne Forest, help FDR design the New Deal, work out the Lend-Lease agreement with Churchill, defend the capitalist system in a debate with Khrushchev, serve as counsel to LBJ, marry a twenty-three-year-old Brazilian tango dancer, lose most of his fortune in a humiliating divorce, take a position as chairman of a venerable Washington bank in order to sustain himself, and end up indicted when the FBI found out that the bank was laundering money for a drug cartel. Cuthbert beat the rap, but, broke and broken at eighty-five, he found himself bitterly eager to unload the family manse, along with all its contents, to an Indonesian banker who offered only a third of the asking price, but in green cash money. "Wog," Cuthbert muttered as he drove away, directing the comment at the small round-faced man with shiny nut-colored skin who had purchased his entire heritage for thirty cents on the dollar, but Roland Vanatua wasn't angered by the insult. Cuthbert Diebold was a bitter husk who smelled of hair tonic and who would be dead within a year; Roland, with his pretty young wife, Penny, on his arm, had so many of his tomorrows still ahead of him, and now had a spectacular mansion in Washington to go along with his magnificent home in Jakarta, the breathtaking vacation compound in Goa, the sprawling apartment in Belgravia, and the luxurious penthouse on Fifth Avenue. Time to look around in Tokyo, he thought.

That was more than twenty years ago. Now the sun never set on the Vanatuas' empire.

But as spectacular as the house was, as good as the food would no doubt be, as fine and as stimulating as the company would surely prove, Godwin would have been just as happy to have let Richie come in his place. And had this been purely a social occasion, Godwin might have done so. But as surely as if he were wearing a mining helmet instead of a tuxedo, he was there to work.

"Roland!" he exclaimed, spying his hosts near the door. "Penny!"

He embraced Penny, a still-attractive woman of a certain age who had squeezed herself into a silken red kimono. One could not tell how old Penny was, neither by looking at her face nor her press clips, which variously had her at forty-eight, fifty-five, and sixty-two. Nor was there any more certainty about her background, apart from narrowing it down to Asian; over the years, it was asserted with great authority that she was the daughter of a Hong Kong broker, a Japanese industrialist, a Korean farmer, and a London dry cleaner. The vagueness never bothered Roland. The Vanatuas had interests everywhere; it was fine that his wife could plausibly come from everywhere, too.

"My dear," he exclaimed, "you look lovely tonight, as usual."

"Oh thank you, Mr. Vice President," she gushed, gently turning the vice president so that her photographers could capture their friendship being sealed with an air kiss. He then manfully grasped Roland's hand. "Roland, my good friend," he said loudly, as though he was on a stage, which in a sense he was. "Thank you so much for once again inviting me to your lovely home. I'm delighted to be here."

"A very mild evening for February, isn't it?" said Penny.

"Indeed. We're fortunate."

"Come in, Mr. Vice President, please," said Roland, guiding him by the elbow. "I'm sure you know a great many people here." Roland was a smiling man, possessed of a big toothy smile that he wore almost constantly, as though life were nothing but an endless supply of delightful surprises. But after giving Godwin a good long look at his pearlies, Roland's grin suddenly imploded and his voice plummeted to a whisper. "I must speak to you soon! Upstairs! Come up soon!" He steered Godwin to a group of guests. "Here, I'm sure you know Mr. Granger of U.S. Bankgroup—"

Only for years, Godwin thought. "George, nice to see you. How's the handicap?"

"Fine, Mr. Vice President, thank you."

"—and Professor Simpkins of Stanford—"

"Professor, nice to see you again. I thought your piece on Third World debt in *The Economist* was most illuminating."

"Thank you, sir."

"Not necessarily correct, but illuminating nonetheless."

"I'll be happy to tutor you on the points you missed, sir."

"I bet you would, thank you."

"And this is Ms. Newbold, the *Newsbreak* correspondent."

Ms. Newbold of *Newsbreak*! Well, well, well. "Yes, we've met," said Godwin. Although on that occasion, she didn't look quite this good. Tonight, Godwin assessed, she's shimmering.

"A pleasant surprise seeing you this evening," she said, smiling that devastating smile, thinking how happy she was that she had splurged a third of her paycheck on a devastatingly elegant little black dress from Diane von Furstenberg.

"Please excuse me," said Roland, leaving the group, though not before nudging Godwin and giving him a nagging look that would have made Godwin laugh out loud if he hadn't known that Roland possessed no sense of humor whatsoever. Instead, he just nodded.

"Mr. Granger was just telling us about some new B2B software that is going to reduce corporate bill paying from seventeen hours per transaction to one-sixteenth of a second," said Professor Simpkins.

"Really!" said Godwin. "Do go on!" Of course, he thought, I'd say "Do go on!" if he was talking about the process by which hogs produce shit. As it was, unless you were as hopelessly behind the cutting edge as Granger here, there wasn't anything radically new in software that was already in its 2.0 version. But it doesn't matter what any of them are saying, he thought. He wasn't here for his personal edification or amusement, nor to admire, as much as he may have wished otherwise, the economical cuteness of Ms. Newbold's nose or the valley between her breasts. He was there as an ornament, a symbol of the Vanatuas' success. Roland and Penny were among the richest people on the planet, huge in the Far East, dominant players in commodities, communications, construction, casinos—everything! What's more, they'd built their fortune the old-fashioned way—by buying access, cashing in favors, making secret deals. No one knew where the family got its money originally— drugs, slaves, black market, pirating the plunder the Japanese looted during the war, whatever—but the reason they had money now was because they had access, and the reason they had access was because they had money. And like a railroad handcart, Roland and Penny never stopped working the two in tandem. Which was why Godwin had to be there. The Vanatuas had given a pile of money to the party last year, which had surely helped elect the Mahone-Pope ticket. I'm here to show our gratitude, Godwin thought. I'm here to show the world that they have an entrée to the White House.

Granger, the banker, stopped talking.

"Fascinating," said Godwin reflexively. He felt a tug at his elbow.

"Excuse me, Mr. Vice President," some functionary said. "Mr. Vanatua wonders if you could please join him for a moment."

Jesus, Roland is impatient, he thought. "Gentlemen, Ms. Newbold, if you'll excuse me—"

Maggie caught his eye as he started to move away, and as she sipped a drink, she smiled.

"Don't disappear," he said.

"You're the one walking away," she replied. He laughed, shrugged, turned, and plowed into a large hairy man, who immediately grabbed Godwin in a bear hug and bellowed, "Duuuuuuuude!"

It was Lowell Mahone, the president's six-foot-two, 270-pound little brother. "Hey man!" he said, punching Godwin in the shoulder. "Whatcha been up to?"

"Just—being vice president."

"How d'ya like doin' that? D'ya ever hafta do anything?"

"Oh, you'd be surprised."

Lowell had been a fixture on his brother's campaign, and everybody liked him. It would have been easy to dismiss him as a simpleton—he was, of course, dumb as wood. But he had a genuine friendliness, like a big dog who just wanted to be petted. Godwin had originally pegged him as Mahone's idiot brother—the Mahone who knew his station in life, which, as it happened, was being a not very good front man for one or another not very good blues bands that frequented the roadhouses in greater Texarkana—and never gave him another thought. But late one night, when Godwin's campaign car broke down after a debate in Ocala, who came chugging down the pike in a Ford F-150 but Lowell Mahone. He gave an exhausted Godwin a ride all the way to Jacksonville, sharing with the famished candidate his Dunkin' Donuts Munchkins and Dr Pepper, and generally behaving as though he had no idea that Godwin should be loathed and despised by all who embraced the cause of his brother Jack.

"How's the singing career?" Godwin asked. Lowell was very dedicated to his profession, a manifest lack of talent and success notwithstanding.

"Slumpin', man, slumpin'," the big man said, his shoulders sagging. "The gigs have trailed off, y'know? I've been thinkin' maybe I oughta try this political shit, y'know? I mean, it worked for Jack."

"Hang in there, Lowell. Your day will come." Yes, Godwin thought, Lowell's day will come, and when it does, it will signal that the apocalypse is nigh. "Now if you'll excuse me, old boy, I've got to see Roland."

GODWIN CLOSED the great doors of Roland Vanatua's study behind him. "Come in, come in." The older man waved impatiently from behind the massive desk that Norbert Diebold had imported from Bavaria in 1895. "Goddammit, Goddy, what the hell is happening with the satellite deal? I'm getting good and goddamned worried, I tell you. It's starting to smell like an old dead fish. Want a drink?"

Roland didn't speak to everyone this way. To those in power, he was obsequious as a footman, and to strangers, he was generally opaquely polite. But he had known Godwin as a businessman, from back when he wanted to license Zephyr software for the computers he was manufacturing in Sumatra, and he always talked to Godwin the way he would talk to anyone with whom he wanted to make a deal—frankly, impatiently, the way one should speak when money's on the table. And Godwin appreciated it.

"Scotch," Godwin said, sliding into the leather wing chair opposite the desk. "And you should be worried. Jack's getting very soft on the idea. He's afraid of being criticized. The administration's made too many mistakes and he thinks he can't afford another. He's going to do whatever's going to cause him the least grief. I would gauge its present chances of survival as teeny-weeny."

"Jackie's lost his goddamn balls, eh?" He handed Godwin his drink. "Well, that's a helluva thing for me. I've spent a shitload of dough securing all the programming that would have gone onto the satellite. English Premier League football, NASCAR, *Soul Train.* I've already got people translating *I Love Lucy* into sixteen goddamn dialects. Helluva lotta goddamn dough. And what about my reputation?"

Now he's finally gotten to the heart of the matter, Godwin thought. Roland doesn't care about losing the money. He's lost money before. What he cares about is his reputation for having influence in Washington. That's the key to thirty more deals Roland's got in the pipeline this year, and a hundred the year after that, and so on, and so on. "Why are you worried about your reputation? Everyone knows how grateful the administration has been for your help. Didn't Jack invite you to watch the NCAA finals at the White House last year?"

"Ah, how many goddamn times can I show that same picture around? Plus, I hate college basketball. I'm much more of a soccer man."

"You know what you ought to do?"

"What?"

"I saw in the paper today that Mariah Carey backed out of headlining the opening of your new casino in Hong Kong in two weeks."

"Yeah, so what? Scratchy throat. Maybe we'll, I dunno, ask whatshisname, the old Beatle, McCartney."

"Good idea. But Paul McCartney's brother isn't the president of the United States."

"Huhn. Lowell Mahone. But doesn't his singing suck?"

Godwin couldn't believe Roland was actually considering the suggestion. Well, let's play with it some more. If I have to spend the night here being Roland's show pony, I may as well have some fun with the old bird. "What do you care if Lowell can sing or not? Suppose he's awful. So half the audience gets up and walks out. Where are they going to go? They're going to go play blackjack. More money for you. But meanwhile, your real audience—the government in Beijing, the officials in Malaysia, Singapore, Mumbai, Tokyo—they're not going to hear Lowell sing. They're just going to see pictures of you arm and arm with the president's brother." Of course, Godwin thought, they probably won't know that the president is fonder of his hemorrhoids than he is of his brother, but that's their bad luck.

"Huhn." Roland had the faraway look of a man solving quadratic equations in his head. "Interesting goddamn idea. You think he's available?"

"I don't know, but I think so. I gather that he's just finished touring."

"How much you think he costs?"

"I don't know. Less than McCartney. What do you care? It's all chicken feed to you. Be generous. Overwhelm him. You'll earn it back ten thousand times."

"Huhn. Interesting idea. I will ponder it. But enough—we better go back to the party."

Godwin paused when he reached the door. Time to play one more card, one for the future. "Look—if it's any consolation to you, I pushed hard for the deal."

"I wish you were president, Goddy. Jack's got no balls. Next time, I'll back you."

"Yeah, well, thanks, Roland. But it's a long time until next time."

They reached the top of the staircase. At the bottom stood Maggie Newbold, affording at that angle a view of her cleavage few others could ascertain. "You want to come to the casino opening?" Roland prattled on. "Maybe you could cook up some trade mission or something. I'll give you a goddamn good discount on the room." Finally, Roland observed what had been occupying Godwin's attention. "Mmh. Ah. Goddamn beautiful woman, eh?"

"Yes. What do you know about her?"

"Nothing, really. Penny said somebody said somebody should invite her. You know how we do these things."

"Right." Godwin saw that a valet was handing Maggie her coat. Leaving Roland without looking back, Godwin double-timed it down the great staircase. About halfway down, it occurred to him that he was setting a clip dangerously un–vice presidential (although amid the highly focused games of networking, sycophancy, and one-upmanship being played by the guests, the comings and goings of a mere vice president barely merited notice). "Ms. Newbold!" he called. He was trying very hard not to seem like he was galloping down the stairs. "Awfully early to be going, isn't it?"

This rich, handsome, powerful man just raced down a flight of stairs to talk to me, she noted. "Well, surprisingly, I heard a thing or two of interest tonight, so I have to go file."

"I thought this issue would be closed."

"This is for the Web site. We're always trying to break stories there."

"I see. What did you hear?"

"Wait a few hours and check out the Web site."

"Did you happen to hear that the president is close to appointing Adrian Simone to the Civil Rights division?"

Maggie's eyes widened. "No. Is that what you're telling me?"

"Oh, I'm not telling you anything." He stood close to her and began murmuring in her ear. What he wanted to say was that he had always heard that only a woman with a long neck ever knew true passion, but he couldn't quite summon the nerve. "I'm just saying that if you called Chet Wetzel and asked who was on the president's helicopter to Camp David this afternoon, and then you called the Four Seasons Hotel and asked for Adrian Simone and then asked him how he found the weather in Catoctin Mountain Park a few hours ago, then *Newsbreak*'s new reporter might have herself a scoop."

"That's going to cause a shitstorm of protest, isn't it?"

"Probably. This wasn't well thought through. Adrian isn't liked. He's pissed too many people off, even people who share his views. This kind of trouble is so avoidable."

"Well, thank you, sir." She couldn't wait to get on her phone.

He went to shake her hand, but at the same time, with his left hand, he gently stroked her elbow. "You're welcome, Ms. Newbold. I'll be in touch."

Watching her slip into the evening, Godwin did briefly consider whether hitting on a reporter could be a mistake. The thought did not linger. He wasn't apt to tell her anything he didn't want her to know, she wasn't apt to expose him in an article or memoir. "I Slept with the Vice President!" Who would care? Besides, he thought, who else was available to him? Lobbyists? Attorneys? Interns? There were a certain number of job seekers, and there were a certain number of married ladies of indeterminable discretion. There was no shortage of women who'd be willing to sleep with him; there was just a shortage of women he'd feel safe waking up with. But there was something about Maggie Newbold—independence? intelligence? self-confidence?—that made him think the revolutionary thought that if she was interested in him, it would be because he was a man and she was a woman.

7

HE SPENT THE NEXT HOUR holding court in Roland's spacious library, chatting up a variety of reasonably powerful people—savvy Washington lawyers, deeply pocketed lobbyists, lupine defense contractors, minor senators. They all offered variations on one of two greetings, either a vaguely warmer-than-cordial greeting (signifying that they thought he might be important to them one day) or a solemn expression of sympathy for the administration's myriad troubles. Only the chipmunk-faced party chairman, Tavis Whouley, dared to tentatively express the thought that all were silently entertaining. "Sometimes I think we all might have been better off if y'all were in the Oval," he muttered discreetly, a mild, well-modified, fully deniable expression of treason, which Godwin pointedly recognized by elaborately ignoring.

Godwin was about to pack it in for the evening, when Roland sidled up behind him. "Goddy, there's somebody here maybe you would like to meet," he whispered in his ear.

Godwin grimaced. "I kind of feel I've flown the flag enough for one night, eh, Roland? But next time."

"Zhang Tian," Roland said.

"Aha." Godwin nodded, recognizing the name of the deputy commerce minister of the People's Republic of China. A hugely influential man, his deliberately insignificant title notwithstanding.

"Big goddamn fish, Goddy. Bigger maybe than you in the scheme of things—pardon me for pointing that out. You don't think the State Department might be a little bit hinky about the two of you, you know—"

"No, not if we're not so public. I'd like to meet him."

"He's back in the sunroom with a whole goddamn trade delegation. Not much of a bunch of minglers. And they're eating all the goddamn shrimp."

Roland had depicted the essence of the scene quite accurately: a handful of Chinese men in regulation Brooks Brothers knockoffs standing amid the bountiful olive trees and imperialistic spider plants in the Vanatuas' sunroom, scarfing down thumb-size shrimp with a hunger that immediately betrayed someone's fundamental failure to understand before arriving that this evening's event offered hors d'oeuvres but not dinner. But as soon as Roland and Godwin entered, the men squared their shoulders, and one stepped forward.

"Mr. Vice President," he said, not waiting for an introduction, extending his hand. "Delighted to make your acquaintance." It was Zhang Tian. Forty years old, hair spiked up, he was the casual, smiling, confident, consciously Western face of tomorrow's China. Assuming he didn't blow it.

"Likewise, sir. And please call me Godwin."

"Thank you. And you, please, feel free to call me—Don." He caught the inquisitive flicker of Godwin's eyebrow. "Long story. From when I was in B school at UCLA. I was a huge Madonna fan, so the guys started calling me Don."

"You got off lucky."

"I know it." He sipped his drink. "Roland and Penny really know how to throw a party, huh?"

"This is small by their standards."

The two stood in silence for a moment, and Godwin took measure of the shorter man. He was not so many years Godwin's junior, but he seemed far more boyish, far less experienced, simply to have less bottom. He wondered what attributes—what cold-bloodedness, what ruthlessness—lay hidden behind his easy manner that allowed him to assume his present level of power. He finally decided to ask.

"So, Don, what's the People's Republic's chief spook doing in these parts?"

Zhang Tian fielded the question with his cool intact, a bemused smile exhibiting neither more nor less surprise than if Godwin had offered him a joint. "You have me confused, Godwin. I'm merely the humble deputy minister for commerce."

"Now, now," Godwin countered, "I'm not talking about what's written on your business card. We have some very conscientious people working for us on the National Security Council who take an interest in these matters, and they're quite sure that your true calling is intelligence. Political and corporate espionage."

"Please, Godwin," said Zhang Tien, using self-effacement to blunt the query, "all that secret agent business is vastly overblown. Your CIA simply wants to increase its budget, and to do that, they need enemies. They're just trying to save the jobs of all those yobs who are three years short of retirement and who have no aptitude for combating Islamic militants. Frankly, it's annoying. Every time somebody in Los Alamos leaves a memo on a copier, they start smelling chow mein. The truth is, we do very little spying anymore."

"Yeah, right. As if you would tell me that you ever did!"

"Oh please. We have had some adventures. But it's not like we can hold a candle to what the Israelis get away with."

"Still—you didn't answer the question."

"What? What I'm doing here? No mystery. I am the deputy commerce minister, whatever else you think I do. I just want to help fast-track the satellite deal if I can. Speaking of which: how's that looking to you?"

It wasn't meant to be a trick question, but Godwin realized that it wouldn't be hard to misplay it into one. A sale that could have security ramifications? Discussed during an unauthorized, ad hoc conversation with an espionage official? Whatever Godwin said could quickly attain a life of its own, meaning that the best play would be simply to ape the line the administration had already taken with the media. "We still have questions about whether you could use them militarily," Godwin said.

"Why the hell would we want to do that?" said Zhang. "All we want is better communications. We want the Internet. Yahoo. QVC. Our women want zirconium earrings from the Home Shopping Network."

"I'd be happy to believe you, Don, if only you had a little more credibility."

Zhang sighed. "That's the trouble with being chief spook. You tell the waitress you want sugar for your tea and instead she brings you atomic secrets." He quickly glanced over his shoulder, then back. "Sir, if you don't mind, I would like very much to present my colleagues. Gua Lian, a cultural attaché at the embassy—"

"How do you do?" said a tall, austere, bald man, presenting his hand.

"Professor Chua-Eon of Tsinghua University in Beijing—"

"Nice to meet you," said a prim man with tortoiseshell glasses.

"Deng Laoping—"

"Ah yes," said Godwin, "I well know the chairman of Yangtze .com, the Chinese Amazon. So how goes it, Deng? Make any profits yet?"

"We're executing our business plan to the letter."

"Splendid!" said Godwin. "Good for you!" He'll never make a dime, he thought.

"And this is—" Zhang pressed forward a young woman but groped for a name. Adroitly, she stepped into the yawning pause.

"Irene Kim, Mr. Vice President," she said. "I'm pleased to make your acquaintance."

It was all Godwin could do to keep from gasping out loud. He was stunned. It was the girl.

It was the girl, it was the girl, it was the exact same girl, the Asian girl, the girl in the pool with Marco McChesney.

It was the same damn girl.

Or an incredible facsimile.

"How do you do, Ms. Kim?"

"Ms. Kim is a student at Georgetown University," said Zhang.

"Actually, sir," she said, correcting him, "I'm at George Washington."

"Sorry, yes, George Washington," said Zhang. "She's actually the niece of an old family friend." The poised spymaster suddenly seemed awkward as he stretched an avuncular arm around her shoulder.

It is her, isn't it? Godwin thought. It has to be. Is there possibly a difference? Certainly the demure way she's wearing her hair is different from the wet and wanton way it draped about her in the pool, and certainly with her wearing this charming little black dress, we can't tell if her ass is comprised of the same grabbable globes or if her titties have the same perky upturned posture and end in nipples that resemble Bing cherries, but gosh, we look to be in the same neighborhood. Try to imagine the broad backside of a fullback next to her face. And on the plus side, just look at the beauty mark, the nape of the neck, the tilt of the head, the luster of her skin, the overall presentation! But what's her story? Is she really here with dear Uncle Don, who has infiltrators telling him about the inner workings of the highest levels of every government in the world but who has no idea of tender Irene's horizontal position in the new global economy? Maybe he doesn't know. Maybe Don just wanted a date, and he's dragging out the old niece cover that was already ineffectually transparent during the Truman administration. Or maybe it was one of these other guys who hired her, a little something to impress Don, to get on his good side, a special treat for his hospitality basket. My God, what if he has no clue? And then what if he were caught? Think of the headlines: INTELLIGENCE MINISTER CAUGHT WITH HOOKER. How would he explain that? That's why those of us in the public eye have to be so careful. That's why it makes your head spin when you see people heedlessly taking chances, like Jack Mahone, for fuck's sake—

Like Jack Mahone—

Jack

Ma

Hone.

He thought of garrulous Jack, garrulous, incompetent Jack with his hungry pecker; then he thought of Irene, this beautiful girl with her graceful neck and her apparent willingness to open her legs whenever somebody of sufficient stature showed signs of having recently visited an ATM. He thought of Richie, lonely Richie, eager Richie, and then he thought of Roland and Penny, conniving Roland and Penny, the most opportunistic couple on land, sea, or air. He thought of Lowell, affable, show-witted, credulous Lowell, and he thought of Don, with his avuncular arm around the shoulders of dear Irene.

My God, he thought, the ingredients are all right here, aren't they? For God's sake, look at them; they are ALL right here, like so many pennies on the sidewalk, just waiting for somebody to scoop them up. Here are the ingredients. The opportunity is in your hands.

He heard Tom Ralston saying, "Look, whatever it takes, we've got to get rid of him and get you in there. The country needs you," and he heard Maggie Newbold saying, "If Jack Mahone's had a couple bad innings, his game might be all over," and finally he heard himself saying, "I think all these things come down to leadership. Whatever you decide, just be strong." Then it was Maggie again, asking this time in a taunting way, "Is this a job that's making the best use of Godwin Pope's talents and abilities?"

All it takes is leadership. Just be strong. The only fucking thing it takes is leadership! Be strong!

If I act, we will be rid of this Mahone. We will be rid of this Mahone, and I will become president.

So lead!

A waiter bearing an empty shrimp platter was heading for the door. Godwin grabbed him. "Excuse me, but earlier I saw a photographer roaming about. Would you please ask him to come over here?"

"Very good, sir," the waiter replied.

Godwin returned his attention to Irene. "I'm sorry, Ms. Kim. Now tell me, what is it that you're studying at George Washington?"

"International relations," she replied.

"Really?" He couldn't resist. "I bet you're the head of your class."

If she got the joke, she ignored it. "I'm doing my best."

"Well, that's splendid. Good luck to you." He was about to ask her other questions, when the waiter returned. "Excuse me, sir— your photographer?"

"Ah yes," said a suddenly animated Godwin, tossing the waiter a twenty. "Listen, I'd like to get a picture with my friends here." He stuffed a wad of cash into the photographer's jacket, a thick wad, multiple hundreds, way more than enough to win the photographer's undivided attention.

"I probably couldn't have prints for you much before noon, sir. I'm way backed up."

"No problem. Do you have a fresh memory card for that thing?"

"Yes, sir."

He shoved more cash at the photographer. "Just give me the whole memory card when we're done, okay?"

"Absolutely."

"Just wait for my say-so before snapping the picture, all right? Got that? Wait for my say-so." The photographer nodded. "Mr. Minister!" Godwin called. "A picture with your party, please." He pulled in the professor and the businessman and the attaché; Irene held herself aloof. "Ms. Kim, please!" He could see her checking Zhang for an indication, but Godwin bulldozed his way through, taking the girl's slender arm and pulling her into the group next to

Zhang, who slipped his arm around her waist as Godwin himself stepped behind the now-smiling group. "How are we doing, Mr. Photographer?"

"All set here, sir, waiting on you."

"All right, then, everyone—think of the Cultural Revolution!"

But at that instant, indeed, at the instant before that instant, just as the photographer depressed his finger and the shutter opened, Godwin dropped his head behind the attaché's back. He heard the click, saw the light of the flash brighten Irene Kim's shapely legs. "Wonderful!" he said, snapping back up. "Thank you all!"

The photographer sidled up. He didn't look happy. "Here's the memory card, sir, but I'm sorry—I don't think you were in the shot."

"I'm sure it was fine."

"It looked like you moved."

"Don't worry about it. Now, was Lowell Mahone still out there when you came in?"

"I'm pretty sure so, sir. There was still food out."

"Excellent!" said Godwin, hurrying to the main room, which was now far emptier than when he'd stepped away to see the Chinese group. Fortunately, Lowell had not yet joined the departed, but he was still planted at the badly depleted food table like Heimdal at the gate of Asgaard, suspiciously poking a smear of goat cheese that alone among the fromages had been ignored by the guests.

"Lowell!" he called out. "Lowell!"

"Heeey, man. Hey, whaddya think this is?"

"Goat cheese."

"Really? Goats have cheese? Hey, could you do me a favor? You know those little creamy crab puffs? I only had a couple; then the guy with the tray left, and they didn't have any out here. But I bet if you asked for some . . ."

"Yes, sure, no problem. I'll find Mrs. Vanatua. But listen. I want to tell you something. Mr. Vanatua might—just might, mind you—have an engagement for you."

"Yeah? No shit!"

"Ssshh. Maybe. But here's the thing. If he does, don't ask for your usual fee."

"Don't worry, he and Mrs. V. are good people. I'll give him a discount."

"No, Lowell, he's rich. If he asks, tell him you want—" Godwin grabbed a cocktail napkin and wrote a number. It was in the middle to high six figures. When he showed it to Lowell, his eyes popped open wide. "Why would he pay me all that?"

"Because he can. Because if you were Sinatra, he'd pay you a million. But you're not as big a star as Sinatra, are you?"

"No."

"So it's less. Okay?"

"Right."

"So now be patient. I have a hunch he'll call. Now, where's Penny?"

"Maybe the kitchen? Remember to ask about the creamy crab puffs."

Godwin's heart was pounding as he crossed the room. It had been a long time since he'd felt this excited about something, this enthused, and he desperately feared that he might appear to people to seem anything but casual. The point of an exercise like this was to make a suggestion so pointedly as to be heard, but so softly, so lightly, so offhandedly that the person receiving the suggestion would forget that you were the one who'd said it. That's not so hard, he thought. Successful people almost always believe that they think of everything by themselves. People like Roland and Penny think that when they open their eyes in the morning, they've caused the sun to rise.

He found Penny in the kitchen, by the sink, furiously rubbing a stain out of a silk shawl she had been wearing earlier in the evening. "The Danish ambassador dribbled wine on me when he was describing the hip-hop dance lessons he takes," she said, shaking her head. "You have to take care of something like that fast. If you don't, wine will never come out."

With her shawl off, he could clearly see the fleshy curve of Penny's shoulders. It occurred to Godwin, not for the first time, that Penny had held herself together pretty well, somehow having negotiated the Scylla and Charybdis of stringy and saggy through which all women eventually had to sail. Still, there was a businesslike hardness about her. He never really thought of making a pass at her. Sex with Penny, he thought, would be fast and order-filled.

"It's time to take my leave," he said. "Thank you again for inviting me. Another lovely party."

"Nice to see you, Godwin," she said. She offered her cheek but kept rubbing.

"Listen, I have bad news. I won't be able to sit at your table at the White House Correspondents' Association dinner. I have to go with the CNN people."

"Oh." She pursed her lips. He knew she'd be perturbed.

"Larry King got all in a twist, so Chet Wetzel practically decreed I go with them. I'm sorry—does it create a problem for you?"

"Well, I have to think of who to invite now, and it's pretty last-minute. It'll be hard to find someone with any celebrity. Damn, I told Roland to ask the guy who's the new James Bond in the first place."

"There's the secretary of the interior—"

"Oh, who wants that old bag?"

"Or, uh—well, never mind."

"Who?"

"Well, I know your penchant for star making. How about a real up-and-comer? There's a speechwriter at the White House, a real ball of fire, named Richard Platt."

"Richard Platt?"

"Yeah. Richie. Richard. He's going to run this town one day."

"Richard Platt. What's he like?"

"Brilliant, for starters. Pretty good-looking. Handsome maybe. But he's catching everybody's eye. He's got real potential."

"Richard Platt." Her eyes narrowed. She was trying the idea on for size, and wasn't sure yet if it fit.

"Or Richie."

"Is he married?"

"No, thank heavens. The poor guy works, like, twenty hours a day. I don't think he's got much of a personal life at all. He really holds that place together. But if word ever leaked out about him, he'd probably be Washington's most eligible bachelor."

"I thought that was you."

"You know what I mean. But maybe you'd be doing him a favor if you invited a young lady—"

"Oh?"

"A daughter of some friend, perhaps, or—in fact, there was somebody here tonight who might be perfect. She's a student at George Washington. Irene something. She came with that Chinese trade mission. Charming girl."

"Richie Platt."

"Right."

"And Irene something."

"Kim, I think."

"Uh-huh. Well, we'll see."

Godwin could tell she was considering the idea. The rubbing had slowed and her eyes lost focus as she weighed the negligible social value of having a fairly invisible garden-variety senator parked at her table, as opposed to causing a head-turning stir by elevating a couple of unknowns. It was time to play a final card. "I'm sure I've heard you and Roland say it a dozen times," Godwin said softly. "It's never too early to start making friends with the next generation of leadership."

He left Penny after that, and slipped out of the party with minimal additional good-byes. Reaching his limousine, he suddenly felt tired, and as he sank back into the seat, he was aware of the tightness in his shoulders and the cold dampness in his armpits, signs of the eagerness and stress he'd been feeling. I hope this worked, he was thinking. He had Roland considering Lowell, and he had Penny considering Platt. The first steps had been taken, and his safety, his deniability, was perfectly secure. There'd be no cost to him if they let the ideas fizzle, nor would there be a problem for him if his name remained conspicuously attached to either idea; the plan just wouldn't work, that's all. And of course, more would have to happen. More things would have to go just right. This wasn't going to be easy; the whole fantastic idea was still a long shot. But if things worked out the way they could, Jack Mahone would soon be accused of treason against his own country, and despite having committed no treason, he would find himself confronted by a web of circumstantial evidence that would hang a saint. Godwin smiled and closed his eyes. And when that happened, Jack Mahone would relinquish the presidency, and would be succeeded by his vice president, Godwin Pope.

8

HAVING PLANTED HIS SEEDS, Godwin left the scene—the farther from sight, the further from mind. There wasn't much more he could do anyway: they would either germinate or they wouldn't, and there was no point dwelling on the matter. Instead, he went to Detroit for two days. He spent one of them in linoleum-floored meeting halls, talking to members of the autoworkers' union, most of whom seemed to be fat or emaciated, eaters or smokers, plagued by clogged arteries or tumorous lungs. He spent the other in carpeted conference rooms, talking to executives from the auto companies, most of whom seemed to ostentatiously fit, with short lacquered hair and industrial-strength smiles. All of them wanted the same thing: to be saved. What from, of course, was a matter of some dispute—candidates included the companies, the unions, the environmentalists, Congress, and the Japanese. What they really wanted to be saved from was themselves, from their mistakes, their bad judgments, their selfishness, their credulity, their fear, and, above all, their responsibility. They all knew a day of reckoning had been coming. They were the ones who built unreliable cars, who lost touch with the consumer, who surrendered initiative, who demanded and awarded generous retirement plans, such that the price of every American car carried an invisible surtax that bought Viagra for their retirees. They all knew they'd have to pay a price for these decisions, but rather than pay the price at a time and place of their choosing, they continued to hide. Now these car men gathered around him, practically tugging on his hems, hoping that he'd tell them that all of Washington had at last agreed to pass the National Relieved of Your Responsibilities Act and they could all continue merrily on their way. The best Godwin could do was nod and listen, nod and listen, and try to remain noncommittal when any of them said, as so many of them did, that Jack Mahone was useless and that they wished Godwin was in the White House.

It was the rankest sort of bullshit, but Godwin appreciated the gesture.

On the flight back to Washington, Godwin's secretary informed him that Ms. Newbold from *Newsbreak* had called. He hadn't been able to tune into the blogosphere to follow all the developments, but evidently she had gone with his tip about Adrian Simone, as he'd known she would, and it had inaugurated a firestorm, as he'd known it would. He phoned her, cell to cell.

"How are you doing today?"

"Fine, sir, thank you."

"I gather you took my advice and called the Four Seasons."

"Something like that." As it happened, she didn't run right out and call Adrian Simone at the hotel. That would have been stupid. Simone would have just denied the story. Instead, she called Mrs. Simone in Macon. It was a little late, but the lady was up, and like many a person who spends time standing in the shadow of another, she was thrilled to pieces to talk about all the good work her husband would be able to do once he was in charge of the commission, and the deadwood he'd get rid of, and all the policies he'd change. She was frankly delighted that at long last someone had decided to recognize her husband for his good points, and not to dwell on superficialities like his outbursts of temper, none of the incidents of which were relevant to this job, and all the accounts of which had him misquoted and were all blown way out of proportion, particularly that one where all he did was put his hands around that man's neck, and never actually choked him. Only with those quotes safely in the can did Maggie then call Adrian, and only when she had recorded his sleepy, reluctant admission did she then wake up Chet Wetzel and lay the hammer onto his head. But until the vice president was prepared to tell her the tricks of his trade, she didn't feel obligated to share hers.

"I'm assuming your little scoop went over well?"

"Quite well. Pat on the back, gold star on my forehead, telephone call from Loomis, the whole deal. How did they go over in the White House?"

"I wasn't there, but I've been led to believe not well. Lots of raised voices behind closed doors. It doesn't seem Adrian Simone will get nominated after all."

"Can I get a quote from you on that?"

"You can quote me as saying that Adrian Simone is a valued friend of this administration, and we treasure his support. Beyond that, I have no comment."

"Well, mush from the veep. That'll get me the cover."

"It's hard to beat me at mush." He laughed. He liked hearing the amusement in her voice. He found it encouraging.

"I'll remember that when I need some. But again, thank you for the tip. If you have anything else, please let me know."

"I'd like to see you."

It never fails, she thought. "I'd like to, but that would be hard for me," she said.

"Am I so unpleasant?"

Perhaps if she told him yes, he'd drop it. But she couldn't bring herself to do it. She liked him. He was interesting. He was funny. He was charming. And the fact was, if he were still chairman of Zephyr Software instead of the vice president, she'd say yes in an instant. But Loomis had given her a second chance, and Maggie didn't want to press her luck. "No, you're not unpleasant. It's just that there are—issues. Can we leave it at that?"

"You know I find you attractive."

"I guess that's why you're giving me tips."

"No, that's just a happy coincidence. I'd find you attractive even if you were, I don't know, an astronaut."

She didn't want to doubt him, but she did. "Hey, if you want me to trust you as a source, you can't be telling me fibs like that, okay? Now I've got to go."

He was a little disappointed, but not really. She would come around plenty soon enough. She was an intelligent person. Stupid people often had trouble budging off a moral precept once they'd latched onto it. Smart people could be counted on to eventually think of some greater good that would be served if only they allowed themselves to do what, upon further review, now seemed like quite the right thing.

Besides, there was work to do. The success of this little scenario we're conjuring up requires people to believe that Jack has committed treason, Godwin thought. But Jack isn't likely to do that on his own; who the hell would? Therefore, the trick is to get Jack to commit something. Later, we'll make it look like treason.

The president's staff was tight-lipped as they arrived for the weekly meeting, but as Jack's customary tardiness drifted past the twenty-minute mark, conversation broke out about the NCAA tournament, and whether or not Jack should put in an appearance if Louisiana State managed to fight its way into the Final Four. Opinion seemed to be that it would do the president a lot of good to be seen rubbing elbows with ordinary folks, but then somebody pointed out that the women's team from Louisiana Tech was apt to make it into the Women's Final Four. Could the president afford to piss off women by not going to the women's game? Maybe he could go to both games. But could the president afford to be seen flying all over the country to college basketball games? What had been a loose, jokey, party-on atmosphere sank into timorous uncertainty, and hit rock bottom when Jack finally arrived and quickly infected his staff with his tight, sour, sullen mood.

At issue was still the satellite sale. Jack's most recent strategy had been to set the thing adrift, hoping that it would catch a current of support from somewhere and gather speed. Or, failing that, that one night it would just sink from sight and everyone would wake up the next day and move on to something else, the whole deal now being unmissed and unremembered. It was a naïve miscalculation. The Republicans had seen the drifting issue and had decided to use it for target practice.

"Our latest polling shows that criticism of the satellite sale is having an effect," summarized Chet Wetzel. "The constant carping by Speaker Vanick and the Republicans, the jabbering on right-wing radio, the attacks on Fox have basically convinced people that the sale is a bad idea. And the issue is bleeding over and killing our favorability rating."

"But we finally got a positive report from the CIA," said National Security Advisor Broyard. "They've given it a clean bill of health."

"It doesn't fucking matter," snapped Jack. "The issue's a fucking loser. Wait 'til Friday afternoon, then have the Commerce Department cancel it."

"It's not going to go well for us, sir," said Wetzel.

"I know," said Jack, a note of weary resignation now coloring his view. "I know we'll get criticism, and the Republicans'll go to town. But after the Adrian Simone thing, I just don't think we can stand another defeat." He let the words sink in for a moment. "We just can't. Anybody disagree?"

A silence cloaked the room. Jack looked into the face of each person at the table, passing Godwin after sharing the briefest of glances. Godwin waited until what he was sure was the last second, until he sensed Jack was again about to speak. Then: show time!

"I disagree, Mr. President," he said firmly, and all eyes fastened on him as though he had fired a pistol. "I disagree. It's true, Mr. President, that this administration has suffered some setbacks in our first few months. Not as bad as some, though. Not as bad as Kennedy's, which had to deal with the Bay of Pigs disaster. Or as bad as Clinton's, which had an awful first year before leading to a tremendous economic revival. Both of those men came back to have some glorious moments and to make enormous contributions to the well-being of our nation. And we can, too.

"Is it true that we can't suffer any more setbacks? Perhaps. More setbacks would be bad. But what I think is indisputably true is that we can't keep going without victories. We need a win. And this satellite sale should be a winner. We have good reasons for doing it. It not only provides a way for us to sell a large variety of our products to the largest market in the world but it is a way of selling to this huge Communist nation lessons about our way of life. We not only want to improve the balance of trade; we want to extend the blessings of democracy and a free market to a great rival, and, in doing so, create a foundation for peaceful relations between our peoples. Now I just don't think we've clearly made this case. Our opponents have criticized us, and we've been mute. Mr. President, you are one of the finest communicators I have ever seen. With you at our forefront, we will have this victory."

For a long time, Jack sat in silence, but as he did so, there was a sense that he was changing. His color returned; he seemed sharper and more alive. When at last he spoke, he was quiet but firm. "Okay, then, let's reconvene here in an hour. At that point, I want to see some serious plans for how we can take back this issue. Thank you, Mr. Vice President."

Don't thank me yet, thought Godwin.

Four hours later, he was on the phone to Maggie. "It'll be all over town soon enough, so you may as well have the scoop. The president is going to fight for the satellite deal."

"Wow. How did that happen?"

"I think he just made up his mind."

"Come on, somebody must have pushed him into it."

"It was all Jack. He made the decision on his own. He was very forceful."

"Think it'll fly?"

"I've never seen him so motivated."

"Wow. Thanks."

"Good night, Ms. Newbold."

Godwin hung up and poured himself a brandy. That was good, he thought. He'd gotten the story out before the White House press operation put anything out. It wasn't like any of Chet's underlings were going to say that Vice President Pope had put some steel in Jack's backbone. And, of course, it wasn't like Godwin had had any of his own aides in the room who could be trusted to leak some behind-the-scenes color to a reporter willing to sprinkle some hero dust on Godwin's shoulders. But somebody in the meeting might have blathered something about Jack and Godwin conferring, and thus diluted the focus. No, he thought, better to make sure Jack gets all the credit in print. Get this story out first, and it becomes the lead dog all the others run behind. The press seldom goes back and says, "Hey, remember that story we ran last week? Here's a slightly more nuanced version."

He had another sip of brandy, then began calculating his next move. Having pushed Jack into the fight, he now had to make sure Jack won. Or at least almost won. He began making a mental list of databases he planned to study in the morning.

9

THERE WAS REALLY ONLY ONE THING Linda Archer had learned about being a Washington bureau chief from watching Bryson Berger for all those years: don't get excited about rumors. Bryson Berger may have been harsh, may have been sarcastic, may have cut corners when he had to, may have had little regard for such niceties as budgets, may have played favorites, may have especially played favorites with reporters of the female type who looked good in a skirt, may have been the prime culprit in the disintegration of four marriages and families, only two of which were his—hey, forget all that *may* crap; he *was*—but he was absolutely dead-on about rumors. And for that matter, tips. And leaks, which usually were no better than rumors anyway. "If true!" she could hear him booming. "If true!" "Save your excitement for stories," he'd say, "for actual, reported stories that have been fact-checked and closed." "Only rookies get excited about leaks," he'd sneer. "Half the time they're simply wrong, half the time they're malicious lies planted to make somebody look bad, and half the time whoever's telling you the story is implicated up to his ears in something worse. That's three halves! That's one hundred and fifty percent of the time that rumors are useless! That's a lot for a rumor to overcome!" Linda thought Bryson would have been especially skeptical about a leak on a major story that had come merrily tra-la-la through the gate after it had been fruitlessly hunted for weeks by two White House correspondents and another five or six veteran Washington reporters from your own magazine, plus the bloodhounds from every other news organization in town. And he would have been even more skeptical when Maggie Newbold, who not only had, shall we say, a bit of history as far as tips go but whose very nice story about Adrian Simone had just hit the jackpot, and as anybody with an ounce of brains could tell you, the guy who hits Lotto doesn't turn around and win Powerball the next friggin' week. Linda called Maggie into her office.

"So who's your source on this, Maggie?"

"Godwin Pope."

"Godwin Pope? And you believe him?"

"I don't know why not. It's not like he's Jack Mahone's butt boy or anything."

"He's invested in the administration's success."

"Well, I don't think he is, particularly, but it seems to me we get a lot of news from sources inside the administration who are invested lock, stock, and barrel in the administration's success, and I don't see us holding our noses at them. But Pope's motivation is irrelevant. I got it all confirmed on the record by Chet Wetzel."

"Speaking of Jack Mahone's butt boy."

"Linda, what on earth is your problem? I'm mystified. Why are we having this discussion? The president's pushing the sale. The story's true, it's accurate, it's fair, and it's ours. Our scoop. We should go with it before it shows up on the Worm Report."

Linda looked Maggie in the eye. "I just hate it when I think people are using us for their ulterior motives."

Maggie held Linda's gaze. Linda knows Godwin wants to sleep with me, Maggie thought. Then it hit her. No, Linda thinks we're already doing it. Well, if she's reached the point of thinking, we're long past the point where it would do me any good to deny it.

"Welcome to the world, Linda," Maggie said quietly. "Everybody's got ulterior motives."

As soon as Maggie left, Linda called Loomis in New York to tell him that it looked like they'd finally broken through with the story, that they could have a scoop up on the Web site in half an hour, light-years before anyone else, and that if Loomis wanted to, he might want to clear some time to go on the political talk shows that evening. Loomis was jubilant, full of praise and affectionate delight, and Linda, who so often had Loomis's anger and frustration and gratuitous nastiness slopped atop her head by the bucketload, was delighted to let his happiness shower upon her. "There's just one thing, Loomis," she said after his enthusiasm seemed to have run its course. "I'm worried about Maggie."

"Yeah, you're right," he said. "We really have to make room for her at our table at the White House correspondents' dinner. She's delivered the goods—we ought to showcase her a little, show her how much we appreciate her performance." Yes, that's the idea, he thought. That's it exactly. Get her out front, get her on TV, raise the magazine's profile, get us some buzz, make us the hot book, increase ad pages, increase the rate base, raise my profile in the corporation, set me up for a big move into the senior hierarchy of Google or Yahoo! or Whoop de damn doo or another one of those corporations with a stratospheric net worth that helps you to find Web sites devoted to Sodoku or chihuahuas in jodhpurs or that downloads TV shows right into your cereal bowl or porn right onto your penis, or whatever they're going to think up next.

For a moment, Linda actually considered correcting him, actually thought of telling him what she'd really been thinking, that she suspected Maggie would soon be or more probably already was spreading her legs for another powerful man. Nah, she decided. That would be the old Linda, not the new, smart Linda.

10

FROM THE TIME MAGGIE'S STORY broke on *Newsbreak*'s Web site, the White House was a hotbed of activity. Not normally a quiet place, not normally a library, there was nonetheless a difference, an accelerated metabolism. For the first time since Jack had become president, there was a drive, a sense of mission. There was no sulking, no vague confusion, no waiting for another shoe to drop. Everyone was busy. The faint drumbeat you might have thought you detected as you wandered the West Wing was simply the elevated blood pressure of those who worked there.

That was not so much the case with Godwin. He wasn't so busy. He went to meetings, lending his support to the troops in the war room who were planning the media blitz and keeping the count in Congress. "I want a full-out effort," Jack said at the Tuesday-morning staff meeting. "I want to make some speeches; I want the cabinet out talking; I want the newspapers blanketed; I want a Web site up and running; I want our supporters to launch a letter-writing campaign; I want the cable outlets so thoroughly covered that if I turn on the Food Network, I want to see Emeril Lagasse talking about cooking by satellite." By Friday, support in the president's party had genuflected into line; the last twenty votes he'd need would have to come from Republicans, and the good news was that a lot of them had waggled their pinkies to subtly signal that their votes would be available for a price. The bad news was that the price was not necessarily an affordable one. But at least dickering could begin. On Friday morning, after letting it be known that he'd be mentioning the issue at the White House correspondents' dinner, Mahone exhorted the troops. "Now let's get out there and twist some arms!" he shouted, and the staff stood and applauded him as they headed for the door. But Mahone did not exit the room directly, detouring instead to Godwin's seat. "Godwin," he said, leaning close and whispering, "I want to thank you for helping me to see what to do here. I'm fortunate to have your support."

"We will succeed, Mr. President," Godwin replied firmly in a moment of manly bonding. It was the least he could do.

Even Richie Platt was busy, scripting statements for presidential surrogates to deliver in support of the sale. Godwin knew that because Richie cheerfully mentioned it as they passed each other in the hall. He also reported another bit of news. "Guess what, sir? Mrs. Vanatua invited me to the White House correspondents' dinner. She said she heard I'm a promising young man!"

Godwin smiled. He wanted to be happy for Richie, who seemed so pleased, so proud, so validated by the invitation. It was, frankly, a bit dismaying to see how his head was turned just by being asked to one of these rituals, as though working in the White House somehow meant less to him than a nod from inveterate wheeler-dealers like Penny and Roland. It showed a lack of moral fiber. Regardless, Richie's moment of high self-regard would soon settle. His own moment of glory, Godwin was sure, was yet approaching. Step by step, his plan was falling into place.

There was one late surprise. On Friday morning, he was cc'ed a copy of the guest list. He noticed that seated at the *Newsbreak* table would be one Ms. Maggie Newbold. For the next thirty-odd hours, his thoughts kept sprinting ahead, and there were only two subjects: his little workshop plot against the president, and whether *love* was the best word for the incredible attraction he was feeling toward her.

11

THIS DINNER WAS NEVER an event Godwin had enjoyed, and as he took his place in the receiving line a few glad-handers away from the president and First Lady, he felt a morbid annoyance souring his disposition. What was the point of this dinner? The media spent 364 days a year actively gunning for Washington's officials, then on the 365th, everybody on each side put on tuxedos and party dresses and pretended to lavish respect on one another, which they did by pointedly mocking the foibles, errors, and gaffes of the other. Why bother? Perhaps because this isn't an event unto itself, Godwin thought, but more a part of our whole dance. We let the press think they really know what's going on, in exchange for not printing what they really know is happening. And if on one night along the way everyone gets dressed up and laughs at one another, if Fox News marks the occasion by inviting as its guest the profane dope fiend rock star who has a hot reality show, or if *Vanity Fair* decides to share its table with the oil heiress with the Texas-size titties whose boyfriend just released an unauthorized video of her in estrus, or if the cavaliers at *The Weekly Standard* think it's the height of good fellowship to host the powder blue tux'ed Lowell Mahone, well, this is the price we pay in order to manipulate a free and independent news media.

Godwin's ruminations were soon interrupted by the arrival of guests, and before long he was stationed in a lineup of media and political eminences and their seldom-exposed spouses, assigned to shake hands and exchange approximately twenty seconds' worth of simulated warmth with each of the paying customers. It was phony, robotic work, and before long Godwin had to resort to testing himself on the various shades of hair dye that were worn by the many blondes (indeed, they were almost all blond) in line: honey-dew yellow, strident gold, silver birch. After fifteen minutes or so, though, his spirits soared: there, at long last, greeting the president was Richie Platt, all tuxed and scrubbed and slicked back, along with his date, the beautiful, the alluring, the perfect Irene Kim. Godwin couldn't quite follow the conversation with the rapt attention he would have preferred to devote—there was static provided by a small, bronzed, hair-plugged, Botoxed network news president who had first attained prominence by producing monster truck rally programming, and was now trying to interest Godwin in making a guest appearance on the network's Navy Seals sitcom—but he could still follow the action. Jack gave Richie a hearty but perfunctory two-handed handshake, then proceeded to beam the full measure of his charm on Irene, who seemed as entranced as an ingenue. For the twenty seconds he held her hand—thirty!—forty!—Jack seemed unaware that there were people getting fidgety while waiting their turn. But he knew. And she knew.

It was a different Irene when she and Richie reached Godwin; Lordy, the girl appeared to have left her mind elsewhere! Godwin had to remind her that they had met just the other week at the Vanatuas', and even then, it certainly seemed to him that the magnitude of that august moment had become eclipsed in her mind. She kept stealing glances back at Jack, and it was all Jack could do to look as though he hadn't been stealing glances at her. When she moved away, Jack's eyes slithered behind her.

Godwin wasn't sure what, if anything, the First Lady thought of Jack's acrobatic eyeballs, or if the old gal was even aware, but personally, he couldn't have been happier. It was just as predicted, and all that he had hoped: the doggy liked the dog food. It was good to know that in this world of woe, some people would never let you down.

Sitting in the back of the Lincoln Town Car the magazine had hired for her, watching the streets between her home and the Hilton peel away like fan dancers in a Busby Berkeley musical, Maggie Newbold laughed at herself. She had been flattered when Linda invited her to the dinner, flattered that hard-to-please Linda had hacked through the thickets of their long, thorny relationship and was finally prepared to honor Maggie with the recognition that was her due. But then Maggie's brand-new friend and protégée Ayisha Mumenyori overheard Linda's perpetually piqued secretary spilling the truth at several indiscreet decibels above conversation level in the employee cafeteria, and Maggie understood that in fact Loomis had been behind the decision, as of course he ultimately was behind all the decisions at the magazine.

That left Maggie with an entirely different feeling. It was a confidence, a renewed confidence, really, a confidence she had not known in nearly a year—coupled with an enormous sense of relief. Ever since she had accepted this job, she had known that all over New York and Washington, invisible eyes were watching her, evaluating her, and now that she had passed the test, Loomis was intent on showcasing her. And himself, of course. It was his way of pointing out that her accomplishment was his genius. After all, anyone could have plucked this jewel from the gutter—Gaffney at the *Times,* McGrady at the *Post,* Edelman at ABC, Vanderdonk at *Time,* Ogilvy at *Newsweek.* Yet it was Loomis and only Loomis, the shrewd editor of *Newsbreak,* who possessed the acumen to scoop her up.

Thus even before Maggie heard that Godwin was attending the event, she had determined to make an impression that would stun the room, if only to demonstrate her gratitude to Loomis. But once she got his E-mail enumerating the dignitaries who were expected— the Honorable Godwin Pope, vice president of the United States, second on the list—she decided to go beyond all out. The conclusion wasn't reached without small, prudent voices in her head putting up a struggle. Her savings, which had been depleted during her enforced vacation, had yet to recover, and she surely didn't think it would be worth the cross-examination she'd get from accounting if she tried to slip the cost of a Badgley Mischka or a Carolina Herrera party frock into her expense report. But investments are important, she thought as she maxed out her credit card for a five-thousand-dollar strapless, body-skimming gold Dolce & Gabbana gown. And as investments went, this one was fun. Far too many people neglected investing in themselves, and besides, this one in particular offered an immediate psychic return to a girl whose best clothes during her hardscrabble Indiana girlhood, and, indeed, all through her self-conscious high school years, were hand-me-downs from a condescending cousin who was rabid about plaids.

Maggie had been irritated when she realized that Linda assumed that she was already sleeping with Godwin. She had thought she had been quite strong, as well as brave and decent and morally upright and ethically pure and all the other things the great world thought she should be, in resisting her powerful inclination to respond to the wildly attractive Godwin Pope. And where had it gotten her? It was true that Maggie had always heard whispers behind her back, murmurs from jealous low-talent sour balls like Linda. But she'd always been careful enough to preserve at least a Brazilian thong's worth of plausible deniability about her romances, thus ensuring that the ostentatiously high-minded individuals above her—people who possessed so much satisfaction in their own fundamental rectitude that they had no room for common sense—had always acted appalled by the gossipmongers. Now Linda had become one of those who ought to be similarly high-minded, but she was showing no sign of bending backward to be fair; so if she wasn't going to improve, why should Maggie?

Maggie never quite subscribed to this doctrine against sleeping with sources. It wasn't like she slunk around swapping hummers for headlines. The truth was at once simpler and more complex. She was just one of those women who had a thing for powerful men, not a weakness, but a taste—a trope, she'd once heard it called—and always had. In college, she was seldom impressed by the guys her own age. The jocks were just muscular animals with too much unfocused testosterone, the sensitive poets were neurasthenic twits with insufficient nerve, and all the rest of the guys, once you got past their lust and bravado, were simply insecure boys who couldn't handle the thought that the great piece of ass they were drooling over could possibly be smarter than they were. She was much more excited by cool Professor Thewlis, with his easy laugh and evocations of Emerson and stories about working at *Rolling Stone.* He recommended to her techniques for interviewing and fellatio, and after he bull-rushed her past other candidates and got her named editor of the school paper as a junior, they celebrated at a Super 8. He got roaring drunk and ended up naked on the end of the bed, weeping because his wife was going to leave him. It was then, at the tender age of twenty, that Maggie realized that men may hold titles and positions but that she held power, and would for the foreseeable future. And so it was, armed with that insight and her other gifts, that two years later she was having an affair with the governor's chief of staff in Springfield and breaking a big prison scandal story, and four years later was heading the *Journal*'s Cairo bureau, from which position she slept with the Arabian oil minister and the Egyptian defense undersecretary and the Israeli intelligence section chief, all men whose assuredness and acuity and verve she found fascinating. And it was simply true that time and again, her proximity to these men, her closeness, her ability to take a morsel from one and a tidbit from another allowed Maggie to end up nailing stories, good stories, important stories, stories that nobody else would have gotten.

But once she won the Pulitzer, somebody got gabby and word sloshed around, and she had to bear the humiliation of being called back to New York and hearing how shocked and appalled her superiors were, how aghast, how disappointed. It was insulting to sit and listen to such perorations from Olivia Britton Kuster, a brilliant journalist who had nonetheless never come close to matching Maggie's body of work, and whose own meteoric rise at the paper coincided with a happy and celebrated courtship and marriage to managing editor Morton Kuster. Maggie refused to go there. "Olivia," Maggie said quietly at what became the pivotal moment of her hearing, "everyone admires those stories you wrote about devious accounting practices and underhanded tax shelters, and the reforms that resulted were much needed and to your credit. But the pieces I wrote led to the smashup of a ring that recruited and financed and equipped suicide bombers, and if because of that there are today children playing in the sun who would otherwise be dead, then I don't think it's anybody else's damn business what I do with my free time." In the end, her sullen chiefs subtly, silently separated her from the paper without relinquishing her Pulitzer.

It all seemed the height of hypocrisy, she thought as the Town Car pulled up to the Hilton. Her driver opened the door, and she planted on the sidewalk a foot elegantly shod in Christian Louboutin, exposing a shapely leg from ankle to middle thigh to the appreciative view of a curbful of men. To hell with them all, she thought. I know what I'm doing.

12

THE RECEIVING LINE had disbanded, leaving Godwin to sip cocktails with assorted members of the political-media complex. Finding himself suddenly gummed up in a conversation with two Heritage Foundation economists and a comely American Idol runner-up about interest rates and the consumer price index, Godwin was relieved to feel a tapping on his shoulder, even when the tapper turned out to be Roland Vanatua. "Goddamn good news about the satellite deal, eh, Goddy?" The little man's smile was so bright that it could have been measured in lumens.

"Yes," Godwin pleasantly agreed. "I think things are falling into place."

"Mahone's not so goddamn worthless after all, eh? I told you he would come around."

"Indeed," said Godwin. You shameless turd.

"So you think we get this sale wrapped up soon, now that Jackie's got his ass in gear? In a week, maybe?"

"More likely two or three," Godwin said. "A lot depends on how hard Herman Vanick wants to fight."

"We want this done pretty damn quick, you know. My new casino's opening in Shanghai in ten days. I can't go until things are settled here."

"I'll bet you'll miss it. Did you get your headliner problem straightened out?"

"Oh, you heard about that, huh? Yeah, we got a real authentic

American country rhythm and blues artist to perform—Lowell Mahone!"

He doesn't remember our talk at all, Godwin thought. "Gee, Roland, do you really think your audiences will appreciate his kind of music?"

"They'll eat him up with a goddamn spoon! He's a real good ol' boy, and when you hear him sing, he sounds practically like he used to be a slave. You know—all spiritual and shit. Ooh, there's Sam Donaldson! I gotta go say hello. He still owes me a tenner!"

Before long, dinner began. The CNN people had been surprised that Godwin's secretary, having rather backhandedly declined their invitation to the vice president to sit at their table, called up sometime later (the Monday after the party at the Vanatuas', to be exact) and asked if the vice president now couldn't pretty please accept. Of course they agreed, apologetically bumping their Supreme Court reporter to the network's kiddie table in the ballroom's boondocks. The meal passed agreeably. Everyone did his or her best to avoid talking shop, and most people were content early on to sit quietly and let Godwin and Christine van den Hurdle (vanilla cream blonde), the network's Eurasian correspondent— that is, the correspondent covering Europe and Asia; Christine herself was from a ranching family in Montana—discuss some relatively new art galleries in London. This subject easily gave way to the matter of bad British food, something with which everyone at the table had experience, and all the guests chimed in with their memories of hideous dining, leaving Godwin momentarily free to scan the room. To his right, he had a clear view of the Vanatuas' table, where he could see Irene Kim basking in all the attention her youthful beauty deserved. Although Richie didn't seem to be doing much, to Godwin's eye he seemed to be doing everything right. The others at the table talked to Irene—Penny and the other women with a mild, auntlike kindness, the men somewhat more avidly. But Richie doted on her, hanging on her every word, anticipating her wants, assuredly beckoning waiters to bring her more of this and another of that. She looked very happy, but there was the tiniest bit of tentativeness in her glances and her smile. Why, it's as though she is worried about something, Godwin thought. Perhaps she's wondering if she should drop Marco McChesney's name in a crowd like this.

Meanwhile, on Godwin's left, at the *Newsbreak* table, a somewhat different dynamic pertained. Like all the tables, theirs was a round one, but one at which Loomis still sat at the indisputable center. Linda and the other subeditors flanked him, tilting his way as though he were projecting a tractor beam. The resultant tableau struck Godwin as looking like an FBI photo of a mob capo surrounded by his crew in a social club on Carmine Street. Okay, this bunch looked a little more bookish. Godwin couldn't hear what was being said at the table, but looking at the movement of Loomis's lips, he seemed to be performing a virtually ceaseless commentary on an apparently bottomless topic. Occasionally he'd pause to ask a question of one of his tablemates, but that was only to allow himself a forkful of meat, which he swallowed almost unchewed before leaping back in and reseizing the conversational wheel.

All the while, Maggie sat 180 degrees away, seemingly floating in her own space, a bemused, indulgent smile on her face. Encased in her magnificent golden gown and propped on a lowly functional chair, she looked as though she was simply biding her time there until something better came along. Several times people came over to say hello to her, most of them taking care to greet Loomis and pay their obeisance to him first. Thus it was nearly newsworthy when the venerable Leonard Dvorcheki, the snowy-haired former secretary of state, trundled over and gave her a warm, rumbling, bear huggy greeting, while sending Loomis the sort of faint four-finger wiggle a seventh-grade girl at a school dance might begrudge her chaperoning mother. Godwin wondered if Loomis had ever seen *A Star Is Born*.

At long last, it was time for the speech making—first, the dusty, obligatory welcome and statement of purpose delivered by the portly president of the White House Correspondents' Association, the *Baltimore Sun*'s Judson Fuller, followed by the occasionally humorous commentary of Gorman Franks, a leathery New York radio personality who attracted political guests, followed by a reply from the president of the United States, Jack Mahone.

Who was funny.

And charming. And self-effacing. He talked about his golf game. "I had the great thrill not long ago of playing a round out at the Congressional with the amazing Tiger Woods. And this is a true story—Herm Vanick can tell you; he was out there, at least for a while. Then it clouded up a bit, and Herm ran home. I said, 'Herm, where you goin'? Got to take care of some vital legislation that would serve the interest of the American people?' He said, 'No sir, it's just with the luck you've been havin', I don't want to be anywhere near you and lightning.' "

All of Mahone's folksy charm had been brought to bear, and the audience was really laughing, not the tolerant, supportive ha-ha-ha of a sympathetic group grading on the curve, but real laughter. Washington insiders seldom require a speaker to have exquisite comic abilities, and often admire a good performance by a game amateur much more than one by a polished pro. But Jack was managing to be game and polished.

"My first shot," Jack continued, "it kind of hooked a little to the left. Hooked a little, then hit a bird. Kind of a big bird, actually, who carried the ball over to the parking lot, where he dropped it into the cab of a UPS truck, which just so happened to deliver it to Republican National Headquarters over there on K Street. Tiger Woods, such a gentleman, said, 'Maybe you should take a mulligan on that shot, Mr. President.' I said, 'I'm glad you said that, Mr. Woods. 'Cause if you made me play that shot, I think the next place you'd be golfing would be Guantánamo.' "

Mahone continued on his roll for quite some time, then brought the speech home in impressive fashion. "It's a good thing that you can get mulligans in golf. I've given a few, and Lord knows, I've gotten more than my share. I don't know if you can get mulligans in politics. I guess that's up to the voters. I know my administration hasn't done so well this first year, and I'm sorry for that. But I feel confident that we have put our act together, that we're going to do what the American people sent us here to do, and that our best days lie in front of us. I've got a great staff, I've got a great cabinet, I've got a great vice president in Godwin Pope, and because of that, you should all expect great things from us in the days to come."

Whether it was a confession or a monologue, or both, it was surprising and captivating theater, and the audience jumped up to applaud. Godwin joined the surge. As he watched Jack negotiate his way through the tables in front of the exit, Godwin felt oddly touched that Jack had bothered to mention him. His eyes stayed on Jack as he moved through the audience, shaking hands as he walked. When he reached the Vanatuas' table, he greeted Penny with a kiss and gave a handshake and a pat on the back to Roland. Godwin expected Jack to move on, but Jack continued around the table—he was heading for Richie! Yes, a handshake with Kerr of Levco, Inc., and Mrs. Kerr, Masur of Morgan and Mrs. Masur, and now he reached Richie. He took Richie's hand and pumped it twice; then he bent down and whispered in Irene Kim's ear. She nodded but still looked baffled, and the president moved on. Richie had never been his target.

Dead man walking, thought Godwin, still applauding. Dead man walking.

Once the president left, a solid half of the crowd split, too. Godwin himself would have been happy to have concluded his evening's labors and hightailed it, but when he saw Maggie settling in with new conversation partners and a fresh drink, he realized that things were going to take awhile, and he told himself to relax a little and dispense some charm. He danced with Charlotte Crispin, the president of CNN and his nominal host (and a white-chocolate cheesecake blonde), then did a few laps with Christine van den

Hurdle and the wives of two other correspondents (champagne on ice, dulce de leche). Cut in on by a gallant husband—awfully tardily, Godwin thought—he jumped at the chance to take a turn with Penny Vanatua, and thereby end all of his obligations within the space of a single Cole Porter medley.

"How were things at your table tonight?" Godwin asked blandly.

"Oh, very nice," Penny said.

"Did your little experiment in matchmaking work out?"

"What?" Penny coyly feigned ignorance, but only for a second. She gestured toward Richie and Irene, who was resting her head against Richie's lapel. "Look at them. See for yourself."

The couples turned, so that the backs of Penny and Irene faced each other. A grinning Richie caught Godwin's eye, waggled his tongue, and flashed a double thumbs-up.

"Yes, I think they're hitting it off," Godwin agreed. Over Richie's shoulder, on the periphery of the dance floor, Godwin could see Maggie shuffling with a short fat man—ah, Leonard Dvorcheki! Now's the time to strike, he thought.

The song ended, and Godwin and Penny politely applauded each other. "Another triumph, Penny," he said, and as swiftly as he could politely move, he crossed the floor to Maggie.

LOOMIS HAD BEEN shrewd to bring Maggie to the party and show her off, but instead of squiring her around the room, he snuggled into the comforting company of his yes-men, leaving Maggie to dangle. She had swatted away an approach from a gnomish man who turned out to be the debonair baritonal voice of NPR in the morning, who wondered if she'd like to join him in a discussion of media ethics—as if!—and another from a lean, handsome lad from an on-line political magazine who felt obliged to recite a list of pieces that he'd written that she'd probably missed, as curious a case of boasting and self-abnegation as she'd ever seen. She kept anticipating Godwin Pope to make his move—he had every other time they'd encountered each other—and although she was quite sure she caught him scanning the room for her, and was absolutely positive on several occasions that she felt his hot eyes on her shoulders, he always seemed jammed up by his companions. Briefly it occurred to her that maybe he wasn't going to make a move, that she had rebuffed him too often, and she felt the cold clutch of disappointment in her stomach.

Thankfully, Leonard Dvorcheki appeared—Leonard Dvorcheki, whom she thought an official war criminal in her youth, but who now seemed cute in his roly-poly way.

"Do you find it's true, Ms. Newbold, that power is an aphrodisiac?"

"Perhaps," she allowed. "It's true that many powerful men are attractive, but many are not. But nearly all powerful men are confident; perhaps it's that confidence that women respond to."

"I'm as confident as I ever was, but I'm no longer powerful." The old man sighed. "And I no longer get the babes."

"Oh, I can't believe that."

"Sometimes graduate students," he said, shrugging. "You know—history, international relations. I tell them about playing Ping-Pong with Gorbachev, and sooner or later, the knickers come off. The girls, that is. The boys just want to know the score. I change it every time. I bet that story is in a hundred graduate theses, and each one has a different score. Did I ever tell you about playing Ping-Pong with Gorbachev?"

"Oh, I'm afraid that wouldn't do you any good, Mr. Secretary," she said. "I'm not much of a sports buff."

"Ah, too bad. But I have other stories. Alas, here comes Godwin Pope. He has the look of a man who hasn't eaten in months, and you look like a cupcake. Mr. Vice President!" the old man boomed, extending his hand. "How wonderful to see you!"

"Mr. Secretary," Godwin acknowledged.

"I was just going to tell Ms. Newbold a hilarious story about what happened to me when I went looking for the water closet at the Nobel Prize awards ceremony, but I think maybe now I'll save that tale for another time. Did you see any graduate students out there?"

"I don't think so, sir."

"Well, I'll go have a look anyway. Maybe one of the waitresses would like to hear a good Gorbachev story. Excuse me."

They watched the small round man waddle off. It made for a fortuitous cover; they both knew what had brought them to this point in the evening, but a smooth transition was essential. When the old man disappeared, Godwin looked back at her. She was wearing a small smile and looking up at him. Her eyes were glistening.

"Did you come to tell me of some exciting personnel changes in the Department of Agriculture?" she asked.

"No," he said. He thought about parrying her joke, but decided to pass. "I just wanted to ask you to dance."

They took to the floor, which was now populated by senior producers and senior editors and Hill staffers, ordinarily somber, competent people in their late thirties who had booked the sitter until two and who were now intent on doing all the things that seemed like fun back in the days when they were young and carefree and were drinking a lot and were overweeningly confident of concluding the evening with some genital friction. Now the dancing and drinking were leaving them merely overheated and footsore, and many were too self-conscious of sweating through their new discount dresses or rented tuxedos to pay attention to Maggie and Godwin. The band was playing something new and Celine Dionish, but he didn't care. He was closer to her than he had ever been before, was holding her close. As always, the actual proximity of a woman, her substance and weight and warmth, was intoxicating. He felt he heard her purr.

"So how does it feel?" he asked.

She lifted her head to look him in the eyes. "To be dancing with the vice president?" she asked with a smile.

"To be the most beautiful woman in the capital of the free world."

She thought she might blush, but resisted. It would be bad form to succumb so easily. "It would probably feel better if the band wasn't playing something so turgid."

"You don't think I'm serious," he said.

"Sorry. I'm just accustomed to discounting everything a politician says."

"Oh, but I'm not a politician."

"No?"

"No, I'm a vice president. My job is to stand close to the ear of the president and whisper the truth. Just as I'm doing now." He pulled her closer.

"You are the ruler of my imagination," he said. "You are the queen of all my thoughts."

She knew he wasn't mocking her, but she was surprised by what for the life of her seemed to be sincerity. She had arrived at the dinner prepared to respond to anything that seemed in the realm of debonair, and now here he was being actually romantic.

And making her feel romantic. "Do you know what I like about this event?" she finally asked.

"What?"

"The sexual tension. The way everyone has to stay polite and apropos. The way you're supposed to pretend that I'm not a woman, the way I'm supposed to ignore that you're a man."

They had stopped dancing and were just holding each other, but then the song ended and they jumped back, as though everyone was now looking at them, and reflexively they pitty-patted applause. But her eyes were electric.

"Let's leave," said Godwin.

13

IT WAS SHE WHO WAS the smarter of them. It was she who told him to go and that she would follow in twenty minutes or so, putting some time and public conversations between their dance and their departures so that all but the most imaginative minds would be lulled. "Go to my house," he told her, writing the address on the back of a place card. There was a time on occasions like this when he would hand the woman a business card that had the address printed on it. Handwriting worked better. It seemed to be so much more spontaneous.

Heading for the door, he ran into a flushed and nearly breathless Richie Platt. "How's it going, lad?"

"Excellent, sir! Really, really excellent! Irene and I have hit it off so well! And you know what the president did?"

"What?"

"He invited me and Irene to come to a screening of a movie at the White House next week."

"Really?"

"See? It's like I told you. Once you come to one of these things, you're in."

Yes, thought Godwin, and once you dangle a T-bone steak before an old hound, he can think of nothing else.

GODWIN INSISTED on maintaining his house in Georgetown—"my own personal reasons," he barked at Chet Wetzel when the issue first arose during the transition period after the election. The Secret Service wasn't happy, and groused about the cost of extra shifts and extra apparatus. Godwin listened to that for about fifteen seconds, then closed off that discussion by whipping out his checkbook and signing a blank check. Now the security detachment sat discreetly outside, front and back. Inside, guests passed through a full-body scan so powerful that the images it generated verged on soft-core.

Godwin surprised himself with his nervousness; it was almost as though he'd never had a woman over before. He puttered around, made sure there was ice—of course there was ice, liquor in the liquor cabinet, fresh flowers in the living room, coffee in the cupboard, fresh everything in the fridge, and all his traps set. He thought of changing (resisted it); thought of loosening his tie (nah). Ultimately, he decided not to alter anything lest the mood be altered with it, and just sat down with a glass of Perrier.

He began to think of Maggie.

It was hard to say why he'd fallen for her the way he had. More than her looks—he'd enjoyed hot-and-cold-running beauties for years, and none had worked her way into his head like this. It was her smarts, of course, but maybe more, it was the way she used them. Look at the way she'd handled herself during that first interview: interested in him, but not impressed. She had confidence. She reminded him so much of Minerva, who was both warm and challenging, whose constant smile made it seem that she was always either being delighted by something really fabulous or mocking some sham. He thought something similar about Maggie, that she seemed like she wouldn't mind spending a great deal of time with him, while at the very same time seeming like she could get a call tomorrow and move to Kuala Lumpur without giving him a second thought. He was intrigued by that quality, bothered by it. He wanted to know what he would have to do to make a difference to her, to make her want to spend her time with him, and to hate the thought of being away from him. Because he knew he wanted to spend time with her.

Which is why he didn't particularly want to use her in his little scheme. Or, to be clearer, why he would never want her to find out that he'd be using her. Because the choice to use her had been made. That ship had sailed.

Or had it? What if he stopped now? What would be the harm? That's an easy one—there would be no harm, he thought. Lowell Mahone would have his gig, the Vanatuas would have their deal, Richie Platt would have a girlfriend with an interesting history, and Jack Mahone would have a real presidency, one in which he'd finally get to use his gifts to build a record of accomplishments.

And Godwin would have been helpful in all that. As if he were an angel, moving secretly behind the scenes. And Jack would be appropriately grateful, nodding to Godwin at gatherings and suggesting a special round of applause for him whenever people would assemble to sing the praises of the Mahone administration.

Not just a round of applause.

A special round of applause.

Oh fuck that, he thought. It's too late.

Jack had a good week. After a bad year, he had one good week. Leopards don't change their spots. He's just not good enough, and he never will be. He has to go before it's too late.

The doorbell rang.

It was already too late.

He opened the door. Maggie was leaning on her elbow against the door frame, grinning. He reached for her to kiss her, but she blocked him and reached for his bow tie. "Wait a minute," she said. "I love untying these things." He stood there without contesting as she tugged at it with both hands, the tip of her tongue peeking between her teeth. "There," she said, and it sprung loose. She looked in his eyes. "Now let's get to it."

They lunged hungrily, pressing against each other and pulling off their clothing. Her dress, stiff and beaded, was heavy; she herself was light. Under his fingertips, her breast was as tender as meringue. He was inside her before they reached the top of the stairs.

They had a night of passion that people over thirty-five who aren't under the sway of powerful stimulants seldom enjoy. Once, twice, a third time to salute the dawn. She was happy with his old-fashioned muscularity, a body not cut and defined like those of modern young men, but just a broad-shouldered slab, with a pinch of flesh at the waist and just enough hair on his chest to put her in mind of William Holden and Robert Mitchum and the other men she saw on the black-and-white portable in her fatherless home when she was a little girl. He liked the bouquet of her breasts and her abundance, more artist's model than aerobics instructor. They communicated well but seldom spoke, emphatic grunts and sighs and trills perfectly replacing poorer, word-bound expressions. It had been months since she'd had sex with a man, not once in the whole time since she'd returned to Washington. It had been years since he had made love to a woman he actually desired, and not simply one whose eager curiosity he had availed himself of. He liked it. He liked it a lot. And as he watched the minutes before eight o'clock count themselves down, he regretted that this moment was coming to an end. But once again, it was show time.

"Fuck!" he shouted, and lurched abruptly to his elbows. "Fuck! Fuck! Don't tell me it's already eight!"

He got to his feet and went hunting for his robe. "I completely forgot I'm supposed to be in Philadelphia this morning! A prayer breakfast! Of course, my staff would ordinarily make sure I was up, but I have issued them standing orders never to bother me here. Aw, fuck!" There were no lines for her in this scene; he knew it was a monologue. The key was to maintain a high level of rushed distress. "I have to shower. I'm not even sure I have the right suit—"

She had sat quietly with the sheet drawn across her breasts, watching in sympathetic silence as his tension built. "Is there anything I can do?" she finally asked.

"No," he said, "nooo. Well yes. If you don't mind, would you put on some coffee? It's all in the kitchen. Coffee's in the cupboard above the coffeemaker. I'd really appreciate it. I hate to ask."

"No problem," she said, easing out of bed and slipping on his tuxedo shirt as a wrap. "I'm happy to help."

He didn't wait for her to exit before heading to the shower. He really did have a prayer breakfast in Philadelphia on his schedule, but people at these things were understanding if a vice president arrived in time for a few "Heavenly Fathers" and photography and skipped the scrambled eggs. Still, he'd have to hurry. He'd laid a trap, and the whole point of setting a trap was to catch somebody, not to get a manly, fresh-all-day feeling while the quarry sneaked off with the cheese.

She padded softly downstairs and headed toward the kitchen, which she was presuming was in the rear of the house. She took note of his artwork as she passed—a Picasso, a Mondrian, some photography—all remarkable pieces, to be sure, but at the same time garden-variety zillionaire art. Ah, here was something out of character, a large labyrinth of white chalk figures on a black background, inscribed "To Minerva, Keith Haring." Maggie didn't think that eighties stuff would catch Godwin's eye. The southwestern Stickley-style furniture in the living room also surprised her, although when she thought about it, the twenty years Godwin had spent in California was ample time to form that taste. There were photos in frames, not many, but well presented: a man and a woman Maggie took to be his parents, young, happy, each with a giddy display of teeth, probably taken not far on one side or the other of their wedding day; the same man twenty or so years later on, thicker, dark rings under his eyes, faded, standing with an attractive, sharply dressed brunette on a city sidewalk somewhere, she with a dazzling smile, his a sincere but more freighted grin. There was a shot of a young hairy Godwin and a young hairy Tom Ralston and three or four other young hairy men, all wearing Zephyr T-shirts, probably at a picnic or a softball game on a sunny Silicon Valley afternoon, and another of Godwin and Tom, shorn and suited, exultantly ringing the opening bell at the New York Stock Exchange on the day, no doubt, that they took the company public. There was a picture of a delighted Godwin sitting at the controls of a single-engine airplane. And that was it. No covers from *Forbes* or *Fortune,* no pictures from his senatorial campaign, no shots of him and President Mahone waving their arms in victory or putting their heads together in an effort to save the world. Nothing like that at all.

She moved to the kitchen. It was mostly neat and clean, with polished satin-steel appliances and clean marble counters, although there was stuff all over the large table—a laptop that had been left up and running, as well as documents and papers. She automatically looked closer.

They were White House papers. White House reports. Doesn't say who sent it, just initials, she thought. Who could P.K. be? The distribution list was also initials and acronyms, but any list that started with POTUS and VPOTUS and moved to COS was not going to be an insignificant document. One report showed a list of congressmen—Republican congressmen—and senators—most of whom she could recognize, though not all. Not completely up-to-date. Douglas Shorto had died last spring. Quinn had retired, and Belden had lost. Next to them were names of corporations—defense contractors mostly, but others, too—conglomerates she couldn't identify, and what seemed to be little companies. Next to them were amounts of money. Campaign contributions? No, the amounts were too large, many in the tens of millions. And not only too large—some were too weirdly precise. Here's the name of a coffee-supply company in Altoona with $12,839.42 next to it. Weird. What year is this list for? she wondered. Last year. And there's another for the year before. There's one for each of the last five years.

She gently poked the ENTER button on the laptop. The screen came alive. It looked to be the same kind of list—names, amounts—but now it was Democrats. And it was a current list. And the numbers were all round numbers. She scrolled to the top of the list. Here's why. "Projected Expenditures." I see, she thought.

Godwin saw, too. Watching from a vantage point in the pantry, into which he had quietly crept, he was struck anew by her sexiness, by her tousled hair and the keen intelligence in her still-sleepy eyes, by the way the tuxedo shirt parted to semireveal the parabolas of her breasts. God, she's beautiful, he sighed. "What the hell are you doing!" he bellowed.

He had expected to see her startled; he had wanted to make her jump. Instead, she flicked her eyeballs in his direction and murmured, "Mmmm," the sort of bare acknowledgment you might offer customers who were impatiently fuming as you stood in line in front of them at the post office indolently affixing stamps. She didn't even bother to close her shirt, and her utter comfort disarmed him. He hadn't toured that landscape so frequently that he could take that vista totally in stride. Silently and apparently ineffectually, he stood waiting as she more closely scanned the paper. Finally, she looked up.

"You know you're not supposed to see that stuff," he said, trying to put an edge in his voice.

She shrugged. "I don't see anything anywhere that says 'Top Secret.'"

"No, but you're in the home of the vice president! You're in his kitchen! This is internal White House material. You're not supposed to be looking at it. It's confidential."

"Yeah, but it won't be for long, will it?"

"I guess not. Not if you intend to write an article about it."

"It won't be confidential for long whether I write about it or not, right? The White House is going to use this, right?"

Godwin shrugged. Best to look a little pouty and recalcitrant, he thought. She was figuring it all out, just as he'd expected she would. Best to do everything to convince her that she's stumbled onto a major scoop.

"This'll steamroll the Republicans, won't it?" Now she closed the shirt and covered herself. She had entered explainer mode. This was the first draft of the pitch she'd give her editors later today—surely no later than first thing tomorrow—about the significance of her discovery. "Correct me if I'm wrong, but what all this data proves is that the Republicans in the House and the Senate supported satellite sales to foreign nations, China included, when the satellites were being built by contractors based in Republican districts. And now that the satellites are going to be built by companies in Democratic districts—"

"Yes," said Godwin. "They oppose it. It has nothing to do with security, just who gets to drink from the government's spiggot. Makes them look a little hypocritical."

"At least!" she said. "Where does all the data come from?"

"I don't really know," said Godwin. "Some analyst in the GAO."

"I want a copy."

"Not from me."

"Please, Godwin!"

"Just wait a few days. We'll schedule a press conference. You and all your colleagues will get them."

"No! Are you joking?"

"We'll put all the information in a nice blue folder with the White House seal embossed on the front."

"I want it first. Make it an exclusive. I can almost guarantee the cover."

Can't make it too easy for her, he thought, and can't make it too hard. "You're putting me in a terrible spot, Maggie," he said, shaking his head. "I don't want it to seem like the White House leaked to *Newsbreak* in advance, if for no other reason than the other outlets might underplay it and we'll lose the impact. Can't you—why don't you do it yourself? There are no secret figures here. As far as I can tell, it's all data that's in government reports that are available on the Web. You just need to go to the right databases."

There was a knock on the door. "That must be my ride. I've got to dash. I'll get some coffee in Philadelphia."

"You're going to leave me here?"

"Shut the back door when you go. Look—about last night—I enjoyed myself tremendously. May I call you?"

Already thinking about her story and distracted by the arrangements of her departure, Maggie took a moment to retrieve the mood of romance. "Absolutely," she said, tilting her head and smiling. "Do it soon."

14

MAGGIE SPENT THE DAY in her apartment in front of her computer, re-creating the GAO data she had seen on Godwin's kitchen table, and taking it a step beyond. It didn't take much time on the Federal Elections Commission's Web site to see that the companies that were building the satellites in the Republican districts were also generous contributors to Republican officials. There wasn't anything corrupt going on—not unusually corrupt anyway—but it did expose Herman Vanick and his claque as two-faced blowhards whose position on an issue was available to anyone with a deep pocket. She didn't mention her findings to Linda Archer before the big 10:00 A.M. conference-call meeting with New York the following day. She didn't want Linda's fingerprints on the story, didn't want Linda sending the report off on some tangent, didn't want her input. Instead, Maggie passed Linda a packet of data just as Loomis called the teleconference to order, about a half hour after she had E-mailed the data to Loomis, just time enough for him to talk to his adjutants about it and get excited before the meeting was to begin.

"This is hot," he said right at the get-go. "I'd like to put this on the cover." He had been thinking about putting another heart disease story on the cover, mostly because stories about heart disease always managed to sell incredibly well to those traveling businessmen who spent their layovers eating pizza in airport Sbarros and drinking six-dollar Budweisers in airport bars. "Maggie, write this up and we'll see how it pans out," he said. "We can always bump heart disease. Linda, make sure Maggie gets whatever help she needs." Ordinarily, Linda would have felt rightly cheesed off by Maggie's naked end around, but since neither she nor anyone else in the bureau had anything that was going to advance the story, and since Loomis was obviously so giddy with joy, she was relieved, if not exactly delighted, to play along.

Maggie spent the week gathering predictable quotes from hemming, hawing Republicans and suddenly pure, happily strutting Democrats. The only quotes that seemed odd to her were from the General Accounting Office, whose bewildered spokeswoman apologetically avowed that nobody there had been working on any data related to satellite design or construction. "No ma'am," she said. "Nobody." Maggie thought the GAO must have been counting on making a big media splash and must be very disappointed that their thunder had been stolen.

By Thursday, Loomis was convinced that Maggie had brought him a major story, so major that he made a virtually unprecedented decision and had the magazine's PR people release the text of her article on Saturday afternoon, allowing it to dominate the Sunday-morning headlines and the Sunday-morning political talk shows. Maggie herself appeared on *Face the Nation* and was asked to join the panel on *Meet the Press,* whose host offered to let her keep her logo coffee mug from the set, a gesture generally regarded among capitol cognoscenti as signaling that she had been readmitted to the set of those who belonged. Not to be forgotten was the story itself: quietly, Republicans from swing districts began letting the White House know that the price of their support was dropping, leaving Herman Vanick, who had pledged to fight the sale until the last dog died, holding an indefensible outpost manned by a diminishing supply of increasingly frightened, panic-stricken curs.

Meanwhile, Godwin sauntered through a fairly slow week. After flying to Philadelphia and injesting some powdered scrambled eggs and double helpings of pieties, he returned to Washington. He put in some time on his sole constitutional responsibility, presiding over the Senate, if only to make sure nobody could ever accuse him of failing to fulfill his sole constitutional responsibility. He dropped by the White House legislative office to see how the vote count on the satellite sale was going. Mahone's people made a show of treating him with respect, a reflection of how his stock had risen in the president's eyes. Still, they really didn't have much for him to do; they calculated that they had enough nod-and-wink deals with the GOP to pass the measure, and they weren't sure what effect Godwin would have on that effort. The only public appearance he kept on his schedule was to make some brief remarks at a meeting of the Democratic Leadership Conference at the Westin, after which he caught the elevator to the forty-first floor and found the room that Maggie had taken. She opened the door wearing tiny French-cut panties and a black corset that pushed her breasts up to her clavicle. "Come on," she said, reaching for his crotch, "let's put some vice in this vice presidency," and before long they were sharing a volcanically shuddering nooner that left him weak-legged and cheerful for the rest of the day.

That happy mood was further elevated later when Jack phoned him and personally invited him to attend a private screening of a new film at the White House that evening. This time no blond doxies needed escorting; this was just Jack recognizing that Godwin's recent contributions had earned him a new, heightened status. Another guest in the small crowd was a beaming Richie Platt, who was accompanied by his very special friend Irene Kim. They made a good-looking couple (in truth, Irene made such a good-looking single that she could average even Andre the Giant into good-looking coupledom). Not too many minutes before the show was set to begin, Godwin could see Chet Wetzel approach Richie. As they spoke, a cloak of seriousness descended upon Richie. His brow furrowed, and he responded to Chet with a series of crisp, assured nods. He then turned to Irene, wearing as he spoke an expression that could only have been apologetic. Then he left. No doubt Chet had asked young Richie to undertake some critical mission vital to the future of the republic. Godwin watched the abandoned beauty for a moment, wondering what she would do. She looked forlorn and uneasy, and Godwin thought that perhaps she was thinking of bolting, when Jack made his entrance, Chet Wetzel in his wake. Shaking hands and patting backs, he made his way through his guests until he at last came upon Irene. He made a show of remembering her, and she seemed flattered. Then Chet leaned in and whispered something to Jack, who struck an expression of sorrow and disappointment, one so broad he might have copied it from something he'd seen in a silent movie. He then gallantly offered his arm to Ms. Kim and escorted her into the screening room. For Godwin's money, it was a better show than the movie. Filing out at the end of the evening, Godwin looked for Richie, but in vain. Neither did he see Jack and Irene; apparently, they'd slipped away early.

That week, Godwin also began spending time at the gym. Specifically, the Capitol Hill gym, the one reserved for members of Congress and the Senate. As an ex-senator, he was still allowed in, and as soon as he was back from Philadelphia, he began taking his workouts there, just so people could get used to seeing him. After five visits spent idling eagle-eyed about the Nautilus machines, he had a fairly good idea of the habits of some of the members, most particularly Herman Vanick, who seemed very attached to a fifteen-minute plod on the treadmill, followed by a steam bath. On Monday—the day following the weekend when Maggie's report had so triumphantly dominated the news, a mere handful of days before the satellite vote that would rescue the Mahone presidency—Godwin decided to join Herman Vanick in the steam room. Having elevated Jack to the brink of victory, it was now time to bring him down.

"Hey, Herm," Godwin nodded through the mist. "How's it hangin'?" Man, look at all the moles Herm's got!

"Hey, Godwin. Haven't seen you around here in awhile."

"I like it here," said Godwin, lying. For a long time he had taken his exercise with a personal trainer named Ingrid. Her, he liked.

"So how's the count looking from your end?" the Speaker asked, not out of any real inquisitiveness, just making polite shop talk.

"I think we have it in the bag," Godwin said with as much affect as he would have had if he were merely clarifying which of them was to be served next at the deli counter.

"Hmmm," Vanick rumbled. "If I believed you, that would mean some other people are lying to me."

Godwin laughed at Vanick's deadpan delivery. "And I bet you have a pretty damn good idea who they are, too."

"Yeah, it's the younger ones. None of these congressmen getting elected today can lie worth a shit. Too many born-again Christians. You ask them what they're going to do on a vote and when they answer, you hear that quavering in their voices, like they think God's stenographer is making a permanent record of everything they say."

"Herm, you should go on tour. You're a funny guy."

Herm himself was pleased with his little joke, and Godwin waited until the last of his self-satisfied chuckles faded away before abruptly changing the subject. "You know, Herm, I've been waiting for a chance like this—to get you alone."

Vanick's brow clouded over, and the furrows between his eyes deepened. Carefully, he turned his head to look over one shoulder, then, with equal deliberateness, he turned to look over the other. "You know I've always found you an attractive man, Godwin," he said at last, "but—why don't we get ourselves a room?"

Godwin didn't know if Herm was joking, but he surely didn't want to laugh at him. It took a moment to decide to just be cool. "I've wanted to get you alone, Herm, because there's something troubling me. A CIA analyst who reviewed the sale said he thought maybe the satellites could be adapted from pure communications to include a military capability."

"Uh-huh, yeah. Which, if you'd ever listen to our speeches, is what we've been saying."

"Jack ordered the report buried."

Herm had too much experience swimming in deep water to leap at a worm the first time it wriggled in front of his face. "The deputy director testified at the hearings. He said there was no danger. I read the transcript myself."

"And maybe there isn't any. But why did Jack bury the report?"

"How the fuck should I know? Maybe because he didn't want to hand us any ammunition."

"Why not?"

"Why do you think, why not?" Herman snapped. He never liked being the party in a conversation who was being asked all the questions, and Godwin's coyness was getting him exasperated. "For an intelligent man, you're asking some damn stupid questions this morning. Maybe you need to drink less decaf."

"I'm certainly not a person you should ask about Jack Mahone's motivations," Godwin said, thinking even as he was speaking those words that actually he had made quite the study of Jack Mahone's motivations. "Maybe the person you should ask is Roland Vanatua."

At the mention of the wily financier's name, Vanick's exasperation vanished, replaced by a mix of confusion and suspicion. This had become a terribly strange conversation. Vice presidents seldom tried to throw a monkey wrench into administration victories. "Why you doin' this, Godwin?" he said. "Jack send you out to pick up his dry cleaning or something?"

Godwin let Vanick's shot hang in the mist until even Herm began to wonder if he had somehow wounded Godwin's feelings. When Godwin finally spoke, he was very quiet. "You ever been to New York City, Herm?"

Herm half-expected a slap, but not a comment on his fly-overland tastes. "Yeah, I've been to New York. My ship had liberty there. I got drunk, banged two hookers, saw a John Wayne movie, then went to the Metropolitan Museum of Art. Yeah, a museum! How do you like that?"

Way to go, Herm, Godwin thought, bringing up your service in the marines. How fortunate. "You know they used to have an elevated train that ran down Sixth Avenue?"

"No. So?"

"They tore it down right before World War Two. Sold it for scrap metal. To a Japanese munitions company. They made machine-gun bullets out of it." He waited a moment for Vanick to absorb the inference. "You know who those bullets were used against, don't you, Herm?"

"Yeah, I think so," said Vanick, looking very grim.

"I mean, if there's any danger these satellites could be used against us . . ." Godwin let his voice trail off. Vanick thought himself the stronger of the two men, the tougher one, the marine, and Godwin had come to him. It was time to let Herman take charge.

"Yeah, I get you," grunted Vanick. "Who knows about this buried report?"

He bought it, Godwin thought. "A lot of people know," he replied. "Certainly the director does. And his deputy. Chet Wetzel. Broyard and the National Security team."

Vanick stood up, rivulets of sweat running off his blubber. "Looks like I got some work to do."

15

A MOTIVATED SPEAKER OF THE HOUSE can be a wonder to behold, and even before Herman Vanick finished toweling off and applying Desenex to his itchy toes, he was on the phone to his right-hand man, Junius Jolivette, a moonfaced Texan with a hairline whose premature retreat outpaced the withdrawal of the Iraqi army, issuing marching orders to his minions in the House. Thus it came to be that a scant twenty-four hours later, the House Foreign Relations Committee was called into session, over the strenuous objections of its members in the Democratic minority, for the purposes of hearing further testimony from the director of the CIA about the hidden report. That was startling enough—committee hearings were seldom such popular events that members wanted to go back and get more information about a subject on which they'd already decided that they'd acquired all the worthwhile human knowledge that could be obtained. But observers were surprised when they saw sitting in the central seat not committee chairwoman Sandra Brick Delaney of Utah, a woman so colorless and reserved that it was said that she did not leave footprints even in the Park City snow, but Herman Vanick. As Speaker of the House, he was an ex officio member of all committees, although he had never so much as dropped in on a hearing since taking up his gavel. But here he was, with a showy sheaf of papers, not merely taking his turn but leading the questioning.

Hunching his shoulders as he did during his schoolboy wrestling days, he bore in on the director of the Central Intelligence Agency, Kenneth Keith Brandt. "And in April of last year, the State Department asked your agency, the Central Intelligence Agency, to produce an analysis of the security ramifications of this sale, is that not correct?"

"Yes, sir," the director replied. The slender, brush-cut Brandt, a former admiral, was none too happy about being shanghaied up to Capitol Hill to discuss this issue, having deemed mastering the details of routine trade arrangements far below his pay grade. Still, since his days at Annapolis, he had been interrogated on all manner of matters, ranging from the name of Admiral Farragut's cabin boy (Clem) to the offensive capabilities of the Iranian navy (negligible), and the same rules always applied: say as little as possible. Try to look ahead to where the questioning was going, but do absolutely nothing to help the questioner make the trip.

"And in the course of things," Vanick continued, "various of your analysts looked at the sale and approved it."

"Yes, sir."

"But a Mr. Kempton also produced an analysis, did he not?"

"Yes, sir."

"Which could be termed negative, wouldn't that be fair to say?"

Brandt pursed his lips. "We don't really characterize analyses negative or positive, sir," he replied, allowing a hint of patronization to creep into his voice.

"No?"

"Negative or positive, that's for policymakers to decide. We just look at the facts."

"Okay, it wasn't negative, but it did suggest that the satellites could be adapted for military purposes."

"Yes, sir, Mr. Kempton's did so. But his was the only one. Another five analysts, all more experienced, reviewed the material and said such risks were minimal."

"Minimal!" Vanick fulminated. "What's minimal? Winning Lotto minimal? Getting hit by lightning minimal? Or getting hit by a car minimal?"

"Mr. Speaker, I think—"

"Tell me this, Admiral Brandt, what will you say when a Chinese ICBM strike wipes out the West Coast between Seattle and San Diego? 'Sorry, we thought the risk was minimal'?"

Way to go, Herm, Godwin thought. He was watching the hearings on his laptop in the West Wing. If you want a policy bombed, send in someone bombastic.

"Now, am I correct in assuming that Mr. Kempton is one of your top analysts?"

"Mr. Kempton is a capable analyst."

"Now, Mr. Director, that's not what I asked you. I assume he's capable. You wouldn't have him in the agency if he wasn't capable. I'm asking if he's one of your top people. Because I mean, it would seem to me that on a matter of national security, you would want to assign your top analysts, would you not?"

"Of course we do."

"So if Mr. Kempton is one of your top analysts, why would you just ignore his views?"

"We didn't!"

"But you didn't listen to them, did you?"

Poor Brandt, Godwin thought. He could end this dog and pony show in about three minutes if he wanted to, just by saying something he can't say, and won't ever, ever say—namely, that we have the capacity to liquefy the circuitry on those birds if the Chinese ever try to use them against us. Nobody will admit this because then the Chinese won't buy satellites from us, but will go get them from the French, at which point everybody else will, too, and then space will be full of birds whose software we can't liquefy. And as much as Brandt would like to get Herman Vanick to shut up and stop bothering him, he'll never say anything, because the CIA never admits anything. He won't even whisper it to Vanick on deep background, because the Republicans leak like frat boys after a kegger. So Brandt just has to sit there and get his ass kicked over a danger that's less remote than a blizzard in Bangkok.

"And so instead of taking Mr. Kempton's analysis and using it as a basis for further study, the president ordered his findings buried. Isn't that right? Buried?" At long last, Vanick had his money quote, the bit of footage that would lead all the network news broadcasts and morning talk shows, and headline all the papers.

Gauging by the look on Brandt's face, he was going to allow Herm about twenty more minutes of fun before some trusty aide was going to perform the time-honored charade of handing Brandt a note that would suggest some crisis had erupted that required his immediate presence in Langley. Vanick's day of grandstanding would come to an end. He would have achieved his public-relations objective, thrown a lot of red meat to the faithful, given the bloggers and the radio talk-show hosts enough raw material to chew on for a week, and laid the cornerstone for the next fund-raising mailing. He would also have firmed up a few shaky votes, but not enough to win the day. All he'd demonstrated was that there was a disagreement among CIA analysts. Well, big whoop. Anybody who had ever been part of a group of hungry people who couldn't decide on a restaurant knew that when human beings disagree, somebody's going to get his way and somebody's going to be disappointed.

And if nothing else was going to happen, that's where things would have ended, with Herm, huffing and puffing, waving a big question mark in the air. But something else is going to happen, thought Godwin, checking the time as he headed for the door. For a man who had nothing to do, all of a sudden, he was shockingly busy.

16

TAVIS WHOULEY, ONE OF THE WORLD'S last three-martini-lunch men, was patiently sipping his Bombay Sapphire special and perusing the menu when Godwin strode into the Willard Room of the Willard Hotel at the impossibly early lunchtime of ten after twelve. Godwin had chosen to invite the chipmunk-cheeked party chairman since, as the very visible figurehead of a declining institution, he offered a nice balance of important and irrelevant, an appropriately credentialed person whose presence with Godwin would arouse no curiosity whatsoever. Tavis was also, almost by definition, available. He'd have to be scheduled for brain surgery to turn down an invitation from a man who was not only the sitting vice president but also a presumptive candidate for Big Cheese at some point down the line.

"Tavis!" boomed Godwin. "How wonderful to see you! Thank you for coming!"

"Well, thank you for asking me," replied Tavis.

"You look like you've gotten some sun. Have you been marlin fishing again?"

In fact, Tavis had been, and much to his surprise, for the next half hour, in between placing their orders and the arrival of the lobster bisque and the oysters on the half shell they had ordered as appetizers, Godwin sat in the grand, gradually filling Beaux Arts dining room and quizzed Tavis about his vacation—where he went and whom he went with, what kind of tackle he used and the benefits of one kind of bait over another. Tavis was accustomed to discovering that few people could stand to listen to him speak about marlin fishing for more than a few minutes, and he could not quite believe that Godwin was so earnestly indulging him.

Godwin wasn't indulging him, really. Godwin couldn't give a rat's ass about marlin fishing, but he didn't have anything he really wanted to talk to Tavis about, so why not let the man blab on about the advantages of Cartagena over Key West, of Daiwa's Sealine reel over Okuma's mighty fine Titus Silver, and of the great new way Tavis had discovered of keeping his coiled pitch-bait leader (whatever that was) tangle-free? No, the real reason he had asked Tavis to lunch was because Godwin wanted to be sitting in the Willard Room at 12:30 when the astonishingly punctual Ralph Grove shuffled past and took his customary seat under the sketches of Buffalo Bill Cody and Lillian Russell in the corner of the Round Robin barroom. Ralph Grove was a Washington fixture, the longest-tenured reporter on staff at the *Post,* now an elderly, virtually out-to-pasture gossip reporter whose continued presence on the payroll could best be attributed to the fact that decades ago he would take the publisher's seven-year-old son to Senators games, and that seven-year-old, having now become publisher himself, could not bring himself to throw the kindly old alcoholic out on his ear. Godwin wanted to talk to Ralph Grove, and promptly at 12:40, just as the crab cakes were arriving and just as Tavis Whouley was about to climax his tale of landing a really big one, Godwin abruptly popped to his feet and excused himself. Heading for the gents', he made a show of greeting a vague face in the Round Robin Room and then shaking a few hands before catching the eye of the solitudinous Ralph Grove.

"Ralph?" he called. "Ralph Grove?"

Grove was a lean gray man with thin white hair. He wore a threadbare plaid shirt with a knotted wool tie and an aged herringbone jacket. He looked up at Godwin with a look of watery recognition that made Godwin fear for a moment that this wasn't going to work, that the old man was too far gone to be of use. But then he cleared his throat. "Hey, lookee here, it's Godwin Pope. What brings the vice president of the United States into this dump? Shouldn't a man of your stature be addressing the Future Futurologists of America or something?"

"Good to see you again," said Godwin, shaking Ralph's hand. Godwin noted that his timing had been impeccable; there was barely a swallow left in Ralph's first round. "Bartender, a drink for my friend here," he called before quietly adding, "A drink for the man who still has the liveliest items in the *Post*."

"Yeah, well, I haven't been—" Ralph's reflexive response was to dismiss the flattery, but lately the compliments had been few and far between, and besides, he couldn't help but agree that his items, when he managed to get them into the paper, showed a lot more style and craft than the ones by those youngsters who were all trying to be wisenheimers and comedians. "Yeah, okay, lively. Thanks."

They chatted about some mutual acquaintances at the paper and on the Hill, and Godwin had to chip in what most of the world considered his privileged insights into what was now officially the Marco McChesney signing. Then, having softened up Ralph, Godwin made his play.

"I bet you're going to have some fun with this Lowell Mahone business," he said.

"What Lowell Mahone business?"

"Yeah, right."

"No, what Lowell Mahone business?"

"Lowell Mahone headlining at the opening of the new luxury Emerald Garden casino in Hong Kong."

Ralph's bloodshot eyes expanded. "Lowell headlining? Like singing headlining?"

"Yeah. At Roland and Penny's new place."

"Headlining."

"Now don't let that famous Ralph Grove wit lacerate the poor boy too deeply. This is his first real payday in awhile."

"Payday?" Ralph said so forcefully that Godwin got a blast of the old man's sour mustard breath. "What's he getting?"

"Oh come now, let's have a little decency. I don't like to talk about another man's business. But I hear it's a bundle."

"Huhn. Might make a little item." Ralph was playing it close to the vest, but Godwin could see the wheels in the old man's head already trying to figure out what time it was in Hong Kong and how long it would be before he could get the gabby Lowell Mahone on the horn. "By the way," Ralph asked, "what are you doing here?"

"Just having lunch with Tavis Whouley."

"Oh. Wouldn't be an item in that, would there be? Something I could sell to the political desk?"

"Nah. Just a couple of guys talking about marlin fishing."

"Yeah? Have fun. I was sort of hoping you'd be telling me that you were meeting that *Newsbreak* broad with the nice legs."

"No. Who?"

"That Maggie whatsername I hear you danced with so nice and close at the dinner."

"No, we're just friends."

"Never mind," the old man said, rolling his eyes. "In the old days, a guy wouldn't bother to lie about nailing a sweet piece like that, because he'd know any decent reporter wouldn't bother to print the story."

"I have to go. It was good to catch up."

"Yeah. Hey, did you know that this is the room where Henry Clay introduced the mint julep to Washington? Yeah! Awful drink, if you ask me, what with the way the mint leaves stick in your teeth and all, but there you have it. I'm full of stuff like that."

"I bet you are."

"Hey, you know Walt Whitman mentioned Willard's?"

"No."

"Yeah, a piece about paper generals. 'There you are, shoulder-straps!—but where are your companies? where are your men? . . . Sneak, blow, put on airs in Willard's sumptuous parlors and bar-rooms, or anywhere—no explanation will save you. Bull Run is your work . . .' Still the same, right? Big shots putting on airs in Willard's sumptuous bar."

"Nice to see you again, Ralph. Hang in there."

"Yeah, I ain't going anywhere. See you around, Godwin."

Godwin went back to the restaurant, where he found his room-temperature crab cakes sitting opposite Tavis, who was allowing himself to appear to seem ever so slightly peeved, which, within the range of emotions someone like himself was permitted to express to a vice president, meant that inside, he was ferociously angry. His plate was empty and so was his drink glass; Godwin couldn't tell whether it was devoid of Tavis's first, second, or third martini.

"Sorry about that, Tavis," he said. "Please finish your story."

"Short and sweet: I caught the fucking fish. Godwin, let me ask y'all a question. Herman Vanick looked pretty comfortable swinging from his heels this morning. I don't think he landed any punches, but what's going on? Is he going to get any traction against the sale?"

"Short and sweet: no. Everybody understands that there can be disagreements over not only technological capabilities but the intentions of our foreign friends. But what Herm is implying, that the president had some ulterior motive for killing that report, is an ugly accusation, mean, nasty, dishonorable, and flat-out untrue. And preposterous besides. But forget all that—forget the plausibility, forget the absence of evidence. Cut to the heart of the matter, and ask yourself the one question that makes the whole discussion absurd on its face."

"What question?"

"What on earth does Jack have to gain from selling out his country? What does he stand to gain?"

"Right. What does Jack stand to gain?"

"Precisely." He pushed the half-eaten crab cakes aside and signaled for the check. "What does Jack get?"

17

SITTING IN THE BACK OF HIS LIMO, taking the short trip back to the White House, Godwin contemplated his efforts. He was fairly confident Ralph Grove would act on the tip, but there was no telling how industrious the old rum pot was anymore. Hong Kong was twelve hours ahead. If Ralph didn't wander too much on his way back to the paper, if he managed to get on the phone, if Lowell had finished his set and finished banging however many cocktail waitresses he would have managed to entice, well, then in all likelihood Lowell would be in his customary chatty mood, and when he heard a friendly voice from home inquiring about his new-won success, there was a decent chance he'd open up. And if nothing else broke on the gossip front, if all of Hollywood's various Brads and Chads and Jennifers managed to suffer one another's company for another day before splitting up, Godwin figured that there was a reasonably good chance that perhaps as early as tomorrow morning, Speaker Vanick and his henchmen would be reading about Lowell with their Cream of Wheat at breakfast. And if not tomorrow, then certainly no later than the next day. If Ralph's editors had half the news judgment that they thought they did.

He called his office for messages. "Richie Platt has been in and out all morning, hoping to see you," Mrs. Gottschalk croaked.

"What kind of mood was he in?" Godwin asked.

"Mood?"

"Mood, Mrs. Gottschalk. Was he happy?"

"Oh, no, sir. He seemed very upset. Emotionally, if you ask me."

Excellent, thought Godwin. One good thing after another. "Call him in, Mrs. Gottschalk. Have him wait. I'll be there directly." It occurred to Godwin that it had been decades since he'd been called upon to console the lovelorn. He was sure he could fake his way through it fine.

HE FOUND RICHIE slouched in a chair next to Mrs. Gottschalk's desk, bleary-eyed, unshaven, unkempt, and not at all the sort of person who should be seen in the Executive Mansion, helping to conduct the nation's business. "Richie!" he called. "How's it going, lad?"

"Fine, Mr. Vice President, thank you," said Richie as morosely as a boy who'd lost his dog.

"Now now, Richie, you can't fool me. What's the matter?"

Richie didn't reply, but instead performed emotional aerobics with his lips, pursing and flattening and pursing and twisting the corners, a kinetic counterpoint to the blank, hurt look in his eyes. Oh for goodness' sake, Godwin thought, he's been moping around all morning and now he's going to make me drag the story out of him while he represses a nervous breakdown. "Come on, is the job okay?"

"The job still sucks, sir, thank you."

"Then it's something else. Come on in and talk to me."

Richie followed Godwin into his office and dropped into a chair in front of the desk. Godwin took a seat, folded his hands in front of him, and offered what he thought was his best imitation of an expression a kindly parish priest would wear. "Let me guess," he said gently. "Things are not going smoothly between you and the beauteous Ms. Kim."

Richie's head dropped. "No," he replied. "I think maybe she likes somebody else."

"Oh? Another boy?"

"Kind of."

"That's too bad. You two seemed very happy."

"Yeah, we've only known each other, like, two weeks, but she and I were going to get married."

"Really?" Godwin was astonished.

"Well, I was going to ask her anyway. Thinking about it anyway. You know, Irene is the first girl I have ever really, really, really loved, with the possible exception of Mary Jane Kozak in junior year, until we got back from the trip to Spain. Irene is so beautiful, so demure, so charming, so clever, and so cute—she's got this little thing where her nose wiggles when she laughs—and she loves puppies, and kittens, and she would just fuck me dry every night, three times, four, every position—"

"Uh-huh."

"You know that expression, that every man wants a woman who's a lady in the living room and a whore in the bedroom?"

"Vaguely."

"Well, that's Irene."

"I would never have guessed. Here, have a tissue."

Richie blew his nose, three great honks. "And now she won't even take my calls."

"Well, why not? What happened?"

"It's because of him."

"Who?"

"Him," said Richie emphatically while pointing repeatedly in the direction of the Oval Office. "Him!"

"Him?" Godwin did his best to sound flabbergasted. "What's it got to do with him?"

"Because the two of them are hooked up now."

"No! You're joking! No, that cannot be. How on earth did that happen?"

"He saw the two of us together at the White House correspondents' dinner."

"Right, I remember."

"Then he invited us to watch a movie at the White House screening room."

"Ohhhh."

"But then I couldn't go. Chet Wetzel pulled me aside to tell me I had to write some emergency remarks for the president to deliver the next morning for the president of Egypt's visit."

"Important remarks!"

"Yes!"

"Just like you were hoping to be assigned!"

"Yes! And the president wanted them to be perfect. Chet sent me back to rewrite them, like, four times. And of course by the time I was finished, the movie was over. And by then, the president had given Irene his personal Oval Office tour."

"Uh-oh. The tour."

"Yeah," said Richie, shaking his head in disgust. "He had that same look he'd have when I'd get him girls during the campaign. What's the word? He overcompensates. He acts all crisp and officious, but it's not like he's been working, because you can, like, see that his hair's all fucked up or something. And meanwhile, Irene was all glowy. I knew what happened. I'm not stupid! I mean, I'm a moron, because I brought it all on myself, but I'm not stupid!"

Godwin allowed the mood to settle for a moment, let Richie compose himself, become more angry than upset, before asking the $64,000 question. "But you sound like you still want her back."

"Yeah!" said Richie instantly. "Yeah, I do. So she gets a little round-heeled around the president. That doesn't mean she wasn't the best thing that ever happened to me. I love that woman! I love her! But she won't even return my calls. I don't know what I'm going to do."

Godwin let the question pregnantly fill the room. Then, quietly, evenly, he said, "You'll just have to get him out of the picture."

Richie snorted. "Yeah, right. What am I supposed to do, beat him up? Ooooh, look, I'm going to catch the president of the United States after gym class and beat the shit out of him because he stole my girlfriend. Yeah, sir, that's good—I'll beat him up after the sock hop."

Godwin let Richie's disdain hang in the air just long enough for him to feel embarrassed. Which was just fine. Now Godwin owned him. "Look—numb nuts—there's only one reason on earth Jack wants her. He wants her because she's there. If you make it too hot for her to be there, he'll send her away. He'll go back to banging Patti in the protocol office. You shine a little sunlight on their relationship, and it's over." He snapped his fingers for effect.

Richie nodded his head as he tried to absorb the prospect of taking on the president. "So, let me get this straight—you want me to leak it."

"No no no no no. I don't want you to do anything. But if a story about the president's girlfriend showed up on somebody's blog—"

"Like the one that that worm Flip Stacks runs—"

"Yeah, the Worm Report, that would do nicely."

"So I should call him?"

"Call, yes, I suppose. If one only knew the phone number. Or perhaps one could simply send him an anonymous E-mail, say from a Hotmail account that one could set up in about five minutes, saying who Irene is and detailing how many times she's been to the Oval Office—what does she do again?"

"She's a student."

"Okay, saying how often she's been to the Oval Office, and wondering what a student is doing there so much."

"Right. Right. I got it."

"That'll be enough. Chet Wetzel will make up some explanation, but that question alone will turn up enough heat. Jack won't have her back."

"Right," said Richie, getting up to go. "Thanks, Mr. Vice President. I really appreciate it."

He was almost out the door when Godwin called him back. "Richie—do you have a picture of Irene?"

"Yeah. Like a hundred. One day, all we did was take pictures of each other with our phones."

"Good. Attach one to the story. It'll add a lot of credibility."

"Right. Gotcha."

"Make sure it's clear. And maybe even a little sexy, right?"

"Right. Okay, gotcha. Thanks."

Godwin leaned back in his chair. He had done nearly all he could for one day. Leading a revolution—that would probably be relentless work. One would have to foment disturbances and rouse the rabble until the czar or whoever was conquered. But this little operation—this was like farming. One had to work very hard getting the seeds into the ground, but then one just had to set back and give the little seeds time to grow. Herman Vanick has to bang his drum, he told himself. Ralph Grove has to make his phone calls. Richie Platt has to spring his leak. It all takes time. Leaving me, Godwin thought, free for a little R&R.

He took out his phone and typed in an E-mail address—mnewbold@Newsbreak.com—and then added a message. "Come with me," he thumbed, "and be my love."

18

SHE WAS TEMPTED to say no. She really did have a pile of work to do. Loomis had assigned her the lead piece in a package about how the satellite sale could revitalize the entire Mahone agenda, with a point-by-point explanation of what that would mean in terms of taxes, entitlement-program reform, foreign policy, and the economy. Ike Gonzalez, the White House correspondent, argued that he should be writing the story, and by rights he should have been, but Loomis was in his star-making mode, and Gonzalez, who fancied himself a gourmand, was mollified with some candy-ass feature story about Tuscan cuisine, which entitled him and his family to spend two weeks in Italy visiting olive groves and vineyards. Which was great for Maggie. But she wasn't quite done with the story, and she was seeing Loomis at six; he'd surely want to see a draft. Plus, she'd been asked to address the Women of Washington luncheon tomorrow, and she hadn't prepared any remarks for that. No, she was going to turn him down, and probably would have done, too, had not Linda Archer wandered past, looking particularly dried up and worn, with her mouth downturned like a croquet wicket, and Maggie, feeling a nudging from her loins, decided to seize the day. Quickly, she changed into the running gear she had stowed in the bottom drawer of her desk, just so she could say she was going for a quick run if anybody asked, and then slipped outside and into a cab. Soon she was striding down M Street (just out for a run, in case anybody asked), which just coincidentally happened to be

Godwin's street (of course it was just coincidentally Godwin's street; what did people think, that she memorized the home addresses of all the public officials in Washington?). It was all too exciting, the irresponsibility and the artifice and the subterfuge, and she nearly climaxed with his first embrace.

After the eruption of their orgasms, they dozed, he more briefly than she. He didn't waken her, but lay still, collecting the scent of her hair, her weight, her warmth, their stickiness, their pungence. He was thinking how much he liked these feelings. He was thinking how he could arrange to feel them more—more frequently, more permanently.

Then she awoke. Leaning up on one elbow, she batted the sand from her eyes and offered him a wholehearted smile. "Hey," she said.

"Hey yourself."

She nuzzled his chest, then half-turned, stretched, licked the fuzz off her teeth, then snuggled back onto his chest. Godwin reached over and brushed some stray hair away from her eyes, and, smiling, she reached up and touched his hand.

"I do love your hands," she said. "They're so—this isn't going to sound right—so soft. But strong, obviously."

"My dear, they are the product of a lifetime of indoor work."

She turned the hand around. On the back of the index finger, running almost the length of all three joints, was a white, not very neat scar. "What happened here?" she asked.

"Knife wound," he said.

She thought he was making a joke, but he didn't change his expression. "Was it a gang fight? A war? Something involving a woman? I feel an adventure story coming on."

"I got it cutting grapefruit. Disappointed?"

"A little. It's pretty deep."

"Do tell. I should have visited a hospital. Instead, I used Band-Aids. That's why it's so visible."

"Hey, where's your ring?"

"What ring?"

"Your school ring."

"Oh, my Princeton ring. I only wear it sometimes. I was actually a dropout. I only put it on when I feel perverse."

"You had it on at the Vanatuas' last month. You were feeling perverse then?"

"I tried to tell you."

"I wish I had listened. This has been very nice, Godwin. Today, these other meetings. You know, a girl could get used to moments like these."

The thought, so surprisingly close to those he'd been thinking, startled him, and all he could do was nod in a vaguely encouraging way. She, of course, took the wrong interpretation from his surprised silence. "Not to suggest anything," she said, quick to ward off every shadow of real feeling.

"No," he said, trying to reassure her. "Suggest away."

Not thinking the reassurance was sincere, she strived to keep the moment light. "Are the other girls who come here as, what shall we say, delighted with the experience as I am?"

"There are no other girls who come here," he replied.

"Oh come on."

"No, not lately, not for a long time. You're it."

This time the mood registered, and she sensed that their relationship had in an ineluctable way changed, that the heat of their sex had somehow passed them through some invisible membrane, and now they were no longer mere lovers, but people who suddenly meant something to each other, people with a connection, people who might be said in a way to love each other. And that made her feel free to explore. "You know what I want to know?" she asked.

"Uh-oh"—he laughed—"here it comes: the interview portion of the competition. Well, if I win, I'd like to help world peace."

"It's not like that." She laughed, but she was already fearing that she'd gone too far.

"It's all right," he said. "I suppose if I dated a chef, I'd have to spend time peeling potatoes."

"Aw, forget it."

"No, go ahead," he said, the steady tone of his earlier comments returning to his voice. "Really. I'll stop kidding."

She searched his face, looking to see if he meant it. "My question . . ." she hesitated. "My question is, What are you doing here? I mean, look around town. There's no shortage of second-raters. And they all want power, the more the better. But almost none of them knows what to do with it. But you already have power—your wealth, your intellect. You don't need public office to do something. Why are you here?"

It was a question Godwin himself had pondered without ever reaching a really satisfactory response. "I don't know what to say," he at last replied, looking her in the eye. "Maybe vanity? Is that the answer? I was never shy about raising my hand in class—I almost always had the right answer. I never knew why other people should get credit for knowing what I knew, and I never thought there was much point in listening to people spout nonsense when I had a good idea. So maybe it's vanity. Is there anything wrong with that?"

"No," she said, but she was less concerned with answering his question than in keeping this conversation somewhere she wanted it to be. "Look, I didn't mean to get serious," she said. "We can keep it light."

"I know," he said, "but we don't have to keep things light, not on my account. I like you quite a lot, Maggie. I'm not afraid of a little complexity between us."

"Okay," she said. "That's good. *Complexity* is a pretty good word for what I'm feeling these days." The moment seemed to call for some gesture, but something dramatic had just happened between them, and she was confused by it, and not a little bit afraid. She reached over and stroked his hair for a moment, then leaned in, gave him a peck on the lips, and then jumped out of bed and went to the bathroom. When she reemerged, she began to dress. "I have to go," she said. "Loomis is in town and I promised I'd have a drink with him to discuss my new piece. He loves to hear new stuff. Got anything on the satellite deal I can tell him?"

"Not really," he said. He was disappointed she was leaving, and he didn't want to help her entertain the man she was leaving him to meet.

Corralling her breasts in her bra, she prodded a little more. "Speaker Vanick's making some headway on that CIA memo, though, don't you think?"

Godwin's ears perked up. Well, he thought, a moment of opportunity. "Nah," he said. "Jack Mahone isn't burdened with an excessive amount of scruples, but you have to ask yourself, Why would he jeopardize the security of the United States? What would he get for it? What's in it for him?"

Originally, Maggie had planned to meet Loomis at the bureau and to leave for a drink from there, but she wasn't entirely surprised when in the cab she got a text message from him asking if it would be okay to meet at his room in the hotel. She wasn't surprised when he had a pitcher of drinks ready, wasn't surprised that his tie was off and collar open (a signal that Loomis was in casual mode), and wasn't surprised that, after telling her that she'd been doing a great job and that she had reenergized the whole bureau and that there was a lot of talk about her moving up in the magazine and that he had been spending a lot of time fondly remembering their wild weekend in Virginia Beach when they were kids, he stuck out his left hand and fondled her right breast. This day had been coming since the moment he hired her. What surprised her, as she unzipped her skirt, was that she was worried what Godwin would think.

She could have turned Loomis down; he was only doing it because he was determined to lead a great life. He had read many, many biographies of great men, and among the lessons he took from them was that many great men have affairs, and therefore he should, too. He chose Maggie because he liked her vitae. Sleeping with her would bolster his own image the way being married to his wife did, with her chic slender figure and her confident manner, her prematurely gray hair and her part-time teaching gig at Columbia, and the way his kids did, with their suitably high grades and suitably cutting-edge aspirations and suitably worrisome piercings and episodes of binge drinking. Had she said no, the moment would have been swiftly forgotten, but as he groped her she saw in his eyes a pathetic dislocation, the sign that he had stopped being a man and had become only his job, and she decided that a mercy fuck in the memory of the lively, ambitious boy he had once been wouldn't be such a terrible thing.

Which is why it bothered her that she kept thinking of Godwin. It angered her that it bothered her. It angered her that he had reached so deep into her head. She would have to think about this; she would have to think whether or not it was a good thing to be falling in love with Godwin Pope.

Fortunately, Loomis did not take a long time, and he did not seem to mind when she began apologizing for having to leave so soon. "I have a dinner myself," he said. "Leonard Dvorcheki is casting about for a biographer, and it might be me. Anyway, he's having some people over. It's a black-tie event."

He said the last words with a grimace, as though wearing a monkey suit presented an imposition, but Maggie knew it was just another way Loomis confirmed his own importance. "Tell Lenny I said hi," she said.

"I suppose everybody's going to be talking about the way Vanick took Kenneth Keith Brandt to the woodshed this morning."

"He accomplished nothing," said Maggie with a striking finality. Suddenly, she felt angry with Loomis, with the way he seemed to know everything but really knew nothing, and her voice took on the kind of edge that it might acquire when speaking to a customer service rep at a bank who seemed to be almost willfully ignoring her question. "Vanick is accusing Jack Mahone of deliberately jeopardizing the security of the United States. It's not enough to say that he killed the report because he's stupid or had bad intelligence or because he's incapable of a higher-order thought process. No, Vanick is saying Mahone is doing this deliberately. Now if you want me to believe that, you'd better tell me why. Jack Mahone isn't burdened with an excessive amount of scruples, but tell me—what's in it for him? If Herman Vanick believes Jack Mahone is selling out the country, he'd better be ready to tell me what Jack's getting out of the deal."

So struck was Loomis with the perspicacity of her words that he later repeated them, as close to word for word and inflection for inflection as he could manage, before the thirty or so dinner guests having coquilles St. Jacques at Dvorcheki's pillared home near the Kennedy Center in Foggy Bottom. He repeated them again the next morning on the *Today* show, even as Dvorcheki was intoning a fairly faithful cover version on *Good Morning America*, even as Tavis Whouley, who had spent the afternoon and evening tossing around the "What's in it for Jack?" question on the phone and at his poker game as though he were a Johnny Appleseed of Godwin-inspired insights, was sharing a version with the listeners of Don Imus. Thereafter, the observation insinuated itself into the comments of pundits and politicos throughout the capital, until by the end of the day they became such conventional wisdom that the guests on *Nightline* were practically chiseling the thought into marble, and the wags on *The Daily Show* were making wisecracks about the lifetime supply of mu shu pork that Jack had required for his acquiescence.

19

UNSURPRISINGLY, HERMAN VANICK woke up feeling glum, as would any man who had fired his final rockets at what he thought was enemy headquarters, only to see them thud harmlessly into the sandbags piled outside. As he sat at the breakfast table with his already-heavily Elizabeth Ardened wife, facing his green tea (for his blood pressure), his fruit compote (for his cholesterol), and the *Washington Post* (for full coverage of his failures), he was already contemplating how to handle his defeat, how to seem to be unbowed but not a sorehead, to seem to be an unreconstructed opponent of the president who was at the same time personally friendly with the man, respectful of his office, and open to bipartisan solutions. This job makes me have more faces than Sybil, he muttered to himself. He forced himself to slog through the front page, found some escape in the sports section (the Nationals' home opener was only weeks away), and finally gave a quick skim to the style section. On the last page, an item caught his eye:

PREZ'S BRO HEADLINES IN HONG KONG
By Ralph Grove

Capital area music lovers can thank their lucky stars that almost an entire half a planet lies between them and Hong Kong's Emerald Garden Resort and Casino, where the brother of the president of the United States, the grizzly-looking Lowell Mahone, is doing grisly-sounding things to tunes once made famous by Elvis Presley, Otis Redding, Simon and Garfunkel, and Olivia Newton-John.

Readers who may have heard Mr. Mahone's warblings at, say, one of his brother's fund-raising pig roasts or at the Big Room in the Holiday Inn in Nacogdoches, Texas, may fear for their correspondent's sanity. Who would hire a singer this sonically scary?

As it turns out, his benefactors are Roland and Penny Vanatua, who have previously hired the likes of Paul McCartney, Michael Jackson, and Britney Spears for the openings of their Asian sin pits. "Penny and Roland have been real good to me," said Mr. Mahone in a telephone interview after his final set on Tuesday. "My closing number is 'America the Beautiful,' and I dedicate it to them every night."

On-the-scene observers tell the *Post* there have been plenty of seats available for Mr. Mahone's performances; the room, they say, is never more than half-full. Mr. Mahone's compensation for his contributions to the spread of American music: $750,000.

Vanick grabbed the phone and called his chief of staff, Junius Jolivette. "It's me. Didja see? Boy, he's in for it now!"

"You're goddamn right he is," said Jolivette. "How did he think he was going to get away with it?"

"Because he's arrogant," said Herm. "Because he thinks we're stupid. Well, we'll see at the hearings who's the stupid one!"

"Yeah? You're going to bring this up at the hearings?"

Vanick was surprised to hear the puzzlement in Jolivette's voice. "What's wrong with you? Fucking-A right we are! You don't think that we should bring up the possibility that the president killed a CIA report and approved a deal that puts our security at risk in exchange for a seven-hundred-and-fifty-thousand-dollar bribe transparently paid by the chief corporate beneficiaries of the sale through his no-talent brother? Yeah, I think we should!"

"Herm, what are you talking about?"

"Ralph Grove's column in the *Post*. What do you think I'm talking about?"

"I haven't seen Ralph Grove's column in the *Post*."

"Then what the fuck are you talking about?"

"The item on the wormreport.com about the president's young mistress. Here, I'll read it to you. The headline reads 'While the Cat's Away,' and it says, 'Everyone from the tour guides to the cafeteria workers to the usual know-nothings in the National Security Council have been buzzing about how terribly, terribly triste the president has seemed since Doris, his lovely First Lady, sloughed off on a State Department goodwill tour. While she's been visiting India, Pakistan, Afghanistan, Turkmenistan, and the Hindu Kush as part of her personal Beautify the World initiative, her desolated hubby has been secluded in his private quarters, reportedly accepting the comfort of only one person. No, not the human canine Chet Wetzel. His close pal has been an alluring young lady named Irene Kim, a lovely young graduate student majoring in personal presidential relations at George Washington University, who has visited the White House twelve times during the First Lady's absence.' There's a picture of her here. Pretty girl. Herm—did you hear me? Are you still there?"

"Yeah, Junius, sorry, I'm here. I was just thinking that all these years I've been saying so many terrible things about Jack Mahone on *Hardball* and *Face the Nation*, I never thought half of them were true. But they were! And worse!"

20

THE MORNING'S REVELATIONS ignited a froth of activity in newsrooms in Washington and New York. The fact that neither story emerged from what anyone would call a traditional source for news about the president prevented everyone from simply piggybacking on the original reports, and everyone was sent back to square one. The *Post* felt especially aggrieved; somehow all of the editors involved failed to realize that they were publishing a major story, and when the livid managing editor at long last grasped that he was sitting on a solid gold scoop, he wasn't able to locate his own reporter. As it turned out, the resolutely old school Ralph Grove had refused to replace the batteries that had burned out in the BlackBerry the paper had insisted on issuing him in 1999. At 12:30, he was hustled out of Willard's by an impress gang consisting of an assistant managing editor and two copy clerks, which only ensured that when he finally showed up at the paper, he would be hungover and unwell, on top of being congenitally uncooperative. Ralph was from an era where reporters regarded editors the way snakes treat mongooses, and his answers to his bosses were curt, though hardly inaccurate. "I heard it from a guy in the bar," he snarled. "I called up Lowell Mahone and he gave me the story and I wrote it. It's what you pay me to do. Here're my notes. Now I've got a splitting headache. I don't suppose any of you Yuppies keep any booze in your desks, do you?"

The press spokesman for the Emerald Garden Casino, a kooky

blond AmerAsian named Patti Cho Choo, was also hit by a barrage of phone calls from journalists in America and Europe, ranging from *The Economist* to *In Touch,* from *Hardball* to *Entertainment Tonight.* Eyes aglow, she took the requests to Lowell. "You're bigger than P. Diddy," she trilled, but Lowell had enough mother wit to smell a rat. One call from old Ralph Grove was all right, he reasoned, but many of the names he recognized on Patti's pink "While You Were Out" slips were not nice people. "I don't want to talk to anybody until I talk to my brother," he told Patti, and nothing she could do could shake him from that vow.

The Vanatuas adopted a similar posture. They had their spokesman, the silver-tongued Sydney Wolfson, issue a statement. "Mr. and Mrs. Vanatua have a high regard for Mr. Mahone's talent and were proud to present him at their casino." They then put on retainer Barnett Gleason, the silkiest defense attorney in Washington. He did not mind it when they told him that they'd hired Lowell to sing, period. All clients, he believed, start out lying.

The vice president for Public Affairs for George Washington University was unhelpfully closedmouthed as well. She confirmed that a part-time student named Irene Kim was enrolled in the School of International Relations. No further information was released. The campus police had a hectic morning escorting reporters out of the IR building, where they were frantically buttonholing students and faculty, hoping to find someone who knew Irene Kim.

Godwin spent the morning in his office, a quiet oasis in a maelstrom. While Chet Wetzel and other top aides, all colored with the clammy pallor of people about to stroke out, ran from office to office to share what piddly bits of information they'd been able to collect, Godwin sat calmly, reading blogs. None of the bloggers had any information, but they all had a take on the story so far. After all, what would be the point of having a twenty-four-hour megaphone if one needed actual information to use it?

At noon, a sweaty Chet Wetzel took the podium in the White House Briefing Room to issue the daily briefing. "The president of

Italy, Umberto Dante, will be coming for a visit next week," he said timorously. He wasn't happy to be doing this. The press secretary ordinarily would have, but she'd collapsed in the bathroom after vomiting for a half hour, something Chet felt as though he might do soon himself. The Q&A session that followed the briefing was customarily contentious; today it promised to be something between a fraternity hazing and a Stasi inquisition, "Housing starts are up. The FCC will be issuing some new rules about station ownership tomorrow. I'll take your questions now. Helen—"

"Chet, did the president arrange for his brother to sing at the Vanatuas' casino?"

"He absolutely did not."

"Then who did?"

"The president has spoken only briefly with his brother, and apparently Lowell negotiated the deal on his own. Indeed, *negotiated* may be too strong a word. As I understand it, Roland Vanatua offered an amount, and Lowell accepted it. David—"

"Chet, who's Irene Kim?"

"A friend of the president's."

"What kind of friend?"

"I guess personal."

"Okay, what does 'personal' mean?"

"It's a common term. If you don't know what it means, it tells us a lot about your personality. Chris—"

"How often has Irene Kim visited the White House?"

"We're putting together that information as we speak."

"The Worm Report said it was a dozen. Can you confirm that number?"

"I won't dignify anything published on that scurrilous Web site with a response. Over here. Matt—"

"Chet, you say Lowell negotiated the deal with the Vanatuas on his own?"

"So I'm told."

"Chet, had the Vanatuas ever heard him sing?"

"I have no knowledge. Scott?"

"When will the tally of Ms. Kim's visits be available?"

"Not long. As soon as possible."

"Is it even possible that Ms. Kim visited the president a dozen times while Mrs. Mahone has been away, as has been reported?"

"I don't know if I've seen the president a dozen times since Mrs. Mahone has been away. A.J.?"

"But she has visited."

"Yes, she has visited."

"A number of times?"

"Yes. In the back—Rocky?"

"Chet, you said you didn't know if the Vanatuas had heard Lowell Mahone sing."

"That's right."

"Have you heard Lowell Mahone sing?"

"I have."

"Would you pay seven hundred and fifty thousand dollars to have him sing?"

"Sorry, I won't even pay full price for a CD. Josh?"

"Chet, where does Irene Kim live?"

"I don't know."

"Does the Secret Service know?"

"There is no record of them knowing."

The room went dead quiet. Every person gathered there, reporter and staffer, knew the scrutiny under which each of them had been placed before being admitted to the White House, and all of them were veteran professionals who had never been in trouble in high school or anything. The idea that some girl would be able to breeze into the Oval Office left them collectively dumbstruck. Finally, the guy from *Time* blurted out, "They didn't check?"

"We're investigating to see exactly what went on. It seems that an address was left, but which perhaps included a typographical error or some such, because there is not only no record of Ms. Kim having ever been in residence at that address; that particular address is at the bottom of the Anacostia River. Nor is she answering her phone. In any event, it does seem that the president waived the normal process, and once it was determined that she wasn't armed and dangerous, she was admitted."

Yes, thought Godwin, watching the press conference on the TV in his office. She wasn't armed, she wasn't dangerous, and soon she wasn't even dressed. Godwin sympathized with the Secret Service's decision. After all, he thought, if they had to perform full background checks on every woman Jack brought into the White House, we'd have to triple their budget.

On TV, Chet apparently had concluded that he'd thrown the wolves all the meat he had, and that next they'd be gnawing on him. "Thank you, ladies and gentlemen," he said abruptly, and fled the podium without even fully detaching his microphone, which caused no small amount of hilarity when the clip showing him being yanked back was endlessly replayed on *Letterman* that evening.

So much for CNN, thought Godwin, switching the channel to C-Span. The committee in charge of the satellite deal was in emergency session, and Alonzo Rotundo, a Pennsylvanian who was one of Vanick's more dependable lieutenants, was holding forth. "And what I find most alarming, Madame Chairman, and indeed most suspicious, is that the president's brother, Mr. Lowell Mahone, would receive a stupendous payment from the very individuals who stand to benefit from the satellite deal. Children can afford to believe in Santa Claus, Madame Chairman, but as representatives of the American public, I don't believe we can. I move we subpoena Mr. Lowell Mahone and have him testify about this arrangement."

"Seconded," cried someone too impatient for the camera to find him.

"All in favor—" There came a drone of ayes, followed by the smack of a gavel. "So moved."

Godwin spent a moment pondering the specter of Lowell Mahone testifying under oath before a congressional committee. It would be like *Dumb and Dumber* set in a civics class. He wondered whether it would be better to watch the proceedings on Comedy Central or CNN.

On TV, the reporters were doing their stand-ups in front of the White House and the Capitol Building, rehashing what had just transpired. Rowe on Fox seemed fixated on the Secret Service's failures to vet Irene Kim. That was a bad sign. The pack is sniffing up the wrong tree, Godwin thought; if that keeps up, they'll spend days on it, and the only pelt they'll end up with is that of the White House Secret Service detail, a decent, dedicated professional who'll probably take a bullet to his reputation rather than blab about Jack Mahone's weakness for female flesh. No, this can't be allowed to become a distraction. The press can't be allowed to wonder why they weren't spoon-fed Irene Kim; the press has to go find her.

Godwin opened his laptop and began typing. Most people think of the Internet, Godwin mused, the way they think of TV. Hit a button, get something on your screen. Hit another button, get something different. In reality, the Internet is a freeway, with a million connections and a billion cars, and every place you take it to has a front door and a back door. Godwin had spent most of his adult life in Silicon Valley working side by side with one of the true genius programmers of his generation; he still couldn't hold a candle to any of the hard-core geeks, but that didn't mean he hadn't picked up a skill or two—like elementary hacking—during those long coke, coffee, and Taco Bell–infused nights the team spent developing software at Zephyr. He hadn't had much practice in the art in the last few years—he doubted whether he could break through the typical university firewall to change anybody's grade transcripts anymore, and he surely no longer sought the cheap thrill of cheating the phone company. But what only a very few people knew about Tom Ralston was that while he was almost paranoiacally cryptic about corporate security, he was almost disdainfully lackadaisical about his personal systems at home. True, he never kept data that he thought was significant—no financial information, no corporate secrets, no Redskins game plans, but in the more than twenty years Godwin had known him, Ralston had never changed his user name or password. Godwin thought it had to do with what the files contained. They were Tom's little secret, and keeping the secret was all the more delicious if there was a chance, however infinitesimal, that there was a risk of being caught.

Godwin entered the same user name Tom had used at Zephyr, followed by the password he had employed for the first twelve years they had been in business. PURINA, if you must know. With that, the contents of Tom's server opened up, and Godwin could read everything his old chum had been up to lately that he wanted hidden from sight.

It was a lot like rummaging through somebody's attic. He found files full of music downloads, and bootleg tapes of what Godwin was sure was every concert the Grateful Dead had ever performed. There was a file full of surveillance reports on about two hundred young men, whom they saw and whom they partied with and what went up their noses. The men were mostly black, but about a quarter were white; Godwin at first took them to be candidates or members of some private army or protection force, but he eventually concluded they were football players. There were no names on the files, just initials, and it would have taken a more knowledgeable fan than Godwin to know if these were Tom's players, or rival players, or former players, or future possible draft choices.

There were other files. There was an undated, unlabeled file that held about a dozen pictures taken with a cell phone, shot up the skirts of women seemingly random and unaware as they rode up escalators in a generic shopping mall. There was another undated, unlabeled file containing about a hundred photos of Karen Armbrister, a league public relations manager Tom had dated for about eighteen months, until she'd dumped him last spring. There was a file full of *Star Trek* stuff.

Finally there was a file labeled "V." Tom, you've never been an enigma, Godwin thought, and indeed, upon inspection, marked "V1" through "V63," were films of people who had dipped in Tom's pool. Some wore trunks; Bill Gates wore a baggy beige pair as he paddled around in the shallow end for three minutes before getting out without having gotten a hair wet. Some skinny-dipped; National Security Advisor Broyard, for example, took two vigorous laps before he and his shrinkage issues escaped inside a fluffy white robe. Then there were more elaborate encounters; on a hunch, Godwin began working from the bottom of the list, and very soon, at V61, he found Mr. Marco McChesney and three very lovely and very gymnastic young women, including one who had been introduced today in most American households as Irene Kim. Godwin took several frame grabs. One showed a nice close-up of Irene's face, with the unique beauty mark next to someone's large flame-tattooed glutes. Another, taken from a camera a little farther away, showed Irene in the same position, but it offered more of the man's back, assorted body parts of the other two women, and a bit of background for mise-en-scène buffs. Godwin was very sure these shots would look especially nice on what would almost certainly be a special keepsake edition of the Worm Report.

21

THE NEW IMAGES OF IRENE circulated on the Worm Report around eight o'clock, too late for the evening news in most places, too late to catch most of the American public while they still possessed some mental acuity, already after the point when for the most part their minds had escaped into their screen of choice. That meant that most people wouldn't be aware of this news until morning, which left the professional spinners just a few precious hours to orchestrate their positions.

But this was a tricky one. It wasn't immediately clear what could be said. Herman Vanick and his gang were happy just to turn the matter over to the religious zealots in their midst, who were enraptured by having the chance to condemn the president for having sex with a woman who not only wasn't his wife but who was also a woman who had sex with yet another man who probably wasn't her husband and with women who were almost certainly not her wives. Meanwhile, Herman sharpened his knives for Lowell Mahone, who was scheduled to appear on the Hill tomorrow afternoon.

In the White House, the president met with Chet Wetzel, Lucas Ivy, his corpulent pollster, and his top political operatives to discuss developments. "Is there any possibility, Mr. President, that this isn't Ms. Kim in this picture?" asked Chet Wetzel.

"Any possibility, Chet? I don't know. You ever watch any of those *CSI* shows? They've got tests that would convince me you're

Mahatma Gandhi. China's got eight hundred bazillion people. Is it possible that two look like this? Yeah, I guess. But short of DNA testing, I think this is the same girl." After a moment, Mahone broke the frustrated silence with an angry coda. "And yeah, before anybody asks, I fucked her."

The silence that then ensued was too painful to be endured. Lucas Ivy, socially inept under the best of situations, picked up one of the photos. "How many people do you think are in that pool?" he asked. "And what do you think they're doing, exactly?"

Mahone shook his head and groaned. "You all can go," he said wearily.

In *Newsbreak*'s Washington bureau, as in newsrooms around the world, the new pictures forced the journalists to reevaluate their coverage plans. Linda Archer, beleaguered and far out of her depth, was struggling to get a grip on the biggest and fastest-breaking story of her career. "The crucial thing," she said to her assembled staff, "is for us to find out whose ass that is."

Congressional correspondent Todd Overton snickered. "Because?"

"Because if we find that ass," said Linda sharply, "we might just find Irene Kim."

"You know, chief," said Overton, amusing himself, "it's not going to be so easy to find an ass."

"Most people keep 'em hidden," said another wag.

"Yeah," Overton said, piling it on, "and there's not exactly a mug book we can send somebody to go through."

Poor Linda, Maggie thought. She is crumbling before our eyes. In about five minutes, Loomis is going to call and ask her what she's got, and she'll have nothing, and he won't be happy. And if he doesn't take personal direction of the story right then and there, he will blame her for not doing everything that he would have. And of course the great Loomis never missed a story and never made a mistake, and unless someone in this room can figure out whose ass that is before some luckier reporter at the *Times* or ABC or the *Manitoba* fucking *Bugle* does, then Linda's ass is fried.

"No, Todd," Maggie said, "there is no book of asses. It is an awfully good ass, though, wouldn't you say? Uncommonly good. And it seems pretty clear it's a man's ass. So what kind of men have asses like that?"

"Not reporters," quipped young Ayisha, getting into it.

"No, not reporters," agreed Maggie. "Not anybody who logs a lot of ass time at a desk. And look at the nice tile pattern in the pool. I don't know where that is, but it's not low-rent. And the girls aren't low-rent. It ain't much, I agree, but it's something to work on."

"Okay," said Linda, a little more forcefully now. "Here's what we'll do. Maggie, follow the money. See what else the Vanatuas have given to the Mahones. You guys try to find the girl."

"Linda," said Maggie in an authoritative tone that was not confrontational but that could not be disobeyed, "I want the girl. I think there's a better chance she'll give her story to a woman."

"If there's a story."

"She hid her address from the Secret Service," said Maggie. "My assumption is that any story worth hiding is a story worth telling."

IT WAS AFTER 11:00 P.M. at the White House. People had hung around to see what the eleven o'clock news would make of the new photos, but in the hands of local newsies, any story other than murder and extreme weather was lucky to appear as a reasonable facsimile of itself. Two of the stations used the old dodge of running out on the street and asking passersby what they thought. Godwin laughed as convenience store clerks and dog walkers tried to evaluate the fate of the nation. Most of them were probably thinking that for once a president has picked a good-looking girlfriend.

After the news, Godwin wandered past the Oval Office. The lights were still on. Clark, the president's body guy, sat outside reading an Elmore Leonard novel. "Is he available for me?" Godwin asked Clark, who checked, then ushered him in.

"Come in, Godwin, come in." There were no papers on Jack's desk, nothing electronic turned on, just a single green-shaded desk lamp. He must have just been staring into space.

"I'm terribly sorry to be bothering you, Mr. President. I won't be a moment."

"No, no, have a seat. Feel like a drink? I do. I haven't had any tonight because I want to be clearheaded, but I think maybe a bourbon would give me just the insights I'm looking for."

"A bourbon would be good."

Godwin waited until they'd had a couple of sips before speaking. "I just want to tell you that I'm here for you, Mr. President. Whatever you need."

"Thanks, Godwin. I can't tell you how much that means to me. This is such a peculiar situation. I've never seen anything like it, have you? I mean, I know politics ain't beanbag, but somebody is really out to get me, Godwin. Somebody wants to see my head mounted on his wall."

"Sure looks that way, sir."

"That CIA analysis was leaked, right? That was a worthless analysis; I don't even know why the director sent it up. And I knew if the Republicans got ahold of it, they would harp on it and harp on it and harp on it, which is exactly what they have done! That's just good old country hardball, son, and Herman Vanick knows how to play it and I know how to play it, and that's why I killed it."

"Anybody would have, sir."

"And now they're making it seem like I got some kind of secret payoff from Roland Vanatua through my brother. I'd sooner put electrodes on my scrotum. How stupid do they think I am?"

"I don't know, sir."

"I haven't had a conversation with Roland Vanatua since I had all those people over to watch that basketball game last year. I told him I liked Gonzaga's chances and that he should have some jambalaya, and we had our picture taken and that was it. And now they're going to twist it, and twist it, and then they're going to throw the girl into it, like she had anything to do with it."

"They're just mudslinging, sir."

"Well, Lowell'll be here in the morning, and then he's going to go up to that hearing and set them straight. You know my brother may not be the sharpest knife in the drawer, but he ain't dishonest."

"No, sir."

"Whoever's behind this is doing this just to hurt me, Godwin. This isn't about policy or philosophy. This is just about ruining me. But you know what? It's going to hurt him more than me. Apparently it's never occurred to whoever is behind these attacks that we live in a democracy, and that for all my flaws—and I am a sinner; God has not finished working on me yet, that's for damn sure—I was elected, legally and constitutionally, by a majority of the people, and they are entitled to their decision."

For an instant, Godwin thought to ask him if they were entitled to destroy themselves in the process, but instead he decided to play along with the mood of the moment. "Mr. President," he said, "may I say something? We've known each other for quite a while now. I've been your rival. I've been part of your government. I've seen you outside and in. I want you to know something: I believe in Jack Mahone."

"Thank you, Godwin. I am a lucky man to have a friend like you." Godwin was very happy to see the tears in Jack's eyes. He was a little sorry that Jack did not break down altogether, but that would have to wait for another day.

22

MAGGIE WOKE EARLY and primed herself for what she expected would be a long and difficult day. She arrived at her desk at eight, armed with an extra-large coffee—not a grande latte or an espresso, but simple awful hard hat coffee truck coffee for what was shaping up to be a hard hat day. She walked her fingers through the modeling agency listings in the Yellow Pages and got nobody who remembered anyone who was named or resembled Irene Kim. Thinking of Irene's international relations background, she called various Asia-related study centers, fellowship groups, and special-interest organizations, and left a lot of messages without getting any leads. She left messages at George Washington; Maggie didn't have the names of any of Irene's teachers, so she simply called everyone in the School of International Relations. She telephoned a vice cop, a sergeant named Dennis, who looked at the pictures of the man's butt and the girls and opined that the pictures had all the earmarks of professional work. The quality of the photos was better than amateur porn: Somebody had paid attention to lighting; someone had thought through the camera angles. Even if the man in the picture was just a player who had hooked up with three lucky ladies, the quality of the setup and the attractiveness of the women argued that the girls, too, were pros. In his opinion, that was good news; there weren't more than twenty-five high-end prostitution rings in the city, and while he couldn't divulge their names, if Maggie was willing to have dinner with him sometime, certain discreet inquiries might be made.

All of which meant that by noon, she had no new leads, and was contemplating how bad a dinner with Sergeant Dennis, along with its inevitable postscript, could turn out to be. At that point, her young protégée, Ayisha, knocked on her door.

"Maggie, I know you're busy," she said, "but there's somebody I think you should meet. It's a guy named Tony Tanous I used to date a little."

"Sure, but for just a second. I'm really busy."

"Well, it's about that. He thinks he knows whose ass it is."

Tony, it turned out, was thin and a little bit cute, with a shaved head and a goatee; Maggie could see why Ayisha had gone out with him. He was one of those young men you saw more and more, who seemed to bob and sway all the time, even when he was standing still. Tony moved so much, one might have thought he had had a boom box surgically implanted in his rump. Everything he said had a slight hip-hop inflection that seemed entirely an affectation, one that Maggie did not doubt became more pronounced whenever the sun wasn't out. She could see why Ayisha had dumped him. But on the question of the day, he turned out to be Mr. Perfect. "See, I know whose rear end that is," he explained. "It's Marco McChesney's."

"I don't know who that is," Maggie said.

"Marco McChesney? You must not write about sports, yo. He's a football player. A running back. The Redskins just signed him to a big contract."

"How do you know it's his?"

"Because I was with him when he got it."

"Tony is a stringer for FootballWorldWeekly.com," explained Ayisha.

"Yeah, I cover the college teams in the area and sometimes the 'Skins. Last January, I lucked into covering the Pro Bowl in Hawaii.

The players who get picked for that, they don't do much practicing, so usually it's a big party. I got to hang with Marco for a day, 'cause I knew there was, like, a good chance he was going to sign with the 'Skins, and I thought I'd get an in with him, see? And one of the things he did was get that tattoo. Place called Rollo's, right near the Hyatt on Waikiki Beach."

"You were in the room with him when he got it?"

"No, ma'am, I was chatting up this hottie who was the cashier at the place. But when he was done, he was so proud of it, he came out and said, 'Check it out, dog,' and dropped his pants and kind of waggled his butt in my face."

"So you got a good look at it."

"Oh yes, ma'am. But the thing is, I don't think too many other people have. He woke up the next day with an infection that was mad painful and didn't play in the game. He couldn't even fly home right away, his ass was so tender. I guess those flames were hot, yo! Anyway, that was the end of the season, and unless he's been to a health club or a gym, I don't think he's been naked in a locker room. Not one full of reporters anyway. Although I guess some people have gotten themselves a look, huh?"

"And you're positive about this?"

"Totally. It's Marco's ass. It's Marco's tattoo. I'm sure."

23

IT TOOK SOME DOING for the White House to extract Lowell from Hong Kong and get him back to Washington for the hearing. A commercial flight was out of the question; reporters would book every other seat and question Lowell to death all the way across the Pacific. The Vanatuas, sotto voce, let Chet Wetzel know that Lowell could use their corporate jet, but that would surely look too collusionary under the circumstances. Fortunately, the Vanatuas secretly controlled the largest air-conditioning company in Kuwait, which was more than happy to volunteer one of its corporate jets to give Lowell a lift. He liked the ride quite a bit, but a lot of the instructions to things were written in Arabic, and he had to push a lot of buttons to make things work. Still, he got to stretch out, and when the jet landed at little Freeway Airport in Bowie, Maryland, a little after dawn, he was fairly well rested, and there wasn't a reporter in sight. He had a couple Egg McMuffins and a hash brown pattie in the car that took him to the White House, and no one was ever happier to be reunited with American food.

He had been feeling fairly placid. He guessed he had done something wrong; that was hardly an unprecedented condition in which to find himself. But usually if it was something big, he had an inkling of how he'd screwed up, and this time he had no clue. A long time ago, he'd been warned about talking to reporters, and he'd learned never to say what he was thinking about anything, particularly the *Protocols of the Elders of Zion*. But it had always been okay to talk about his singing career, and that's all he'd talked to Ralph Grove about. Now, as the Capitol Building and the Washington Monument poked up over the tree line on the horizon, he felt himself growing agitated. It didn't help when he was finally admitted into the Oval Office. It was only Jack there, and Jack had on his real scary face.

"Come on in here now, Lowell," said Jack. "There's a storm brewing out there, and we got to get to the bottom of some things in order to set everything right. Now, tell me—no bullshit, hear?—how did you get this deal to sing at this casino?"

"Roland ran into me at the White House correspondents' dinner. He asked me to come sing."

"That's it?"

"He said he was in a bind because he'd booked Mariah Carey, but now she had a cold and couldn't do it, and he asked me if I could fill in. And I said sure."

"And what about the money?"

"He said, 'I'll pay you seven hundred and fifty thousand,' and I said sure."

"And that was it?"

"I said I'd have to find somebody to watch my dogs. I got Uncle Merle. He said to say hello."

Jack couldn't quite believe in the simplicity of the story, but he did believe in the simplicity of his brother. Fucking Roland! He should have asked permission before doing anything like this! "And that's all there was to it?"

"It was a straight-up deal, Jack. I play, they pay. It wasn't even anything complicated, like I get the door money and he gets the bar, and then you have to have somebody count the crowd to make sure he's not gypping you. This was all businesslike. The check cleared, no problem."

"And Roland never said anything like 'Talk to your brother about the satellite deal'?"

"No! Why, were you supposed to buy a satellite dish from him?"

"Oh, Lowell."

"I had no idea that was his business."

"It's not his business!" Jack fairly exploded, and Lowell hung his head in fear and incomprehension. "Oh, Goober," said Jack, bringing out the nickname he'd given his brother in the crib, "I'm so sorry. Things have been stressful here."

"I'm sorry, too, Jack. I didn't mean to hurt you. It was just a great deal. I thought my turn had come."

"No, no apologies," said Jack, coming around his desk and embracing his ursine younger sibling. "This is not your fault. Some bad people are out to hurt me, and you're in the middle."

"Who are they, Jack? Let's go whup 'em, like we did the Chacon brothers back home. Come on, Jack—nobody fucks with the Mahone boys!"

"No, old son, I can't do that anymore. Wouldn't be dignified. And now you have to go up the street and talk to Congress. Just remember, all you have to do is sit there and tell the truth. You'll be like Daniel in the lion's den. A righteous man need fear no evil when he walks in the sight of the Lord."

24

IT DIDN'T TAKE LONG TO DISCOVER where Marco McChesney lived. The realtor who'd sold him his McMansion in Montgomery County managed to get a story planted in the real estate section of the *Post,* and Ayisha was able to get her on the horn and, in the course of pretending to be looking for some quotes for a story about housing trends she was working on, managed to wheedle McChesney's address out of the all-too-cooperative woman. A couple more calls and she ascertained from Mrs. McChesney that her husband was presently not home, but was out signing autographs at the opening of an electronics store in Rockville.

Maggie floored it all the way to the mall. There were about seventy-five people waiting outside the store for him, most of them wearing newly minted Redskins jerseys with the name McChesney and the number 44 printed on them. The crowd was mostly male, grown men and schoolboys, even though this was no holiday, combined with a smattering of limp-haired women, all of whom seemed to be wearing jeans and smoking. Although some of them had been waiting for McChesney for three hours, Maggie saw him first, spotting his Escalade as it pulled into a handicapped spot. She went at him like a linebacker.

"Mr. McChesney, I'm Maggie Newbold—"

"You're going to wait with everybody else, Maggie," he said, moving straight for her.

"I'm with *Newsbreak,*" she continued.

"Oh, no media here today," he said. "I'm not talking to any media today." He was just about upon her, and shifted to his right and accelerated, as he had done so often to get into the clear.

Maggie, far outsized, shifted to meet him, steering him toward a puddle of water that would have ruined his pebble-grain shoes. He pulled up, and Maggie pulled out the photograph of his emblazoned butt and flashed it before his eyes. "I have some questions about this."

McChesney stopped. A behemoth used to blowing through opponents, he had never bothered to develop a poker face, and a look of pure horror overtook him. "I, eh, don't know anything," he stammered.

"There's no point in denying it. This is you."

"No, it's, no—"

"It's your tattoo, babe. Don't lie to me about it."

"You don't understand."

"Yeah I do. It's not that complex. I bet anybody over there with a forty-four on his back will understand what this is a picture of."

"Stop! You don't understand! I'm the Brotherhood of Evangelical Christian Athletes' Man of the Year! There can't be any magazine stories about me! I'm a role model!"

The bigger they are, Maggie thought, the faster they give it up. Now she could deal. "Look, Mr. McChesney, it's not personal. You have fans who root for you. I don't root for anybody. I'm a journalist. I root for stories. And right now, a role model caught in an orgy is a pretty good story. But if you can tell me a better story, I'll root for that one and forget all about you."

"I don't know a better story."

"Are you sure?"

His face lit up. "How about steroids? When I was a rookie—"

"I don't give a shit about steroids. Tell me about the girl."

"I didn't know any of the girls! They were at the house when I got there. They asked me to go swimming."

"Were they call girls?"

"I don't know. I thought they were fans."

"Yeah, right. Catch any names?"

"Uh, Barbie, maybe? The blonde. Like I said, I just met her at the house that day."

"Whose house?"

"Mr. Ralston's house. He flew me in right before he signed me. The girls were there. Never saw them since. See the tile pattern? That's his pool. That's all I know."

"Did the Asian girl ever say anything about the president?"

"What president? President Mahone? Like what?"

"Never mind. Go sign some autographs."

"Are you still going to do a story about me?"

"I don't know," she said. Suddenly, she was much more interested in Tom Ralston. "We'll see."

OUT OF RESPECT for the Congress, Lowell wore a corduroy sports coat and his clean pair of Dockers to the hearing. He approached the moment with some trepidation, but when he reached the hearing room and saw the cameras and the crowds, he began to relax. He had always liked performing, and never felt any nerves. This would be just another show, although it wouldn't be his usual crowd. Lowell had never liked visiting his brother on Capitol Hill; he knew he wasn't the smartest man on earth, but he knew when he was being talked down to. People there acted like they were better than him, like none of them ever went to a bar and had a few drinks and played some Percy Sledge records and went outside and got into the back of the Buick with whoever else in the joint seemed willing. He didn't like these people; they didn't like him. When the chairman rapped his gavel, Lowell was ready to roll.

"The committee will come to order," said Bennet Peskoe, a sharp-featured former federal prosecutor with a laughable comb-over, who a decade before had made his name reducing a steely mafioso to tears under his relentless cross-examination. "Mr. Mahone, thank you for coming in today."

"And thank you, sir, for issuing me that nice subpoena."

Tittering ran through the crowd. Lowell felt emboldened.

"Mr. Mahone, how did you come to headline at the Emerald Garden Casino in Hong Kong?" Peskoe's voice had an airy, cultivated tone, almost like the host of the Metropolitan Opera broadcasts on radio.

"Mr. Roland Vanatua offered me a booking."

"And you accepted?"

"Yes, sir."

"Did you take a long time to think about it?"

"No, sir."

"And why was that?"

"I didn't have much else to do."

"Plus, he offered to pay you, right?"

"Yep."

"How much were you paid?"

"Seven hundred and fifty thousand dollars."

The amount had been published and had been quoted on television and the radio for days, but here was Lowell confirming it in public, and a buzz ran through the room.

"So let me get this straight," said Peskoe, his tone now less like an opera host's and more like a late-night talk-show comedian's. "One minute, you're standing there, not doing anything, with no prospects. A minute later, you've got a deal for seven hundred and fifty thousand dollars."

"That's right."

"Doesn't that seem like an awful lot of money?"

"I don't know," said Lowell. "If Roland had hired Frank Sinatra, he would have had to pay him a couple mil."

Peskoe offered a line reading Olivier would have envied. "Surely you're not comparing yourself to Frank Sinatra, are you?" He underscored the question with an exaggerated eyebrow wiggle that he thought would wear well on the evening news. People in the audience chuckled.

"No, sir, our styles are very different," said Lowell. "But I can tell you this—Roland Vanatua could have paid Frank Sinatra a thousand times what he paid me, and he still wouldn't have done as good a job as I did."

"Oh? And why is that, Mr. Mahone?"

" 'Cause Frank Sinatra can't sing no more. He's dead!"

The room erupted in laughter, and Lowell, grinning from ear to ear, twisted around in his seat to bask in their adulation. In the White House, Jack Mahone whooped. "Attaboy, Goober!" he cried. In his office, Godwin chuckled. "Touché!" he said quietly.

But this was not the first time Bennet Peskoe had worked in the glare of the national spotlight, and he waited patiently, if grimly, for the laughing to die down. When it stopped, he began again; the tone of his voice had more of an edge than before. The class had had its amusement. The schoolmaster was back in charge.

"Prior to the casino, Mr. Mahone, when was the last time you worked?"

"Last September."

"Six months ago. And where was that?"

"Greasy Johnny's Rib Room and Juke Joint, Bogalusa, Louisiana."

"And how much did you make there?"

"It depended on the door. One week I made one ninety."

"A hundred and ninety thousand, did you say?"

"No, one hundred and ninety."

"Gosh," said Peskoe, laying it on thick, "that's lots less than Roland Vanatua paid you. Can you explain the gap?"

"Stuff like that happens in show business all the time. Haven't you ever seen *American Idol*? Nobodies become stars overnight. It was just my time."

"It was just your time."

"That's right."

"You finally got lucky."

"I guess."

"It didn't have anything to do with the satellite deal."

"Sorry, I don't know anything about that. What deal?"

"An agreement wherein the United States will sell the People's Republic of China some satellites. It's been all over the news."

"Yeah, I never watch the news."

"Well, let me help you catch up. You've heard that your brother is now the president of the United States?"

"Yeah, I know that."

Godwin cringed at the sarcastic question. Lowell is a dope; people will figure that out. But if you're mean to him, the way Peskoe's being, you'll look like a bully picking on the slow kid in the school yard.

"And do you know who the biggest beneficiary of that satellite deal will be?"

Lowell searched his mind before answering. "No, I don't."

"Roland Vanatua."

"Really?" Lowell's face brightened. "Hey, that's great! He's a nice man."

"Yes, a nice man who hired you out of the blue and paid you three-quarters of a million dollars to sing for him. Mr. Mahone, I know your band isn't here, but I was wondering—would you favor us with a song?"

Lowell didn't expect that question, and he stammered as he tried to think.

"Just a few bars, Mr. Mahone. Something from your act."

"Well, uh, okay," Lowell said, feeling compelled to cooperate. "You know, I usually get to warm up my voice—"

"That's okay. This isn't a competition."

"All right," agreed Lowell. He hesitated, cleared his throat, and began to sing. "Sometimes when we touch, the honesty's too much, and I have to hold my head, and cry." More of the lyrics followed. Bennet Peskoe, a hard man, did not stop Lowell, but let him go on until he finished.

Congress is a place where bipartisan agreement is a rare commodity, usually reserved for items such as resolutions against dingoes eating babies and so on. But on that day, there was no one to be found—neither man nor woman, liberal nor conservative, Democrat nor Republican nor unreconstructed Whig—who would say a kind word for Lowell Mahone's singing. He was off-key, out of tune, and out of time. He missed notes and got the words wrong. He was so bad, the audience could not bring themselves to laugh, because Lowell wasn't bad in a laughable way; instead, his singing verged on abusive. On the bright side, he entered the lexicon, and for the next half century, anyone manifesting stupendous incompetence in a field would be said to have "lowelled" it.

Watching from his television, Godwin thought Peskoe looked like a man in the throes of temptation. Don't do it, thought Godwin. Don't ask for an encore. You'll look like Torquemada.

Peskoe calmed down. "Thank you, Mr. Mahone," he said, resuming. "Just a few more questions. Did you ever discuss this booking with the president?"

"No, sir."

"Ever discuss the terms of your deal?"

"No, sir."

"Never?"

"Never."

"Not once?"

"No."

"But it was understood that you had to give him a cut."

"What? No."

"So you didn't give him a cut?"

"No!"

"So you gave him nothing?"

"No, not yet."

"What does 'not yet' mean?"

"Well, I took half the money and bought some Vanatua Corporation stock for him and set it aside. I was going to surprise him with it later, when he leaves office." But even as Lowell was talking, the reaction in the room overrode him, and the flurry of people running out of the room to use their phones caused a great disruption. "What? You know, he ain't a rich man. He's got kids to send to college." Bennet Peskoe banged the gavel for order, but the turmoil would not cease, and the uncomprehending Lowell, with increasing anguish, just kept asking, "What?" Behind closed doors in the White House, Jack Mahone hung his head and moaned. Twenty yards away, behind closed doors in his office, Godwin Pope laughed. Poor bastard, he thought. Ensnared in a web of truth. The game, he knew, was all but over. He'd better start thinking about whom he wanted in his cabinet.

25

AFTER SPEAKING TO MARCO MCCHESNEY, Maggie asked Ayisha to track down the whereabouts of Tom Ralston. Ten minutes later, she called Maggie with the news that Ralston was spending the day at Redskins Park, the team's practice facility in Ashburn, Virginia, just a rip around the Beltway from her location at the electronics store in Rockville.

Waving her magazine ID and batting her baby blues, she managed to charm her way past the grandpa of a guard at the gate. Lucky she got through fast—if she'd been held up any longer, she might have missed Ralston. He was standing outside the front entrance of the training center building, his car and driver waiting, talking to four stoic-looking middle-aged men. Ralston's outfit, she noted, was semi-color-coordinated: his burgundy-and-gold satin jacket with the Redskins insignia was perfectly accessorized by his burgundy-and-gold baseball cap adorned with a large signature *R*. Underneath, he had on a pink Ralph Lauren Polo shirt and a pair of wrinkled brown pants he might have wrestled off a UPS guy, finished off with black-and-white basketball sneakers so bulky that they made it seem as if he were standing on tugboats. Ralston gave every indication of being unhappy; he was scowling and wagging his finger at the men like a truncheon. When she got out of her car, the sideways glances of his underlings caused Ralston to pause, and when he saw her, a stranger, he abruptly corked his soliloquy. "Just take care of it," he said with a terminal snarl, and turned toward his car, shooting her a sideways glance of his own.

"Mr. Ralston, I'm Maggie Newbold from *Newsbreak,*" she said, walking toward him with the same single-mindedness as when she'd approached McChesney.

"Talk to Fred Pinto. He handles all the media requests."

"This isn't really a request," she said, close enough now to be surprised at the dinginess of his teeth. Didn't the dude ever brush? Deftly, she flipped open a folder that contained the picture of Irene and McChesney's flaming rump. She watched to see what he would do, and obligingly, he blanched, then quickly collected himself.

"Flashing dirty pictures? Is that what journalists do nowadays? That's real Woodward and Bernstein of you." There was already a snottiness imbuing his voice. The veneer was off; he was using the coping skills he'd relied on as a teenager.

"Who's the girl, Mr. Ralston?"

"How should I know?"

"Because she was in your pool."

"Was she?"

"See the tiles?"

"I can't be the only pool owner in America with tiles like that."

This is going to be easy, thought Maggie. There are a handful of Hall of Fame liars whom you can never touch, but Ralston's like most people, as false and unpolished as a karaoke singer who's working on his fourth beer. He's crawled himself out on a limb, and he will fall with a crack. "No, Mr. Ralston, you are not alone in owning that *type* of tile. But those? Those are your tiles. And that's your fullback. Marco told me this encounter took place when he visited your home just a few weeks ago. That's your fullback, and this is a girl you paid to fuck him."

Tom had lost touch with snotty and had now acquired a nervous, embarrassed look. Time to go for the kill, she thought.

"You know what surprised me, Mr. Ralston? Marco is so worried about this story not becoming public that he doesn't quite realize that you're the one who took this picture. Imagine what'll happen when he does. He'll probably sue you for invasion of privacy. The league will probably investigate. There might be criminal charges. You may well lose your franchise. But listen carefully: I'm not really interested in that story. I just want to find the girl."

Now it was cop-a-plea time. "You know this is just standard operating procedure," Tom explained. "You want to sign these players, you've got to treat them well. Get them a suite, get them a limo, wine and dine them. In New York, they get to go to a Broadway show. In Miami, it's South Beach. Here, I show them some monuments, the Capitol, the White House, introduce them to some senators or the vice president, somebody whose name they know or have seen on TV. A fellow celebrity, if you will. And then they meet some ladies. I'm just being hospitable."

"I want the girl."

"I don't know the girl. Not that girl. I hired the blonde. She brought the other girls. I can give you her contact information."

The blonde—Ralston said her name was Brandy—had an address out by the Pentagon. It wasn't far. She was driving there even before she could call Ayisha and get her to set up an appointment. It was a pretty funny thought, Godwin being one of the attractions on the Redskins recruiting tour. She wondered if he ever stuck around for the girls. It doesn't seem like his way to play, she thought, but who the hell knows?

26

ABOUT TWO HOURS AFTER the Lowell Mahone testimony wrapped up, Herman Vanick convened a council of his chief lieutenants. "I hate to say this," he began, "but I think it's time we asked ourselves if we should start drawing up some articles of impeachment."

Vanick wasn't lying about hating to broach the subject of impeachment. For him, Jack Mahone had been a great president—weak, ineffectual, needy, unable to launch any expensive big-government initiatives, a tackling dummy to pile onto whenever the party wanted to raise money (which was always), a large, easy-to-hit target that could be carted out whenever blame for something needed to be assigned. Best of all, Mahone's weakness wasn't Herm's problem. It was Jack's problem, and it was the Democrats' problem, but it wasn't Herm's. But just as soon as articles of impeachment were filed, Herm would start to take ownership of Jack. The politics of Washington would become even more partisan, even more poisonous. If Jack survived, Herm would forever be known as the man who took a shot at the president and missed. He could say good-bye to any claims of effectiveness he ever hoped to make. And if Jack lost, Herm would be the man who'd brought Jack down, a villain in the eyes of many, a hero to only a few.

Because the bigger hero, Herm knew, would be Godwin Pope. He'd be the new president, the fresh face, the media darling. Herm could remember being a political science major at Youngstown State, fresh out of the marines, when Jerry Ford succeeded Richard

Nixon. Look at him! the press sang. He makes his own toast! He cleans up his dog's poo!

And the worst part, Herm thought, the very worst part, is that Godwin might make a pretty successful president. Godwin is too chilly a customer ever to win a national election. Elite. Aloof. Not cuddly enough. One-on-one, he can be charming enough, but on a large scale, his flame burns blue. But the son of a bitch is smart as hell. If he ever got in and got to run things, well, he could probably govern. If that happened, people could get used to him, and the popularity problem might take care of itself. Then where the hell would we be? Fucking Jack Mahone!

"I don't see how we can avoid impeachment," said Alonzo Rotundo. "I can't believe Jack Mahone would take a bribe, but Lowell's story is just preposterous. It's like asking us to believe in the Tooth Fairy."

"I, on the other hand, can easily believe he'd take a bribe," said Bennet Peskoe. "What I can't believe is that he'd sell himself so cheap."

"People who are inclined to be corrupt aren't pure until you hit the right dollar amount," said Rotundo. "People often sell cheap. Every one of those guys they caught in Abscam destroyed their careers for twenty-five thousand dollars."

"Noted," said Sandra Brick Delaney. "And at the same time, maybe he didn't sell himself so cheap. Maybe there's more. Maybe he's done this before. Maybe he's got other conduits that we haven't discovered."

"Now that's an intriguing possibility!" said Alonzo Rotundo. "The problem with this deal is that it's so obvious! Jack Mahone is a crafty bastard, but this is so wide open."

"So what you're thinking is that maybe he just got too cocky," said Bennet Peskoe. "Maybe he's been stealing left and right and he just thought it was too easy and thought he could get away with anything and got careless. That strikes me as very credible. You ask anybody in law enforcement, and they'll tell you that happens all the time. There aren't very many supersleuths out there unmasking criminals. Usually, bad guys don't get caught until they screw up or get overconfident or piss somebody off who rats them out. Smart people—smart people get away with murder. It's true."

"So you're envisioning an investigation," said Herm glumly, now realizing that not only was he going to be forced into doing something but he was going to have to do it for most of the next year.

"Sure," chirped Bennet Peskoe, already seeing himself in the role of Jack Mahone's prosecutor, a role that, if he played his cards right, could set him up for a Senate seat and maybe even more. "We'll subpoena all his financial records, and his wife's, and Lowell's. We'll question all his campaign contributors. We'll examine the contracts he awarded when he was governor of Louisiana, in hopes of finding patterns of favoritism. Don't worry, we'll find stuff. Send a proctologist up somebody's ass, he almost always finds shit."

"Oh, Bennet, don't be crude!" said Sandra Brick Delaney.

"Sorry."

Herm had left orders to hold all calls, but nonetheless the phone rang, and Herm's chief of staff, Junius Jolivette, answered. "Mr. Speaker, Sally says we should turn on the TV," he said. "She says there's something on we're really going to want to see."

They picked up the CBS story mid-broadcast, Brent Hemple reporting. "Ismail Chacon says it comes as no surprise to him to hear that President Mahone may have pressured someone to get his brother a job."

Cut to a wrinkled, snaggletoothed man with a graying greasy pompadour. "Oh, yeah," he said, "back when Jack wuz de gubnor, everybody wit' a club knew dat if you wanted to get your liquor license renewed, you had to hire his brother's band for a couple weeks."

Cut to Hemple: "Mr. Chacon says that on three occasions he succumbed to pressure and hired Lowell Mahone."

Cut to Chacon: "And dem boys wuz bad. Dey wuzn't no musicians. Didn't know no zydeco. I always thought Jack must have took a cut of Lowell's take."

In his office, Godwin couldn't believe what he had just seen. Amazing, he thought. Now people are crawling out of the woodwork to accuse Jack of malfeasance. It just goes to show that if you live right, good things will happen to you.

In his office, Herman Vanick groaned. "Oh for sweet fuck's sake. All right, Junius, call Doreen Wasserman in the White House Counsel's Office and tell her"—Here we go, he thought—"tell her we're starting to launch impeachment proceedings, and that she should take steps to preserve all E-mail records, phone logs, visitor logs, and everything else that might constitute evidence in a constitutional proceeding."

27

"HI," THE TALL BLONDE WAS SAYING as she opened the door to her apartment. "Come in. You're a little late."

"Yeah," Maggie said, "I'm sorry. Traffic. I'm Maggie Newbold from *Newsbreak*."

The blonde took her hand. "Nice to meet you. I'm Brandy. Look, I've got to make this quick, I've got a five o'clock coming. Come in and sit down."

Maggie had only seen parts of her in the photos—a shoulder, the crown of her head, some underboobage. She was struck by the fact that the girl was so attractive, with wide blue eyes and a toothy smile. She was wearing pink cotton shorts that said JUICY across her full round bottom and a baby blue tank top that revealed her to be a most buxom lass, though Maggie speculated that the fleshy parapets on her chest were in all likelihood man-made. She didn't look desperate or coked-out, and Maggie wondered how Brandy found herself in this profession. "I'm just curious—is your name really Brandy?"

"Uh-huh!"

Well, that might start to explain things. "First, Brandy, I just want to say that I really appreciate your taking the time to talk to me."

"No problem. As soon as I saw the picture on the Internet, I assumed that sooner or later somebody was going to find me. Can I get you some water?"

"No thanks. I won't take much of your time. What can you tell me about her?"

"Well, for starters I can tell you that Irene isn't her real name. It's Mingsha or something, like Mingsha Gi Pan or something. She was real nice."

"How'd you meet?"

"A client called me last November, around Thanksgiving, said he wanted a three-way. I went to his hotel, and she was there. We got along, and after that, she and I worked together eight or ten times. Anytime a guy wanted a new girl, I called her, and once or twice she called me. I liked working with her. She was clean, she used mouthwash, she kept her nails short. And she was very punctual."

"Did you have any idea she was seeing the president?"

"Sorry, hon, we just worked together," said Brandy. "We didn't swap makeup tips."

"I'd like her phone number."

The doorbell rang. "Excuse me," said Brandy, "that's my five o'clock."

She went to the door and admitted a gray-haired, gray-faced man who smelled of smoke and talc. "Hi, hon," she said quietly. "I'm just finishing something up. Why don't you have a seat in the kitchen for a second." The man eyed Maggie and smiled.

Brandy took the man into the kitchen, went into her bedroom, and returned to Maggie, handing her a piece of baby blue paper adorned with flowers and balloons. "Here's her address and phone number."

"Thanks, Brandy," said Maggie. "You've been very helpful."

"Sure," said Brandy, ushering Maggie to the door. "Look, one thing, about using my name—"

"I know," said Maggie, "I'll try to keep it out of the magazine."

"No," said Brandy, "feel free. Can you also put in the number of my fantasy phone line? And another thing, hon—" She leaned in close. "You ever do any girl-on-girl stuff? Barry thinks you're hot, and he'd pay."

"Oh, you're very flattering," said Maggie. "But a three-way? In these shoes?"

28

DARKNESS FELL ON WASHINGTON, and like Dracula's little children of the night, the pundits came out to feed on the weak and dying. And from the *NewsHour* to *Larry King* to *Nightline,* the general feeling was that Jack Mahone was toast.

"I don't think an American president has ever had a worse week," said Harvard presidential historian Cameron Hetherington, appearing on an ABC prime-time special all about the growing scandal. "Well, I suppose Pearl Harbor ruined FDR's week. But even the week Abraham Lincoln was assassinated started off with him receiving the news that Robert E. Lee had surrendered and that the Civil War was at an end."

"Cameron's right," said Landon Donlon, the celebrated correspondent famous for braying questions at the president over the whirring blades of a helicopter, and for the impressive inauthenticity of his toupee. "President Mahone is being whipsawed. It would be bad enough for him if it was just the alleged personal scandal, bringing a hooker into the Oval Office. He might well be able to survive that. But there is the other alleged scandal, the implication of which is that President Mahone has committed treason by jeopardizing the security of the United States for cash."

"One of the problems with a scandal this complex is that there's no simple name for it," said Bitsey O'Hara, the soft-spoken, self-consciously poetic former speechwriter whose vacuous turns of phrase lived on long after the vacuous presidents for whom she wrote them. "The good scandals have simple names. Watergate. Travelgate. Troopergate. Iran-Contra had such a clumsy name that it was like it wasn't even a real scandal. I suppose this will be something like Hooker-Kickbackgate. It's not a good name."

"How about Pander-Bribegate?" suggested Donlon.

"That's horrible," said Elena Dover of the *Post*, a staunch Mahone supporter early and late, "but what's even worse is that there's no proof of any malfeasance. We hear that the Republicans are already talking about impeachment, but where is there actual evidence? Bennet Peskoe asked Lowell Mahone all the questions we wanted to hear, and Lowell Mahone answered them. You may not like Lowell's answers. You might even think he's lying, but where is your proof?"

"What kind of proof do you want?" boomed Antonio Rasa, editor of Washington's conservative Moonie paper. "A tape of Mahone negotiating with that sleazeball Roland Vanatua? Let's be realistic. There's a mountain of circumstantial evidence, coupled with an utter paucity of credible explanations. And besides, we know the man has no moral fiber, conducting a cheap, disgusting liaison in the Oval Office."

"The problem is bigger than a matter of proof," pronounced Cameron Hetherington. "There may not be proof, as we understand it in a legal, courtroom sense. The problem now is trust. Nobody has any more trust in this man."

"Cameron, once again, is right," said Landon Donlon. "And this brings us to our most vexatious problem. In our society, we believe a person is innocent until proven guilty. President Mahone deserves the presumption of innocence as much as any garden-variety murderer, rapist, or thief. But the presumption of innocence applies to criminal law. This is politics. He simply can't stay in office while he's being investigated or while his trial is going on. He might be innocent, in which case it's a terrible shame to destroy a man and his reputation over nothing. But if he is guilty, if he has acted at the behest of a foreign power, think how much damage he could do during the weeks and months that it will take us to work through the process. The mind reels."

"You've put your finger on it," said Moonie editor Antonio Rasa. "We can live with a president who's been molesting the interns while his case is heard. But how do you live for even a minute with a president who may be a traitor?"

While pundits spouted forth, the weary reporter Maggie Newbold trudged down the streetlight-illuminated concrete of a now nearly empty Fifteenth Street, showed her ID to a nightshift guard whom she didn't recognize and who didn't recognize her, took the elevator to the bureau's offices, and slowly moved down the long corridor to Linda Archer's office. Her shoulders were stiff from all the driving and her stomach, which churned from all the coffee she had gulped in her travels, craved something benign and comforting, like scrambled eggs or chocolate cake. As she moved along the corridor, the few colleagues who were laboring late on the story—Ayisha, Todd Overton, Gonzalez, who had rushed back from Tuscany, one or two others—jumped up from their desks and followed her into Linda's office, where she plopped into a chair and unceremoniously began her report.

"Good news and bad news," she said. "I found her, and I didn't find her. Good news first. Her name is not Irene Kim, but Mingsha Gua, age and nationality to be determined. She lives—lived, past tense—in the first-floor rear room of a shotgun tenement on Potomac Street, just a couple blocks from the Navy Yard, legal ownership to be determined in the morning. She appears to live there no longer. The drawers of her bureau and her closets are empty, there're no bags left, nothing of value remaining—a Nike T-shirt, a pair of flip-flops, a well-thumbed copy of Elena Dover's campaign biography of Jack Mahone—that's about it. It looked like she left in a hurry. Here, I took photos of the place on my phone. The quality's not so good, but then how sharp does a picture need to be to establish that this is an empty bedroom?"

"All right, good," said Linda flatly. "But how—"

"One more thing," said Maggie, interrupting. "I guess I buried my lead. She's a call girl. Tom Ralston hired her."

Gonzalez whistled and Overton grinned, but Linda was underwhelmed. "What I was going to ask you is, How did you get into her apartment?"

Are you shitting me? Maggie thought. "Her landlord," she said. "Mr. Estrada let me in."

"How'd you get him to do that?"

"I guess he somehow got the impression I was from the INS."

"You didn't!" said Linda, who was actually shocked at Maggie until she heard knowing, appreciative chuckles from others in the room, at which point Linda became shocked at them.

"Jesus, Linda, be happy," said Maggie. "This is a twenty-four-karat scoop, and it's all ours. I have it cold, with on-the-record quotes from one of the girls she worked with. I don't know if even the Secret Service is yet aware that her name is Mingsha Gua, and I'm positive no other news organization knows that the president's mistress is a high-end call girl. If we get any further ahead of these people, we're going to lap them."

Linda sighed heavily. "Just be careful. Remember, just because she prostituted herself with some men doesn't mean she prostituted herself with President Mahone. We don't know that he actually paid her, right?"

"True," Maggie agreed. God, is Linda uncomfortable, she thought. Give her some complicated policy story, and she can decipher it with the best of them. Hand her a platinum-grade scandal, and she's lost. No feeling for the story. No taste. She wants a justification for wanting to find out what happened. She doesn't realize that the game is to find out the story first, and roll out the justifications later. "But Linda, does it really matter whether technically the woman prostituted herself with Mahone? I mean, does it matter now? Because right now, it walks like a duck and it quacks like a duck, and I think that's enough to put it up on the Web site."

"Fine," said Linda, rolling her eyes. Outwardly, she seemed exasperated. Inside, she was cheering. Linda grasped that she was like a person who hated racing but who happened to own a thoroughbred, and knew that her only intelligent move, finding herself pressed against the side rails at Santa Anita, was to let Maggie run. Back in her office, Linda dialed Loomis. He'll be very happy, she thought as she waited on hold. Tomorrow morning, he'll be the envy of every news executive in America, and he won't think of firing me, at least not until the next news cycle begins.

WHILE THAT WAS GOING ON, Jack Mahone convened a meeting of his senior staff and political advisers. It was nearly midnight, not a typical time for a meeting to be held, but the president wanted Lucas Ivy to get some polling data after the evening news ran. Had the question at hand yielded more ambiguous findings, Ivy would have been reluctant to state his credibility on the rushed results. As it was, plus or minus six points, plus or minus twelve, the answer was clear.

"Lucas," said Chet, dispensing with all folderol, "what do you have for us?"

"Mr. President, your approval rate tonight stands at eleven percent, the lowest of any president since data was kept. Seventy-three percent of our respondents believe that you have accepted a bribe. Sixty-six percent believe that you have committed treason. Fifty-eight percent think you should resign, sixty-five percent say you should be impeached, and sixty-six percent say both. Thirty-one percent think you should be arrested for soliciting a prostitute. Of course, under the Constitution, that could never happen."

"Thank you, Lucas," said Chet Wetzel. "For any of you—"

"Oh, by the way, bear in mind that we took this poll before *Newsbreak* published the story that Irene Kim was a call girl."

"Right, Lucas, thank—"

"Oh, just remember, there is, of course, a margin of error."

"Thank you, Lucas," said Chet, glaring the pollster into silence. "Now, for those of you who somehow missed the news, Herman

Vanick has notified the White House Counsel's Office that he will commence the impeachment process forthwith, and that we can expect articles of impeachment to be introduced by early next week."

"But I have done nothing wrong!" cried Jack Mahone. The president, who had been morosely silent all day, ever since his brother crashed and burned before the committee, now roared like a wounded bear. "I did nothing wrong! I did nothing close to wrong! I did not compromise our security one whit! I cut no deals! Where are their witnesses to my transgressions, their documents, the records of my meetings, of my phone calls, of my shady transactions? Where is their proof? Yes—I did bury a useless report. Was that a crime? Or was that my duty? And yes, I slept with that girl. Did I know she was a prostitute? No. Did that come as an unpleasant surprise? You bet it did. But my God, it's like they are criminalizing what it means to be who I am!"

"Y'all will have to fight them, Mr. President," said Tavis Whouley. "Stand your ground, sir, dig your trenches, and resist their assaults. The American people are intelligent and fair, Mr. President. After a few days, they will wonder why Herman Vanick is trying to bumrush you out of Washington, and they will return to your side."

"What does anybody think of Tavis's advice?" asked Chet Wetzel.

Lucas Ivy cleared his throat, a signal that he was reluctant to speak because he was going to say something unpopular. "Go ahead," Chet said.

"I'd have more confidence in Mr. Whouley's position if the data showed that we still retained a core of support. Alas, that does not seem to be the case. The president is weak across the board, weak among groups where he was previously strong. There is a strong undercurrent of anger in these results. We know many voters felt they were giving you the benefit of the doubt in the last election; now they feel you've betrayed that, Mr. President. You've betrayed their trust."

"Well, what do you people think I should do about it?" Mahone asked, and the exasperation that was on his face when he spoke the question turned to wounded sorrow when he looked into his followers' eyes and saw nothing but pity and fear. Their silence provoked the kind of tension that makes men want to disappear, as though someone in the room had drawn a gun and nobody wanted to be the next man to move.

"You think I'm lost," Jack at long last said, and the silence that followed was filled with a shame that indicated that no one disagreed. Which meant that once again, as at the cabinet meeting where sticking with the satellite sale was discussed, it fell to Godwin to break the gloom.

"Mr. President," he said, his voice strong, clear, confident, leaderly. "You have only one recourse. Though wise as Tavis usually is, I'm afraid this time he is wrong. You cannot sit and allow them to besiege you. They will nip and nibble, and we will rot if we try to wait them out. Even if you prevail, you will have lost your presidency. No, sir. You must take the fight to them. You must go testify on the Hill."

"Oh, I don't know, Godwin," said Tavis, so aghast that he interrupted. "A president going up to the Hill? It's almost completely unprecedented. It would be embarrassing, the head of one branch kowtowing before another. You'd lose face."

"Ford did it once," said Lucas Ivy. "Kinda took the steam out of his Nixon pardon problem."

"President Bartlet did it on *The West Wing* once, too," said Chet Wetzel.

"What a perfect precedent," said Godwin. "We need something with a little drama, a little flair. I'm not talking about the president going up there and tugging on his forelock and saying, 'Oh please, Great Wise Men, do not impeach me.' Nonsense. The president should go up there and spit in their eyes. Face them down, tell them the truth, and challenge them to prove that a syllable of what he has said is false. Get up in their faces. Humble them in their audacity." Now Godwin spun around and faced the president, working to an audience of one, "Remember, Jack, who you are. You are not merely a gifted politician who had the strength and toughness to win this office in an election. You ARE the president of the United States, the only official in this country who is chosen by all the people. And these pantywaists, these midgets, these termites are trying to throw you out. Now you owe it to the people, to future presidents, and to our Constitution to go into that arena and beat them."

Once again, Godwin could see the persuasive effect his words had had on the president. Mahone's color brightened, his posture straightened, and traces of that ineffable quality called fight filled his spirit. "And you think that would work?"

Godwin waited for effect. "Perhaps not in the hands of a lesser man," he said quietly. "But if you were to do it, hell yeah it would work."

Jack laughed, at first quietly and then loudly, and then his advisers began laughing, too, strongly, confidently, a laughter that was filled with courage. "Chet," the president said when the sound subsided, "call Herman Vanick. Ask him to convene a committee. Tell him the president of the United States—the head of government, the commander in chief of the armed forces, the man who has pledged to faithfully execute the laws of this nation and to preserve, protect, and defend the Constitution—is coming to pay a call."

Godwin leaped to his feet and applauded. It all comes down to this, he was thinking as he madly clapped. If you're going to shoot at the king, you better make sure he ends up dead.

IT WAS AFTER ONE when Godwin finally left the White House. It was a clear March night, chilly but no longer winter, invigorating, an occasional clue of spring in a wind that no longer pushed but now patted. He had told his driver to take him to his residence at the Observatory, but he reconsidered, and called Maggie on her cell.

"Feel like coming over?" he asked.

"Oh, I'm in bed already. I'm nearly asleep."

"Hard day?"

"Exhausting. Name a suburb, and I was in a traffic jam in it."

"That's too bad. If you knew any important people, you might be able to talk to them about fixing that."

"Ha ha. Hey, I was giving some thought of turning Easter into a four-day weekend and going someplace. Would you be able to get away?"

"I don't know. Possibly."

He sounded uncommonly vague for him, but she didn't have the energy to pursue the point. "I'm envisioning swimsuits and umbrella drinks," she said. "Does the Caribbean pique your interest?"

"Maybe. Soon my choices might be limited to the mountains for a while. But we'll talk about it. You should go back to sleep."

She had almost done so when a question elbowed in: Was he talking about Camp David?

WHEN GODWIN ARRIVED HOME, he dressed for bed, but he had too much on his mind to feel sleepy. Padding downstairs, he poured himself three fingers of Macallan and sat back in his big leather armchair. Tomorrow he'd be very busy; he'd have to work fast. But if all went as he foresaw, mere hours from now Jack Mahone's presidency would be in shambles, and in no more than a day or two, his would begin. Yet for all that, for all his burgeoning responsibilities, all he could think about was Maggie. Sitting across the room from the photograph of the vivacious Minerva and the sad-eyed Chesbro Pope—no older in that picture than Godwin was today, yet looking substantially beset—Godwin knew that Maggie was the woman he'd been waiting to meet. And yet, once he was president, there would be no dating a reporter. Unwise as it would be for him to have a professional tattletale as a lover, it would be utterly impossible for her employers to condone it. And he and

Maggie could hardly keep seeing each other in secret. That would be foolhardy, even if he thought he could stand it. But what to do?

A preemptive offer. At Zephyr, he and Tom had learned the hard way that when they wanted something, really wanted it, there was no point in haggling about the cost. The smart approach was to put so much on the table that the proposition was soon stripped of expressions like *yes, but,* and *no, unless.* Make the right offer, and the decision becomes clear: up or down, in or out, yes or no.

Very well, he thought. A preemptive offer it will be.

29

AT 6:00 A.M., MAGGIE'S EYES abruptly opened. Lying in the watery gray darkness, listening to a robin chirping in search of another early bird who'd rushed the season, thoughts about the day's work ahead began collecting in her head. Yesterday, she thought, we discovered that the poised, polished Irene Kim is really Mingsha Gua, origins unknown. Today, we'll figure out how she got into this country. We'll also have to suss out how she became Irene Kim, and if one development is related to the other. And then there's what might be the juiciest question of all: How did Irene Kim get into the White House?

How did she get into the White House? How exactly did it happen? She is obviously a pretty girl; that's been known to open all kinds of doors, no further explanation necessary. But Jack didn't do it himself. There aren't streetwalkers on the stroll in Lafayette Park whom the president could turn a telescope onto, and even a hound like Jack Mahone would be unlikely to go to the "Escorts" entry in the Yellow Pages and place an order for a delivery with Hos "R" Us. No, Maggie was certain, somebody had engineered her access to Jack Mahone. There would be a story in that.

At 6:08, she got out of bed, slipped on a robe, turned on the coffeemaker, picked up the phone, and called Chet Wetzel's cell. Only his rather boring voice mail responded. She left a message, but she also kept calling, every ten or fifteen minutes, until at 8:58, as she was stepping into *Newsbreak* offices that she didn't think she'd really left, he called her back.

"You have a lot of nerve calling. I saw what you put up on the Web site."

She couldn't believe she was hearing him right. "What's wrong with what I put up on the Web site? Was I wrong?"

"It just wasn't very helpful, now was it?"

She felt like asking where on earth he got the idea that she had any desire to be helpful to anybody, but she thought better of it. After all, she wanted him to be helpful to her, more than she wanted to cream him. "Chet, sweetie, let's not fight. It looks to me like the *Titanic*'s in real danger of going down, and what's more, Leonardo DiCaprio ain't playing you in the movie. You may want friends later, and all I have is a simple question."

"Oh for Chrissakes, what is it?"

"How did the president meet Irene?"

"Don't you mean Mingsha Gua?" he said snidely.

"Chet, I'm honored. You did read the Web site! Okay, how did he meet Mingsha?"

The delay was brief but measurable, exactly equivalent to the length of time it takes a faithful squire to finally decide to start squealing on his liege. Maggie heard a protracted sigh. "It's a little embarrassing," he said.

"Come on, dear," she said, "you are all way past embarrassing, don't you think?"

"Still. All right, look—she was dating a staffer. Richie Platt. And the president big-footed him."

"So to speak."

"Yeah, so to speak."

"Is the president in the habit—"

"That's enough. They're calling me." The phone went dead.

She strolled up the hallway. The door to Ayisha's office was open. She was putting on eyeliner. "You slept here?" Maggie asked.

"It's going to be a big day. I didn't want to risk oversleeping."

"Good girl," Maggie said. No, we certainly don't want to miss any of this. "Hey, does the name Richie Platt mean anything to you?"

"Yeah, he's the third-string speechwriter at the White House. Worked in the campaign as an advance man."

"You know him?"

"Oh yeah. He was on Pope's staff; then he switched over. Remember when a police car in Cleveland ran over the foot of one of Mahone's advance men? They asked Richie to fill that vacancy. We were on the same plane sometimes. He's funny. He does an imitation of Pope that's hysterical. You know—saying, 'Let's move on,' with that stick up his ass?"

Maggie was tempted for a moment to ask Ayisha if she really thought Godwin had a stick up his ass, but she kept focus. "Do you know Richie dated Irene Kim?"

"Really?" She laughed.

"Why is that so funny?"

"That's the old story with Jack Mahone and Richie. Richie would get Jack girls during the campaign all the time. That was the rumor anyway."

"But you believed it."

"We'd kid him about it, and he'd get really angry, which made me think there was something to it."

"Were the women prostitutes?"

"No. No! I never thought so. Coeds mostly, a few desperate housewives. They just seemed like women who would get turned on by the thought of being with a celebrity. There was a lot of talk about it, but I think the talk made it seem like it happened six times a day. It didn't happen that much. Maybe a handful of times. That I was aware of anyway."

"And Richie was good at this recruitment?"

"Richie's really cute, in a surfer-slacker way. Some women want to seduce him, and other women want to comb his hair. And the other advance men were these scary-looking potbellied Louisiana state troopers who wore mirrored sunglasses."

"But the key thing is that Jack and Richie had some kind of modus operandi. And that's important, because the president might not have thought he was having a transaction with a prostitute. He might have just thought Irene was one of Richie's girls."

"And that he would be able to exercise his right of eminent domain or whatever. That could be, sure."

"We should talk to him," Maggie said. "Will he take your call?"

"He might," said Ayisha.

Less trouble for Jack in one way, Maggie was thinking; it wouldn't seem so trashy if he didn't know Irene was a prostitute. More trouble in another way, though. It's not good form to keep your personal party-girl recruiter on the government payroll. Might even be some kind of indictable offense.

She had barely begun culling her accumulated E-mail messages when Ayisha stuck her head back in the door. "Richie's out sick," she said. "Apparently, he has the flu. He's been out the last three days."

"Mmmh," said Maggie, doing math in her head. "It's been three days since the Irene Kim story broke in the Worm Report."

"The same thought occurred to me."

"Maybe I should take him some chicken soup," said Maggie. "You don't happen to have a picture of him? And his address?"

"We took some funny snapshots on the campaign plane. I'll see if he's in any."

AS IT TURNED OUT, Maggie had a harder time finding a parking place near Richie's condo in the Rock Creek Park area than she did finding him. Just as she at last squeezed into an empty space that left the rear bumper of her Camry perilously close to a fire hydrant, she saw Richie walking down the opposite side of the street. Head down, collar up, lips locked in an intense duck pucker, brow furrowed under a beige cap that said AUDIOSLAVE, Richie was lost in some deeply gripping thought. Following him at a distance, Maggie was intent on giving him plenty of space, hoping that he wasn't heading for the Metro or somewhere equally inaccessible. She was greatly relieved to see that he had targeted Starbucks. Lurking behind other customers, she waited until he had paid for his venti espresso Macchiato and two blueberry scones and had his hands clumsily full with food and change. Then she walked up and spoke to him from behind.

"Breakfast of champions, eh?"

He was smiling when he turned around to find out who had authored this friendly comment. "Shit!" he said when he saw her. "Oh, shit, shit fuck!"

"Hi, Richie, I'm Maggie Newbold of *Newsbreak*."

"Ah, fuck, I know who you are and I have nothing to say." The natural ruddiness of his face took on a nasty purple tinge.

"Now now, don't you want some sugar for that? Let's move over here." She ever so lightly guided him by the elbow away from the other customers, who were nosily eyeing him as he walked toward the milk and sugar station. The move allowed him to collect himself for a second, an opportunity that Maggie used to draw Richie closer into her web. "Come, let's sit down and talk like civilized people," she said, and gently she pointed him to a pair of comfy foam chairs near the music rack. But after he sat down, she pounced the moment he took his first sip. "Richie, you know pimping is a crime in the District of Columbia. Now when you introduced Irene Kim to the president, did you know she was a prostitute?"

"When I introduced— No. No! She was just a girl I was dating."

"So the president didn't know."

"Not from me. I mean, I didn't know she was a prostitute, so I don't see how the president could have known."

"Okay, good—good for you, good for the president. Your attorney will be able to use that in your defense."

"Defense?"

"Next question: When did you introduce her to the president?"

"At the White House correspondents' dinner. It was just a formal thing. We shook hands with him in the reception line."

"Was that some prearranged way you would have of showcasing a girl to him?"

"What are you talking about?"

"When you get a girl for him." She gave him a schoolteacherish look of exasperation. "Come on, Richie. Everybody knows you get girls for Mahone."

"I don't!" he said, his voice not quite rising to a shout, but filled with enough violent intensity that heads turned throughout the café. "I don't," he said again, more quietly but just as firmly. "I introduced him to some girls during the campaign, okay? But not this time. Not anymore. When I introduced Irene to the president, I had just met her myself. And then we started dating. And then he took her from me."

Richie's vehemence was bracing. People lie, Maggie thought, but seldom so stridently. Perhaps this was, after all, simply a classic case of boy meets girl, president steals girl, boy is fucked. "So let me get this straight. Mahone meets her at the dinner, and then what? He calls her?"

"No, I don't think he called her, but who the hell knows? At the dinner, he said 'You seem like a nice couple, and Richie here has been doing such a great job. Why don't you come to the next screening we have?' "

"And then?"

"We went. But then all of a sudden, there was an emergency, and there was some work I had to do. So I left, and I guess they started talking or something, and—things happened."

"Right," she said. Pretty smooth of old Jack. "Now, had the two of you been going out a long time?"

"No. We only met at the White House correspondents' dinner ourselves."

"You were there helping the president with his remarks or something?"

"No, I was a guest. I was there with the Vanatuas."

Now this was a surprise. "Are you old friends of theirs or something?"

"No. Actually, I met them for the first time at the White House correspondents' dinner, too."

"No disrespect, but you're not exactly the type of high roller they usually ask. Especially unmet."

He shrugged. "Penny said Vice President Pope had been telling her that I was a young man with a lot of promise, and that if she and Roland wanted to get to know the leaders of tomorrow, they might consider inviting me."

"Huh." Maggie had heard enough bullshit being slung to find the smell of this suspicious, but she wasn't going to challenge him here. "And that's where you met Irene, too."

"Yes. She was at the table."

"The Vanatuas' table. Now how did they know her?"

"I don't know. I don't know that they did know her. Penny was asking her the same kinds of questions she asked me."

"Like . . . ?"

"Like where we went to school, and what we did. Basic stuff."

"And Vice President Pope is the one who brought you to their attention."

"Yeah, I guess you could say he's been sort of my mentor. I mentioned to him once that I wanted to go to an event like that, and I think he helped arrange it."

"Any idea who brought Irene to their attention?"

"I have no clue," Richie said.

All of this seemed too strange for Maggie to believe. The president met Irene on the night she met Richie on the night they each met the Vanatuas. That's a lot of fast action. If nobody knew anybody, somebody must have known something. "Richie, were you being set up?"

"Like, by who?"

"Like by the Vanatuas, maybe. It's suspected that money they paid Lowell Mahone was actually meant to be a bribe for Jack. Maybe you're supposed to be an intermediary, too. Maybe they were trying to slip a girl to Jack, and you were the beard."

"Ya think?"

"Maybe."

"I don't know, you're pretty smart, but that makes no sense to me. I don't know why they'd want a beard, but if they did, I'm pretty sure they could have found somebody better than me."

30

JACK MAHONE STOOD AT THE SINK in his private bathroom off of the Oval Office and splashed cold water on his face. It was a ritual; he didn't need to be cleansed, nor did he need to be awakened. It was just a last step before saying "Let's go."

He stepped back and checked himself out in the mirror. He wore a charcoal Bill Blass suit with a light gray pinstripe, vaguely military in its cut, bankerish, prosperous, serious in its overall display. In between her self-pitying sobs and rancorous outbursts, Mrs. Mahone, bless her heart, her Middle Eastern tour abruptly halted, suggested that he go to the Hill dressed all in white, looking like the painting of the Lord after his Resurrection that served as the frontpiece of her personal Bible. "They would not dare harm you then," she proclaimed before tearfully running back to her bedroom and the ministrations of her social secretary, a sorority sister from Tulane. But Jack didn't want to look like the Lord. He wanted to look like a man. He wanted them to remember that he was the Man, that of all of them, all of them who scorned him and disdained him and ridiculed him, he alone had the courage and the stamina and the gumption and the wit to convince a majority of their fellow citizens to put him in the big white house on Pennsylvania Avenue. He wanted them to feel the power that that victory had given him. Anyone who wants to take a swing at Jack Mahone should come ahead, he wanted them to think. Just do it in the ring. Don't make some damn sneak attack.

He looked around the little room once more. He liked having a private bathroom. The first time when he truly had one all to himself, long ago, when he was elected state attorney, his first big post, he scoffed at the idea. The Mahones were numerous and poor; at various times, with visiting cousins lodged in semipermanent residency, ten of them shared a bathroom. Nobody could hide much when there were ten to a bathroom; nobody could pretend to be shy about basic human parts and basic human functions. Piss, shit, blood, cum—nobody had secrets. Giving a man a private bathroom was like inviting him to pretend that his shit didn't stink. The pretense could go to his head. In the early days of his presidency, Jack would hide in his bathroom, hide on days when he didn't feel that he could be president or deserved to be president or needed time to muster the courage to act the part. He didn't feel that he needed to hide anymore.

He opened the door and walked out. "Let's go," he said, and began marching toward the portico where his car would be waiting, his retinue of aides and bodyguards quickly falling into step behind him. As he moved through the corridors of the White House, staffers hovering in doorways bid him good luck. By the door, cabinet secretaries and senior officials stood in a row, offering expressions of encouragement and support. Standing last in line was Godwin Pope, who reached out and gripped the president's hand.

"Good luck, Mr. President," he said. Then, spontaneously, Godwin reached around and embraced Jack. "We'll be here when you get back."

A surge of emotion welled up in Jack, and all he could do was offer what he felt was a meaningful nod of solidarity before stepping toward the car.

Good, Godwin was thinking. I thought he'd never leave. Now we can get down to work.

31

IT WAS A NICE COMPACT THEORY, the idea that the Vanatuas sent money to Mahone through his brother and girls to him through Richie Platt, and Maggie was loathe to relinquish it too easily. Yet for all its elegance, Maggie reluctantly had to admit that it made no sense. They had any number of more efficient, better-protected routes at their disposal. If they were going to use Richie Platt, they would have done just as well to stick a stamp on the girl's forehead and ship her parcel post. Well, better ask the source. She trolled back through her E-mail until she found the invitation Penny had sent her to the party back in February, the party where Godwin had given her that useful tip about Adrian Simone. Yes, just as she had remembered, it included Penny's personal number. Penny would be protected by a phalanx of mouthpieces, but surely an independent woman like Penny would not be capable of leaving all her talking to intermediaries.

Maggie got her on the first ring. She couldn't tell whether Penny was pretending to be aghast that a reporter would have the temerity to call her private number, or if she had turned into a fourteen-karat megalomaniac who no longer felt subject to any of the normal processes of society. Maggie felt that she had no choice but to lead with trumps.

"Please talk to me," she said. "I have no questions about Lowell Mahone. But surely you realize that they're going to try and say you supplied Irene Kim to the president as part of your bribe."

"That's outrageous," shrieked Penny, who proceeded to fill the air with a long stream of curses in at least two languages.

"But I don't think you did that," Maggie at last squeezed in edgewise. "And I'll write that. But I need you to tell me exactly how things came together."

"What do you want to know?" said Penny.

"Why did you invite Richie Platt to the correspondents' dinner?"

"That's what you want to know?" Her incredulity only strengthened Maggie's sense that Penny had nothing to do with this part of the escapade. "Well, we first invited Vice President Pope—you know, he's a good friend; in fact, Jack is, too—but Godwin couldn't do it; he had another commitment. So that left us with a vacancy, and Godwin mentioned Richie. I guess he's Godwin's protégé or something."

"Yeah, I gather he worked in the Pope for President campaign, and Godwin set him up in his job in the White House."

"Something like that." Clearly, Penny kept a firm grasp on social geography but didn't dwell on the nuts and bolts of things.

"So where did you know Irene from?" Maggie asked.

"I didn't know Irene. She just came to my party."

Again, the easy access the Vanatuas seemed to grant one and all struck Maggie as slightly ridiculous. "Do a lot of people you don't know just come to your parties?"

"Of course. I didn't know you, and you came to my party. Roland and I, we like to meet new people. Although, funny thing. I don't think I was ever introduced to Irene Kim that night."

"But you invited her to this big event."

"Well, Godwin said Richie was working very hard and wasn't seeing anyone, and he said, 'Why don't you invite someone for him,' and he pointed out Ms. Kim. She was clearly an attractive young woman, and let's not kid one another, that's as much of a résumé as a young lady needs sometimes, is it not?"

"So it was the vice president who pointed out Ms. Kim?"

"He said she was a charming young lady, so I sent Claudette, my social secretary, over to get her phone number. But I didn't meet her until the dinner."

A thought slowly gripped Maggie by the throat. Godwin nominated Richie. Godwin nominated Irene. Godwin knew Tom Ralston, who had procured Irene.

"You're sure Vice President Pope made these suggestions?" she asked once more. Penny's blithe "Of course" landed like a stone.

THE PRESIDENT'S MOTORCADE took only moments to make the short trip from the White House to the Capitol Building. Reflexively, the Secret Service had planned to park the president's car in the building's underground garage, but Jack nixed that proposal out of hand. No theater, he thought, no message. "I want to walk in the front door with my head up," he said, thinking of himself as Gary Cooper in *High Noon*. "I want everybody to see me." Once the decision had been made, Chet Wetzel alerted the media, and they were present in force to record the instant he stepped out of the car. Like MacArthur in the Philippines, Jack was thinking as the flashes fired and the cameras rolled. Deal with me, he thought, marching with steel-eyed determination up the Capitol steps. I am here.

IN HIS OFFICE in the White House, Godwin was busy typing on his laptop as fast as his fingers could fly. There was an E-mail form on his screen. In the SUBJECT window he had typed "EMERGENCY! OPEN IMMEDIATELY!" and he kept adding names to the infinitely capacious address box: Herman_Vanick@USHouse.gov; Bennet_Peskoe@USHouse.gov; Alonzo_Rotundo@USHouse.gov; Jack_Goldstock@USHouse.gov; MaryJane_Abbott@USHouse.gov; Harlan_Brewer@USHouse.gov. Godwin did not rest; he had many names to go.

IT TOOK FOUR CALLS to Tom Ralston's expensive gatekeepers, four calls in which Maggie made it clear to them that he had to call her, that he truly would want to speak to her, that seeing the line "Mr. Ralston would not return phone calls requesting comment" on the Web site or in the magazine would only make him seem guilty and cowardly. "Guilty and cowardly," she emphasized to the last PR man, "and enmeshed in a conspiracy." Within five minutes, Ralston was phoning her cell.

"You said you were going to leave me alone!" he snarled.

"No, I said I'd try to keep your name out of the story, and guess what? It keeps wanting to get back in. Now here's the question: Were you serious the other day when you said that part of the free agent welcome wagon was taking a meeting with the vice president?"

"Yeah. I mean, not every time, but when he can, which I guess is pretty often. Obviously, we go way back. He does me the favor, and I help him."

"Where did he meet Marco McChesney? In his office?"

"No, here. My home."

"On the same day Irene Kim was there?"

"I guess it must have been. Marco was only here one day. Everything happened that day. It was a couple of days after the State of the Union address."

Now for the payoff. "Did Irene and the vice president meet?"

"No."

"Don't lie to me now. This is important."

"No!"

Shit, she thought. What's going on? "Not like in the driveway or in a hallway or something?" she asked, pressing him.

"No. It's a big place, and we keep guests well separated from the entertainment."

"Yeah, right. Like Marco."

"Well, not Marco."

"Maybe he saw her. Did he even see her?"

Ralston's hesitancy gave the answer away. "Well, I don't really recall . . ."

"Do not fucking lie to me," Maggie said sharply. "You will be humiliated."

"I guess he might have seen her," Ralston allowed.

With that tentative admission, the game was over. Maggie went for the kill. "How?"

"Rooms in the house overlook the pool. He could have seen the girls."

"In action. With Marco."

"I suppose."

"No suppose, right? You know he saw them. You were there when he saw them."

"Could be." Ralston could barely bring himself to give voice to the words.

"Let's recap. You had Godwin come over to meet Marco Mc-Chesney, and sometime before the meeting, or after the meeting, you introduced Marco to the girls. They went off and partied, and because you like to create these little moments and show them off, you showed them to your old buddy Godwin."

"All right, goddammit, yes. But Godwin wasn't interested. All he wanted to do was gripe about Jack Mahone and how awful he is and how much he'd like to get rid of him but that that would be impossible, which is hugely ironic, because three weeks later, the asshole's getting rid of himself, right?"

"Now here's the kicker," said Maggie, feeling that she was about to drop the winning card. "A couple days after the meeting, Godwin called you and asked you to call Irene Kim for him, or hire her for him, or arrange something involving her."

"No," said Ralston. The answer killed her, killed her and perplexed her, because she knew he wouldn't bother lying at this point, and he repeated it, piercing her with each iteration. "No. No. Nothing like that, no. In fact, I haven't spoken to him since that day."

Hurrying back to her car, she wondered if Ralston would call Godwin and tell him about her interest. Maybe—they are pretty close. But right now, Tom is more worried about getting in trouble with the league than about my questions concerning Godwin, who, as far as Tom knows, is an innocent bystander. No, he doesn't want any of this known, and it's hardly likely he'll be the first to let the cat out of the bag, to Godwin or to anyone.

32

APART FROM THE MURMURED WHIR of the video cameras and the cricket chirp of print photographers' Canons and Nikons, the august hearing room, jam-packed with media and officials and Washington's elite, was as quiet as a cathedral during the elevation of a cardinal. Herman Vanick himself administered the oath.

"Mr. President, do you solemnly swear to tell the truth, the whole truth, and nothing but the truth?"

"So help me God."

There was a sudden rasp of chair legs being scraped across the floor as the entire assemblage took their seats; then Herm began. "Mr. President, we're going to proceed with questioning from Mr. Peskoe, and when he's finished, we'll call on the ranking member of the minority, Ms. Miller, who'll be followed by—"

"Let's just cut to it, huh, Herm?" The president's interruption shocked and surprised the room, but he didn't wait for their whispers to subside, or for Herman Vanick to gavel the proceedings to order and thus regain the initiative. Jack wanted control of these hearings, and just then he had seized it by the throat. He wasn't about to give it back. "I'll answer questions from you and from anybody else on the committee, all day, all night, as long as you people want. But let's not get ourselves lost in one of these ornate pageants that get produced up here from time to time. Let's just get to it.

"I've known most of you for years," he said, slowly standing and walking to the center of the open space before the seated panel. He began pointing to individual members. "We've known each other eight years, right, Angela? Twelve years, Lyle, right? We were on that Mississippi River Trade Commission together, right? John, we worked hand in hand to help President Clinton get the authorization he needed to sort out that mess in Bosnia. I've known you, Bert, since you were an assistant attorney general in the Carter administration and I was Louisiana state attorney general and we had to figure out what to do with those Marielitos Castro sent over. You had more hair then, Bert. Chris, I've known you since you were four, when your father, who was a great and honorable man, used to bring you to his office and let you play under his desk. And Herm—Herm, I reckon I've got as many tire tracks on my back from you as you've got tire tracks on your back from me. So let's just cut all this lawyerly rigmarole and media posturing and just get to it, huh?

"I believe I am being buffaloed by you people. I believe you all are leaping from conclusion to conclusion like alpine goats that got firecrackers tied to their tails. So I'll start with a simple point. There is nothing to your accusations. Nothing."

IN HIS OFFICE, Godwin continued to add addresses to his E-mail: Jonathan_Simpson@USSenate.gov; Logan_Amos@USSenate.gov; Laurence_Cragan@USSenate.gov. Jack has started off well, he thought. A little Oprahish, but perhaps that's what plays these days.

He cracked his knuckles. He still had a lot of names to add.

AT FIRST, Maggie cursed when she saw the giant moving van blocking her way to the Vanatuas' big house in Chevy Chase. Then she realized the Vanatuas themselves were moving. No time for niceties, she thought, and drove right up onto the lawn. Roland Vanatua ran out of the house yelling.

"No, no, no, you'll ruin the grass! You goddamn crazy woman, you're going to pay the damn landscaping bill!"

"No problem," she said, perfectly willing to become a legend among *Newsbreak*'s expense managers. "Roland, what's going on?"

"Oh nothing. Just taking an overdue vacation."

"Now? And with all your property?"

"Oh, no time to wait. Lawyer says by end of the goddamn day, I may be the target of a goddamn federal investigation."

"Roland—"

"Bad goddamn time to chat with the news media. You understand. I have lots of goddamn packing."

"Two minutes. Two minutes that could keep your ass out of jail. Did you see Lowell Mahone's testimony?"

"Sure."

"Do you agree with his story?"

"Every goddamn word. I asked him to sing."

"Didn't you know how that would look?"

"Now I know how that was going to look, but it didn't look like it was going to look that way at the time I asked. The goddamn satellite deal was in a coma, Jack was running away from it like he was O. J. Simpson. He was giving me a goddamn serious problem. I needed to reassure a lot of people in Asia that I was still a goddamn player in Washington."

"So you thought signing Lowell would show you were close to—"

"Absofuckinglutely."

"But with no strings attached, no bribe to do something."

"No, you don't bribe these people to do something. You go to jail for that. What you got to do is figure out how to give them money all year long, then maybe they think of you when your issue comes up. One gift, one time—that's bribery. Lots of gifts over a long time—that's politics."

"But hiring Lowell—that was your idea."

"Yeah. I dunno. Yeah. Somebody's."

"Whose? Think. It's important."

"We had a big party. Lowell was there. You were there, too. Maybe it was one of Penny's stupid ideas."

"Penny?"

"No, now I remember," he said, his face lighting up. "It was Goddy Pope."

"Vice President Pope?" She felt her stomach clench. It was the name she had come for. It was also the name she feared.

"Yeah. I was pumping him for info about the deal and he said it was going to take time and I said I was going to lose a lot of goddamn face and he said sign Lowell."

"Just like that?"

"I think maybe he meant it as a joke, but it was really a good idea, and it probably would have stayed a good idea until you came along."

"Me?" In her shock, she spoke so loudly that movers carrying a Louis Quatorze divan twenty feet away turned their heads in her direction.

"Yeah, you," Roland said pointedly. "The deal was up for grabs. Then you did all that research and wrote that big goddamn article about how the opponents were all goddamn hypocrites, and everything fell into place."

"Right," she said in a voice suddenly faint and faraway. It came back to her all at once how she had found that information, how on a morning when she was buoyed on a cloud of romantic rapture and postcoital bliss, she had stumbled on the data lying nakedly on his breakfast table, just as naked as she was. He could have placed neon arrows around it and it wouldn't have been more obvious. He could have slapped the word *trap* above it in ten-foot letters and she would have missed that completely, as well.

"It was you," Roland reiterated. "You changed everything."

GODWIN CONTINUED to type. Roger_Archer@ABCNews.com; Rose_Quinn@NBCNEWS.com; Djones@timemagazine.com.

"THERE IS NOTHING to your accusations," said President Mahone. "Nothing."

"Let's pick one to start. You say I buried a CIA report that was critical of the satellite sale. Okay, yeah, I did. It was a bad report, a stupid report, and as the chief executive of the government, as that analyst's boss, I didn't want that report released. Why not? Because, Herm, I knew that you and my other dear friends in the loyal opposition would turn it into a club and beat me about the head with it. Because life in Washington ain't all about policy. It's also about beating your opponent. It's about denying the results of elections and the choice of the people. And I just didn't want to be a victim of that anymore.

"Did the Vanatuas have a lot of influence over my decisions? Not really. But none of us are children, here, are we? Over the years, I took their contributions and I ate their food and I drank their liquor and I sat on their sand and soaked up their portion of the Caribbean sun. Usually it was under the guise of some study conference, so I went and heard some distinguished speaker or two talk about something, before I hit the beach. That makes me about the same as about a million other people in this country who take tax-deductible vacations to Cabo San Lucas to learn about some new development in law or medicine, information about which is no doubt available on-line. I took from them, and from a whole lot of other people like them, just like you, and you, and you, and you, and you. And so when they talk to me, I listen. Just like you do. Do I do what they want? Sometimes—just like you do. I assume the Vanatuas will make a pile of money off this deal. But that's not why I'm in favor of it. I'm in favor of it because it's good policy for America. What's particularly galling is to see all of you sitting there like Claude Rains in that *Casablanca* movie, shocked—shocked!— to find gambling going on. Spare me.

"Why did Roland hire my brother? To curry favor, I assume. But I knew nothing about it, and I have gained nothing from it. It was a complete shock that my brother bought that stock for me. But if it looks bad to you, it's because my brother's not like you. Or me, for that matter. He's honest. If he wants to give somebody something, he does it—no strings. And if somebody offers him money to sing, he'll sing. Was he supposed to be surprised that somebody offered so much money to sing? I sure was. I think his singing sucks. But we live in a world where high school dropouts get ninety-five million for dribbling a basketball, and a girl who didn't do anything with her life but perform fellatio on the president got a million for her memoirs. Hell, three-quarters of a million for singing in a posh casino for a whole bunch of high rollers seems like ditchdigger's wages.

"And I'm supposed to have sold out for a piece of that. Shoot, even if you think I'm dishonest, you ought to have a higher regard for my ability to negotiate a deal."

MAGGIE KNEW what she had to do. Somehow, Godwin had manipulated this whole thing, herself included. She would have to go to Linda—fucking Linda, of all people—lay out the story, confess how literally embedded she was in the plot, and simultaneously break the biggest story of her life while consigning herself to professional oblivion.

She got off the elevator and began the long, slow slog to Linda's office. The door to every office was open, and in each room the television was on, tuned to Mahone's testimony, so that she was able to hear the president's defense in a long, unbroken relay that ended at Linda's office, where Linda and three or four colleagues were watching what was shaping up to be one of the signature moments in American political history.

"Linda—"

"Shh!"

"Linda, this is all a setup."

"Christ, Maggie, I'm watching! Mahone is giving a virtuoso performance!"

"But it's all a setup!"

"I'm watching! Talk to me after."

So Maggie returned to her office and waited.

HE HAS WON, Herman Vanick was thinking. He has come up here and stepped onto our floor and has cleaned our clocks. We have nothing to say. We have no documents to contradict what he's said; we have no witnesses. People can either believe him or not, but the way he has stood here and confessed his transgressions and pointed a finger at all of us, well, what can we do? The best card in our hand was panic, the public's susceptibility to leap to some conclusion. No more. He has reassured them. No more.

"Now let's talk about the real red herring," said Jack. "I'm talking about Ms. Irene Kim. Did I sleep with her? Yeah. Am I a fool? Yeah. Did I have even the slightest inkling that she was a prostitute? No. So am I an even bigger fool? Yes, I am. I'm not proud of it. In fact, I'm damned ashamed of it, and I apologize with all my heart to Mrs. Mahone, who is the love of my life. But I'm willing to bet the vast majority of you have been foolish in some similar way. So let me ask you—who among you doesn't have something you wouldn't want the world to know? How unusual am I? How big a fool does this make me?"

IN HIS OFFICE, Godwin at long last finished filling out the TO box on his E-mail. He then attached a wordless message consisting of a single image. Those receiving the E-mail would see that the sender was thewormreport.com. This looks like a good moment, he thought, and clicked on SEND.

"HOW BIG a fool does this make me?" Jack asked again. "Am I a bigger fool than I was a month ago? A more dangerous fool? Someone unfit to be entrusted with the welfare of the American people?"

He was about to wrap things up, to close the sale. He knew he had been doing well, and he felt that with a plea for forgiveness and a pledge to reform the cesspool in which he had so long swum, he would leave the building with the support and encouragement of every American who had ever sinned and pledged to improve, of every loser who regretted his failures and yearned for a second chance, of every woman and man who wanted to believe that people could repent and be better. But just as he opened his mouth, he heard a cell phone go off, and then another, then a beeper and a buzzer and dings and pings, and suddenly the whole room exploded in Mozart and Sibelius and James Brown and Coldplay, ring tones of every type, and one after another people looked at phones and BlackBerrys and laptops and pagers, and somebody gasped and somebody else cried, "Holy shit!" and then the whole room erupted as people in the audience, no less than the members of the panel, stretched and craned to get a look at the nearest screen.

Jack Mahone was flummoxed. He looked left, then right, found the eye of a bug-eyed Chet Wetzel, who did nothing but shrug. Slowly, he became aware that now the room had quieted, and everyone was looking at him. Finally, Herm, who was now standing in a cluster of congressmen, looking at a laptop, spoke. "Mr. President, is there someone near you with a screen? Would you please take a look?"

Chet Wetzel arrived with a laptop. On it Jack could see a photograph of Irene Kim wearing a black dress and standing with four Asian men. They were in somebody's living room, at some kind of party. One of them was holding a plate of shrimp.

"Mr. President," said Herm, "can you identify those people?"

"Well, that's Irene Kim."

"And . . ."

"I don't recognize the men."

"Mr. President, take a close look at the man next to Irene Kim, the one who has his arm around her waist."

Jack peered at the photo more intently. "I can't say I've never met him," Jack said, "I've met so many folks. But his face doesn't seem familiar."

"It's Zhang Tian," said Herman Vanick, but Jack still looked blank. "China's deputy commerce minister."

"Perhaps at some reception," offered Jack, trying to oblige.

"He's the head of China's intelligence agency. He's their chief spook, Mr. President. He runs all their spies."

No roundhouse right by Dempsey or Louis or Marciano ever poleaxed a man so completely as did Vanick's last words. If he's a spy, that might mean she's a— All at once, Jack tried to think of every conversation he'd ever had with Irene Kim, of every moment they'd spent together, trying to plumb his brain for anything he'd said, for everything that she'd said, of any briefing book or document or piece of paper that might have been lying in the room. It was no use. She was a spy, and if she wasn't a spy, she may as well have been, and he was now a man who could never be trusted again.

"I—I'm sorry, Mr. Chairman," he said, "I don't know the man, and I can answer no questions about him. I'm sorry. Please excuse me. I'm sorry, and I have to go. I'm sorry."

And with that, he turned and headed for the door. People weren't sure what he was up to; they thought he was looking for someone or something, to talk to an aide or get a piece of paper. But he passed his aides and pushed through the media. Cameramen tripped over themselves to make a path for the president, and he himself stumbled over their baggage but never slowed down, and it dawned on Chet Wetzel and the other aides that the hearing was over, that the president was leaving, and they leaped to their feet and went after him, pushing and shoving people out of their way. In the tumult, the media finally grasped what was happening. "He's leaving," someone shouted, and they all jumped to their feet and followed. Jack was already in the hallway, with maybe thirty feet on them, but when they broke out of the hearing room with shouts of "There he is!" and "Go! Go! Go!" Jack began moving faster. He broke into a trot, and then a run, and the media pursued. Jack raced through the corridors of the Capitol and out the door, the pack in full bellowing pursuit. Outside, a Secret Service agent threw himself in front of the pursuing journalists, and with a rolling block that even Vince Lombardi would have awarded a standing O, he spilled a half dozen cameramen and their equipment all over the long marble staircase. Still, a local traffic copter broke the no-fly rule over the Capitol, and at the cost of a massive fine and a lengthy suspension of his pilot's license, the reporter recorded a historically iconographic aerial view of Jack Mahone's flight into ignominy.

33

WELL, THOUGHT GODWIN, there's a spectacle that will live forever in history. It's a little more than I planned, but sometimes these things take on a life of their own. I should get out of here. This isn't going to be a pretty place to be. There's going to be lots of emotion here this afternoon. Great weeping and wailing and gnashing of teeth. I'll go to the Observatory. If anybody wants me, I'll be there. But there should be some distance between Jack and me right now. Jack has to resign, and he has to resign today. I shouldn't be around to talk to him about it.

Quickly, he threw some papers into his briefcase and unplugged his laptop. But instead of slipping it into its case, he took a screwdriver out of its drawer and removed the laptop's hard drive. Time for this to disappear, he was thinking. In a day or two or seven, but in any event, before long, somebody's going to wonder where that picture came from. Perhaps even at the president's instigation—by my very order!—the FBI will investigate. The photographer's going to claim to have taken the shot, but having been overpaid in cash and without a copy, there will be no proof.

Then they'll try to find Flip Stacks of the wormreport.com. They'll begin with all those people who were rumored to be Flip Stacks, and who, because they enjoyed the cachet and interest, played along with the idea, but who will now vehemently deny having any connection. Many will be believed; some will always be suspected. After about a thousand more unproductive leads—assuming the

FBI is this good, which one shouldn't automatically do—they'll finally trace the E-mails, which will all lead back to a computer system sitting in the attic in a home in Biglerville, Pennsylvania, belonging to a man named Peter Gelheim, whom, oddly, no one has ever met, but whose taxes, utilities, home-maintenance, phone, and AOL bills are punctually paid from an account maintained by a small law firm in Harrisburg, whose chief partner is in the throes of Alzheimer's, and who no longer quite remembers the pleasant young man who came in more than six years ago with a million in cash and set up a trust for his aging uncle Peter.

Creating a fictitious identity, Godwin thought. It's the kind of thing you can do when you're rich and bored and infinitely patient.

He took a hammer out of the bottom drawer of his desk. So long, Flip, he thought, and repeatedly beat on the hard drive until he had smashed it to bits.

34

LINDA ARCHER WONDERED what she had done to deserve this. In the middle of the biggest story of her lifetime, the person who is arguably her best reporter comes in talking like she's just eaten some magic mushrooms. "Jesus Christ, Maggie, please! We've just witnessed the first presidential implosion in history! Don't you think our readers would like us to cover it a little?"

"That's what I'm trying to tell you, Linda! I've got the story! The story behind the story! This whole thing was a setup!"

"Oh for Chrissakes, how?"

"Godwin Pope did it," said Maggie, gushing facts. "Godwin Pope knew Irene was a hooker, 'cause he'd seen her at Tom Ralston's house the day Marco McChesney was there. And he knew Mahone used to get girls during the campaign through Richie Platt, a White House speechwriter who was close to Godwin. So Godwin persuaded Penny Vanatua to play matchmaker and set up Irene and Richie at the White House correspondents' dinner, knowing that Jack would hit on her."

"Knowing Jack would hit on her," Linda repeated, shaking her head. "Jesus Christ, Maggie, come on. You know, when I was ten years old, I was sure that if I said three Hail Marys, I could make the deejay play 'My Sharona.' But you know what I found out later? He did it on his own!"

"He also suggested to Roland that he hire Lowell."

"So how did that go? Did he say, 'Roland, old boy, why don't you take leave of your senses for a moment and make this highly suspicious payment to the president's brother'?"

"No, because when he made the offer, it wasn't that suspicious. At that point, Roland thought the satellite deal was a loser. But then Jack resurrected it."

"Which I guess Godwin made him do," said Linda sarcastically.

"I don't know if Godwin made him, but he helped him."

"Yeah? And how, pray tell, did he do that?"

Here comes the hard part, thought Maggie. "By setting me up to do my story on how the Republican opposition was based on partisan politics—contracts and contributions—which made them all look like hypocrites."

"He set you up to do that."

"Yeah. By leaving the data on his kitchen table, where he knew I would find it."

"Oh, so that wasn't just intrepid research on your part."

Linda said that snidely; it hurt Maggie to realize that she deserved it.

"What else?" Linda demanded. "Did Pope mesmerize the president into killing the CIA report?"

"I don't know. I don't know how that happened."

"And I suppose he leaked Irene's picture to the Worm Report."

"I don't know. I always assumed Richie did that, but Godwin might have."

"And somehow he got Irene to pose with Zhang Tian."

"Again, I don't know. Maybe he did! Maybe we'll have to do some reporting and figure it all out!"

"Yes, that's right, that's exactly right, we're going to have to do some reporting," Linda shouted. "We're going to stop playing connect the dots and do some reporting on the major story of our lives, a good, clean, important story about influence and misjudgment and self-delusion, a story that's sitting right here in front of us."

"No, Linda, there's more."

"No, Maggie, there isn't. Now I can use you on this story, Maggie, because you're the best that we've got. But if you're hell-bent on pursuing this cockamamie theory, have at it. I'll be sorry to lose you, and I'm sure Loomis will, as well. But right now I need a reporter. I don't need a fucking novelist. Now, once and for all, which are you?"

I can't do this, Maggie thought. I know I'm right, but I cannot stand here and destroy myself today just so people know that I have a sense of conviction. I cannot just ruin myself.

"What do you want me to do for you, Linda?"

"Good. I'm glad that's what you decided. Now go back to your office and pull yourself together. I'll be there in a minute." Maggie nodded and headed for the door. Just before she got to it, Linda spoke again. "Just one more thing. Later, when we're not so busy, I'll probably ask you how you found yourself looking at papers on Godwin Pope's kitchen table, where he knew you'd find them. You be sure to tell me something that won't leave both of us embarrassed, okay?"

Already exhausted by the half day's events, Maggie headed for her little office. She seemed to be moving in slow motion, in marked contrast to her colleagues, who were hustling around in overdrive. On her left, one of the art directors, Max, was working on a design for the cover. He was playing around with the most emblematic images of the day: Jack during his testimony, at that striking moment when the wormreport.com E-mail came in; Jack, in a shot from the helicopter, fleeing down the Capitol steps; Irene Kim and Zhang Tian and their colleagues in the incriminating photograph. Maggie stopped to watch him work. He was fiddling with the photo with Irene—tilting it left, right, zooming in on her, on her and Zhang.

Ever since she was a little girl, Maggie had been fascinated by games and totally uninterested in puzzles. Crosswords were too cute, Sudoku too tricky, and jigsaws so unchallenging. Shapes and colors were no mystery to her, subtle details were plain, and patterns proclaimed their presence. Looking at the photo, something seemed amiss.

"Max, besides Irene and Zhang, who else is in that picture?"

"He's the deputy of the legation. That's a businessman. This is some professor."

Who else is there? she wanted to ask again. Wasn't there somebody else back there, somebody mostly hidden except for a hand left resting on Zhang Tian's shoulder? Shouldn't bring that up, though, she thought, not here in the art department, not with Linda apt to come down the hallway at any minute and see me doing the very thing she practically commanded me to stop doing. That would be the end of me. She'd throw me out. And yet—

"Max, are all these pictures on the server?"

"Uh-huh."

"I just want to—kind of study them. They're great photos."

"Yeah, they're all in this week's Mahone folder."

Maggie quick-stepped to her office, locked the door, logged on to the art department server, and found the picture she was seeking. There it was, the hand on Zhang Tian's shoulder, unpaired and unattached, at least to anyone whose face could be seen. She used a design program to zoom in on and focus on the hand, magnifying once, twice, three times, four. By the fifth magnitude, the hand filled the twenty-one-inch screen of her monitor, and she could see that on the third finger of the hand was a ring, a big ring, chunky like a school ring, the right size and shape to be a Princeton ring, if she remembered the last one she'd seen correctly. And on the index finger was a scar, thin and white and long, just the sort of thing you might inflict upon yourself if you'd ever taken on a grapefruit and lost.

35

BY MIDAFTERNOON THE CITY and, through the media based there, the entire nation and huge chunks of the rest of the world were locked solidly into death-watch mode. Reporters outside the White House somberly and dutifully observed the arrival of the president's pastor, his children, and assorted dignitaries, and otherwise noted the gradual accumulation of a crowd that had assembled in Lafayette Park as though on retainer, bringing with them the atmosphere of a freaky holiday, as though they were waiting for the presidential mansion to suddenly rise up on one corner and Electric Slide its way across town.

On Capitol Hill, the only people who were working were the members of the House Judiciary Committee, who were with some haste drawing up articles of impeachment. Herman Vanick was certain that all the labor was pointless, that Jack would resign before the articles could be introduced into committee, but he nonetheless wanted them ready for the next morning in case he was wrong. All this time would be better spent getting ready to deal with President Pope, he told himself, but he was simply too tired to think about that. All the years he had spent warring with Jack Mahone and the Democrats, and now Jack had been destroyed. Never did Herm think things would come to this, and realizing that they had left him spent and dismayed.

Inside the White House, Jack spent the early part of the afternoon secreted in his bathroom, using half a bottle of bourbon to anesthetize himself against the memory of the morning, and to steel himself for the ordeals ahead. After a time, he emerged, calm and collected, and frankly a bit surprised to find Tavis Whouley, Leonard Dvorcheki, and a half dozen other party elders patiently parked in the Roosevelt Room, bidding for a moment of his time. Surprised by how quickly they'd gotten there, not surprised by what they had to say.

"Mr. President, I'm afraid that your position has become politically untenable," said Tavis. "Vanick will introduce articles of impeachment by morning."

"There's even talk Vanick will call the House into session tonight and introduce the articles just as soon as they finish printing!" said a shocked Leonard Dvorcheki.

"Y'all don't really have any support left in Congress," said Tavis. "Y'all will be lucky to have half a dozen votes. Even the staunchest of the staunch are talking about just voting 'present' rather than casting any vote on your behalf."

"And here I thought we lived in a land where a man was innocent until proven guilty," said Jack. There was no self-pity in his observation, more a tone of curiosity.

"True enough, Mr. President," said Tavis, "but truth be told, y'all kind of had your trial this morning. I mean, it would be one thing if there was a mechanism in the Constitution that would let you take a leave of absence while your case was being adjudicated, but apart from disability, there's not."

Not unless I drank myself into a coma, thought Jack.

"And let's face it, Mr. President," said old Corn Peavy, the oldest living ambulatory senator, "it would still take a miracle for you to turn this around."

"To be truthful, Mr. President," said raspy-voiced congressman Francis Patrick McGinley, who broke into politics before he could shave, bribing voters for FDR and who often went skirt-chasing with JFK when they were freshmen together in the House, "even a miracle would be useless to you. You need the Second Coming of Christ."

The silence that followed was on the verge of becoming uncomfortable when Tavis played his hole card. "It may be, sir, that the last service for your country y'all are in a position to perform is to spare it the great pain of dismissing you. In coming days, I'm sure people would appreciate the dignity you'd be showing."

Jack nodded. If there was anything he'd always been able to do in politics, it was to sense the glimmer of possibility in a situation when no one else could see it, and to tease that glimmer into life. This was over. It was time to think about the future. It was time to move on. "Thank you for stopping by, gentlemen," he said. "I need to speak to my wife and children."

While this was happening, Godwin sat at his kitchen table and worked. He reviewed and reconsidered the key cabinet choices he would have to make. He was pretty sure he knew whom he wanted, but he had to project the illusion of having an open mind and consulting with people, so he thought he might as well go all the way and actually keep an open mind when he met with candidates. He knew which foreign leaders he wanted to see first, and he was fairly sure he knew which bills he was going to push in these sweet, early days. (He knew one thing he was going to do: cancel that damn satellite sale. There was no way he could support it, although he might see if he could figure out some way to entertain it again next year.) He thought of asking Maggie to become his press secretary; then he thought of asking her something else. Late in the afternoon, he heard from Chet Wetzel, who confided the president's plan. They agreed that Godwin needed to return to the White House.

After all the drama of the morning, Maggie ended up having a placid afternoon. Gonzalez and the magazine's other White House correspondents were covering the story from the White House, and Overton and the other congressional correspondents were all over on the Hill. Linda rightly judged that it would be insulting to send Maggie out to get man in the street reactions. Around four o'clock, Linda asked Maggie if she could try to get a statement or a quote out of the vice president, and Maggie obliged, but Godwin's office was all but shut down, refusing all comment until Jack did whatever he was going to do.

Later, when every unofficial word was screaming that the president would go on TV during prime time and resign, Linda called Maggie again. "Maybe you should go over to the White House, see if you can get something from your friend Godwin Pope. If he's president tomorrow, we'll be thrilled to be able to run something up close and personal."

36

THE WHITE HOUSE WAS the kind of place that couldn't help but reflect the tone of the moment, and Maggie had seen a number of days when the set mouths and furrowed brows were affixed not only to the president and his advisers but to the marine guards and receptionists and the others who walked the halls, as well. Today, people were crying, holding one another and crying. Even the young lady at the press desk was teary.

"Would you please ask if I could see Vice President Pope for a few minutes?"

"I'm sorry, ma'am, he's not taking any interviews."

"I understand. Please tell him I'm here. Maggie Newbold from *Newsbreak*. Could you please ask?"

While she waited, she watched CNN's pundits dissect the last twenty-four hours.

"I just don't see how he survives," said witty ex-speechwriter Bitsey O'Hara.

"It's like the Profumo scandal of 1963," offered historian Cameron Hetherington. "There's no question. He's got to go."

"Excuse me, Cameron," said CNN's Christine van den Hurdle, "this just in. Sky TV is reporting from Shanghai, China, that in her first interview, Mingsha Gua, the woman known here as Irene Kim, says that President Mahone was unaware that she was a prostitute. She also denies that she took instruction from or passed any information to any Chinese official."

"Fine," said the *Post*'s Elena Dover, "but that's too little, too late to help Jack Mahone."

"Too little, too late," said Antonio Rasa, "and if she's telling the truth, why'd she run to Shanghai? Why doesn't she come back here and answer questions? I want to know how she got out of the country. Did the president help her?"

Stupid blowhards, thought Maggie. All spin, no facts. Of course, this is a story totally built on spin.

"Excuse me, again," said van den Hurdle. "This is also just in. What we've been hearing all day is now official. The White House has asked the networks for time for the president to address the country at eight o'clock this evening. That's just thirty minutes from now."

The young lady from the press desk returned. "The vice president will see you now," she said, smiling.

"THANK YOU, Mrs. Gottschalk," Godwin said as his ancient secretary admitted Maggie. "Would you please close the door behind you?"

As soon as it was closed, Godwin stepped briskly from behind his desk. "Darling!" he said, spreading wide his arms. "It feels like years since I've seen you." He embraced her and then kissed her hard. She didn't want to respond—he was manipulating her and using her, and for Chrissakes, he was overthrowing the president. Yet somehow when her lips found his, her pulse quickened.

"God, I've missed you," he said. "Where have you been? I've beeped you a thousand times."

"There's a lot going on," she said.

"I know," he said seriously.

"The president's addressing the nation."

"Yes—he's resigning."

"Well then. I guess congratulations are in order."

"Thank you, Maggie. It's been a terribly difficult couple of weeks. But it's over now, and I'm glad, because now I feel free to ask you—"

"It's an awful damn shame, though," she said, interrupting him. "Don't you think it's a shame?"

Godwin didn't think it was a shame on any level, of course, but he felt obliged to follow her lead, if only vaguely, just for the sake of sociability. "Yes, it's too bad," he quietly agreed. He was listening for a way to get back to what he wanted to talk about.

"Yes, and what makes it a shame is that there's no proof."

"Well, whatever you call it, it seems to have convinced most people," he said.

"We know certain things happened, yes. But there's no proof they're connected."

"You don't think so?"

"Two men have sex with the same woman, it means they know somebody in common. It doesn't mean they're connected. It doesn't mean they've had a mind meld."

"But you have to admit the pile of coincidences looks awfully damning," he said, trying to sound reasonable. When did this chick turn into such a buzzkill? he wondered. It's my night, and she wants to argue like she's on *Pardon the Interruption*.

"Sure," she said, seeing that she was succeeding in getting him irked. "But they're still just coincidences. There's no real proof."

"You're being surprisingly legalistic, darling. There was tons of proof against Clinton, and he survived. Why? Because people liked him, and they hated his enemies."

"So what you're saying is that people didn't like Jack. Let's say for the sake of argument you're right, even though fifty million people voted for him. But I don't get your other point—you don't think people hated his enemies?"

"No, people may not like Herm, but they don't hate him."

"But Herm wasn't really his enemy, not really."

"Maybe you're right," he said. Why were they talking about this? "Maybe Jack's biggest enemy was himself."

"You think so?" she said.

"Sure," he said. The way she was looking at him made him feel terribly uneasy.

"You really think he wasn't up against some other enemy, some extremely clever, extremely resourceful, maybe even brilliant enemy?"

She knows, Godwin thought.

"See," Maggie suddenly said, "what I really wonder is how you got the picture."

"What?"

"I've thought about it and thought about it, and I can't figure it out."

"What picture?"

"The picture of Irene and Marco McChesney. Because that's what made the story get up and go. Because whatever stories the media may have heard about Jack's private life, we wouldn't have gone after that too hard. 'Leave it alone, it's a rumor.' Or 'Leave it alone, it's the man's private life.' That's what we would have said. But the picture—oh boy, that picture, that beautiful girl's almond eyes, that big gluteus maximus with flames on it—that picture made the story irresistible."

Unsure what to say, ignorant of what she knew, Godwin tried to buy time by playing dumb. "I'm just not following you, dear," he said.

"Try this. You're at Tom Ralston's. It's right after the State of the Union address, and maybe you're sick and tired of being most bored supporting actor. Tom said you were griping, that you wanted to get rid of Jack, so—something happened. You saw something or you realized something. I guess you saw them all in the pool. Maybe you were in the pool yourself."

"Hardly."

"And you realized that there was a tape. Maybe Tom showed it to you. Did he offer you a copy? No, he'd know that's not your kink.

And you wouldn't ask for it—you don't like accomplices. Besides, everything else you've done has been subtle, unobtrusive, forgettable, and completely deniable. Asking for a tape would be too memorable. Having a tape would be physical evidence. So how did you get it? Could you have gone back to steal a copy?"

"Check my logs. I've been out to Tom's only once this year."

"So there—you have me. I've figured out most of the rest of the game, but I can't figure out that."

Excellent, thought Godwin. It would have been fun to have pulled this off with no one knowing, but somehow it's better to have someone in on it, someone who will be able to appreciate the sheer ingenuity of the whole thing. Should I share the secret? "Tell me, darling," he said with a smile. "Why does it have to be a tape?"

She didn't follow immediately, and he continued. "Think about it," he said. "Would Tom Ralston, of all people, be a tape kind of guy?"

"No," she said, catching on. "He'd be a digital guy. So you downloaded a copy that day onto a disk."

"You're getting colder—"

"Or maybe you hacked into his files."

His smile was full of self-satisfaction. "You give a person a lot of credit."

"A pioneer of the computer software industry? Yeah, I'll give you some credit."

"How will you prove it?" he asked.

"I guess prosecutors could seize Tom Ralston's server."

"Prosecutors? What's the charge?"

"Try sedition."

"Well, good luck making that charge stick. Besides, don't you think I would have covered my tracks?"

"You might have made a mistake," she said evenly.

"I don't think so."

"You made one," she said, "with the picture of Irene Kim and

Zhang Tian." She pointed to a late copy of the *Post,* an afternoon extra. "There're five people in that picture."

"Uh-huh."

"And eleven hands."

He hated being confronted with evidence of his error, but he played it cool. "So?"

"The eleventh hand—which belongs to someone standing in the rear of the group—is wearing a Princeton ring, like you do sometimes, and has a two-inch scar along one finger. Like you do." She paused, gauging his reaction. So far, so cool. "Already four paparazzi are arguing over who owns the rights to that picture. It won't take much for one of them to remember that you were in it, that you probably asked to have it taken, that you're there with Zhang Tian and Irene. How long will it be before somebody suggests that you and the Chinese cooked this from the get-go?"

"Hah! Where is the proof of that?"

"I hear that proof is vastly overrated. All I know is that once Penny testifies how you got her to invite Richie and Irene, and Roland testifies how you got him to book Lowell—"

At last, Godwin began feeling the pressure. "I suppose next you'll be saying that I'm the one who screwed Irene."

"No, I think you're the one who screwed Jack."

Suddenly, there was a knock on the door. Not Mrs. Gottschalk's gentle rap, but a quick, forceful trio of bangs. Before Godwin could speak, Chet Wetzel let himself in. "I'm so sorry to intrude, Mr. Vice President. The president is going on the air momentarily, and he's asked to see you first."

"Thank you, Chet, I'll be along in just a moment." Wetzel closed the door, and Godwin continued. "You know, Maggie, in every relationship, no matter how much the people love each other, they always find out stuff about each other they aren't too crazy to learn."

"This is a little more serious than snoring, don't you think?"

"Jack Mahone was a lousy president. I could have sat by and been loyal and had a front-row seat as he ruined our economy and gave our worst enemies issues to use against us."

"Or you could have taken it upon yourself to do something about it."

"Yes. And I did. And as a result, I'm going to become president, and I'm going to be a great one, and the country's going to be better off with me in charge. You said so yourself."

"Yes, I did," she said, feeling she had to admit it.

There was another rap. "Mr. Vice President!" Wetzel called.

"Just a minute!" shouted Godwin. Time for the preemptive offer. "But Maggie, here's the other part. I want you with me. I think you're the smartest, savviest, sexiest, most stimulating woman I have ever known, and I want to share this experience with you."

He reached into his pocket and pulled out a ring box from Van Cleef & Arpels. "I love you, Maggie," he said, "and I want you to be my wife."

"Godwin!" she said, exasperated. "Don't you understand? You used me!"

"I know," he said. "I didn't think you'd really mind. I mean, isn't that what friends are for?"

"Mr. Vice President," called Wetzel again, "we really have to go now!"

He stole a quick kiss from her. "I'll be back in a flash."

WHEN GODWIN ENTERED the room, Jack was heading for the desk from which he would be addressing the nation within the minute. "Mr. President, I'm sorry I'm late," Godwin said.

"Oh, Godwin, I'm just glad you made it. I have to go speak to the nation in a minute, and then this will all be yours. I just wanted to thank you for the way you stood by me."

"It was my honor, Mr. President."

"You're a good man and I know you'll do a good job," he managed to get out, and then he began to lose it. "The damn thing is, I'm innocent! I did nothing wrong!"

"I know, Mr. President," said Godwin. He pulled Jack close and whispered in his ear. "I have total faith in your innocence. And I want to make you this promise. No matter how many investigators come after you, no matter how many prosecutors file how many charges, no matter how many juries find you guilty of how many crimes—I promise I'll give you a full and complete pardon. You'll never spend a day in jail."

"Thank you, Godwin," said Jack, holding in the tears and taking Godwin's hand and kissing it. "Thank you."

"I guess, Jack, this is just one of those times—"

Jack stood up. The comment distracted him from his grief. "What times?"

"It's one of those times when you have to ask yourself, How come there's no almonds in my chocolate bar?"

Jack laughed, a quizzical half-choked laugh, then looked at Godwin hard, as though he were seeing Godwin for the first time.

"It's time, Mr. President," said Chet Wetzel, tugging Mahone by the sleeve, pulling him to the desk.

"I'll wait in the Oval Office," Godwin told the remaining aides. "Now would one of you please go back to my old office and ask Ms. Newbold if she would please join me here?"

ONLY AFTER GODWIN LEFT did Maggie open the box and actually look at the ring. It was breathtaking, significant in size and cut, but not ostentatious. It was the kind of ring that never had to boast about being perfect, because it indisputably was. She sighed and closed the box.

This is one of those crossroads moments, she thought. One of those occasions when you have to look into your heart and look into your soul and ask yourself, Who are you, really?

I'm a journalist, she thought. Now what does that mean?

Ask most people, and they'll tell you journalists are interested in right and wrong, in helping good guys and exposing bad guys, and in rooting for the underdog.

Sometimes that's true.

But mostly what journalists are interested in are stories. We like good stories, she thought. We don't like bad stories.

Right now, she thought, I have to choose between two stories. I have to ask myself, Which one is better?

One story is about Maggie, the girl who came from nothing, who had to work for everything she ever got, who built a great career and then fell in love with a handsome, clever multimillionaire who became the president.

The other story is about Maggie, a well-known reporter who broke a lot of rules that damaged her credibility, who got hooked on a story that nobody else believed, and who became a burned-out conspiracy zealot who squandered what still could have been a distinguished career trying to hang some unlikely and unprovable plot on a well-liked and successful president.

Which story is better? Not to write, she thought. That's too easy. The tragedy would be better to write. But to live?

Through the door, on a television down the hall, she heard the sound of Jack Mahone's resignation.

She opened the ring box again and beheld the rock.

It's incredible, she thought. It's almost like a fairy tale. And for once I'll be in a position of influence, and be able to push and prod and help the poor and downtrodden. But for all that, the question remains: Can I trust him?

No, of course not. But, she thought as she reached into her purse, at the same time—

There was a knock on the door. It was one of Chet Wetzel's aides. "Ms. Newbold? President-designate Pope would like you to join him in the Oval Office for his swearing-in."

"Just a minute," she said. She reached into her purse and at the bottom found exactly what she'd been looking for, her voice-activated microcassette recorder that looked like a pen, which her old friend in the Mossad had given her. She could see that it had been running for the last thirty-six minutes. Old reliable.

No, she thought as she rose to her feet. No, I can't trust him. But this isn't one of those relationships that is going to be overly dependent on trust.

"Ms. Newbold!"

37

SHE MADE IT IN TIME for the swearing-in. Godwin had made them wait for her. There was going to be another one, right the next day, at noon in the Rose Garden, in chilly, breezy March sunshine, something if not exactly celebratory, then at least full of hope and good wishes. Still, the White House counsel, Doreen Wasserman, wanted a swearing-in immediately, not because it was exactly necessary, but because lawyerly punctiliousness was what White House counsels were at the White House for, and if she wasn't going to dot every *i* and cross every *t* and take every precaution under these circumstances, well then, why was she there? Besides, what if, God forbid, Godwin had to launch a massive nuclear strike that evening? What would the World Court in The Hague think if he hadn't been sworn in?

And so it was Godwin and the chief justice of the Supreme Court, with the cabinet and Chet and Mrs. Gottschalk and, of course, Maggie as witnesses, in a moment preserved by Jim Spinner, the longtime White House photographer, and the pictures turned out great. Lit by a single desk lamp—Doreen Wasserman rushed everybody so much that nobody bothered to turn up the lights—the event looked like it had taken place over a cauldron. All Godwin could think was that the moment wasn't exactly as he had envisioned it, but at least it was all his.

Congratulations were offered, sincere but subdued. There was sort of an awkward moment when Chet Wetzel had stewards wheel in champagne, but it would have been absurdly awkward to have done nothing. The men and women of the cabinet raised their glasses in a solemn toast, and Godwin thanked them and told them he'd see them all again tomorrow afternoon at the first cabinet meeting of his administration. Of course he didn't tell them that he'd be asking all of them for their resignations at that point, or that all but three would be accepted.

While they emptied their glasses, Maggie sat in Chet Wetzel's office and phoned in her story to Linda Archer. Maggie stressed the gravity and the solemnity, the sorrowful but unchallenged commitment to a government of laws over a government of men. She had details: the color of Godwin's tie, the chief justice's Reeboks, Mrs. Gottschalk's tears, the year the champagne had been bottled. "There was a nobility to it," she concluded. "Kind of a courage against the storm thing."

"Nobility, yeah!" exulted Linda. "Loomis is going to eat this up. Exclusive, girl! Exclusive! Please remember the little people you met along the way. You're going to be able to write your own ticket now." Nice, Maggie thought. Just when that door had closed.

She reentered the Oval Office. The cabinet hadn't lingered, and Mrs. Gottschalk and Chet had been dismissed. She was all alone with President Pope.

"You're wearing your ring," he said.

"No one noticed," she said in the silly way shy schoolgirls deflect compliments.

"I did. I saw it while I was taking the oath of office. I was thrilled."

And indeed he was thrilled. Becoming president would have been a peerless moment for any man, but the satisfaction Godwin felt was surpassed by the exultation sparked by the knowledge that he had secured an even rarer prize. "Maggie," he said, "I really do love you."

Slowly, she strolled across the room. She wished she had been wearing something she could use to show the warmth she was feeling now, a strand of pearls she could tug at as she approached him, or a scarf she could ostentatiously undo. Unfortunately, all she had on was the prosaic reporter's uniform she'd been wearing all day—black blazer, gray skirt—so all she could do was fix him with her eyes as she neared him.

Godwin got the message. No sooner did she get within reach than he placed his hands on her hips and drew her close. "Oh, Mr. President," she said, cooing like Marilyn. He pulled her closer and tugged at her clothes. "Here?" she asked.

"Hell yeah, here," he said. "Just push those papers aside." Jack had been using Harry Truman's famous "The buck stops here" desk. Godwin thought it was ugly, boxy, and he meant to replace it with one of FDR's. But it would do now.

"Here, turn around," he said, twisting her. From behind, she felt one hand flip up her skirt and another tiptoe up her belly toward her bra. Pushing her rump back into him, she tried to brace her hands on the desk, but they slid on the papers. Looking to move them, she saw their subject: supplemental budget requests. The first appropriation: infant mortality in Africa. The amount: absurd.

"Darling," she said, turning abruptly around and pressing into him, "that's not all we're going to give to Africa, is it?"

ACKNOWLEDGMENTS

Thanks to Amy Grace Loyd, my first reader, for her editorial and practical guidance; to Jennifer Ryan Jones, for her fashion consultation; to David McCormick and Gerry Howard, for their perspicacity; to Jim Noonan, for his friendship and patronage; to Chris Napolitano, for all the opportunities; to Kurt Andersen and Graydon Carter, for encouragement at the turning point; to all my colleagues, past and present, for their fellowship; and to Ginny, Molly, and Cara—it's all for you.

ABOUT THE AUTHOR

Jamie Malanowski is currently the managing editor of *Play-boy*. Previously, he held senior editorial positions at *Spy*, where he wrote the magazine's signature "Fine Print" column, as well as at *Time* and *Esquire*. He is also the coauthor of the HBO film *Pentagon Wars* and author of the novel *Mr. Stupid Goes to Washington*.